T H E
CHILD BUYER

THE
CHILD BUYER

A Novel *in the Form of* Hearings
before the Standing Committee *on Education,*
Welfare, & Public Morality of a certain
State Senate, *Investigating the conspiracy*
of Mr. Wissey Jones, *with others,*
to Purchase *a* Male Child

---

by John Hersey

ALFRED·A·KNOPF   *New York*   1960

L. C. catalog card number: 60–13850

THIS IS A BORZOI BOOK,
PUBLISHED BY ALFRED A. KNOPF, INC.

FIRST EDITION

T O

Grace Baird Hersey:

*"Cheerfulness keeps up a kind of daylight
in the mind, and fills it with a steady
and perpetual serenity."*
—JOSEPH ADDISON,
The Spectator, May 17, 1712

THE
CHILD BUYER

Purchase of BOY CHILD,

TOWN of PEQUOT

STATE SENATE

STANDING COMMITTEE

ON EDUCATION, WELFARE, AND

PUBLIC MORALITY

THURSDAY, OCTOBER 24, 19—

(The committee met, pursuant to call, at 4:20 p.m., in Room 429, Capitol Offices, Senator Aaron Mansfield presiding. Present: Senators Mansfield, Skypack, and Voyolko; also present, Mr. Donald R. Broadbent, committee counsel.)

Senator MANSFIELD. The committee will come to order in Executive Session. Mr. Broadbent, will you please explain the purpose and intent of the hearings we will begin tomorrow morning?

Mr. BROADBENT. Gladly, Mr. Chairman. Tomorrow we will begin to look into a situation that has developed in the last few days in the township of Pequot. It is alleged that on October sixteenth, that is, one week ago yesterday, a certain Mr. Wissey Jones entered the town of Pequot from out of State, and that

3

he did conspire with persons in the town in an attempt to purchase a male white child, ten years of age, named Barry Rudd,
advancing unspecified educational and patriotic purposes for
the proposed transaction.

Senator SKYPACK. Was the deal completed?

Mr. BROADBENT. If you'd let me finish my—

Senator SKYPACK. All right. All right.

Mr. BROADBENT. This matter falls within the competence and
purview of this committee on three accounts. First, a State law
of 1829, still on the books, prohibits the purchase or sale of persons. The Pequot case now raises the question whether this
committee should recommend that the law be repealed, or mod-
ified in any way, or let stand and be strictly enforced. I should
warn you, the Federal people may get into the act, on a Thirteenth Amendment involvement; I advert to a possible allega-
tion of 'involuntary servitude,' as it is put. Second, there is a
possible morals angle, though we aren't quite untangled about
this part of it; our investigator is trying to run it down today.
Third, we have the responsibility of this committee for the field
of education, and we are confronted by these assertions by the
man Wissey Jones that he has quote educational unquote reasons for the proposed transaction. The exact nature of these reasons, together with the quote patriotic unquote purposes of the
deal—we're not clear on them. The man Wissey Jones represents himself as an executive of the United Lymphomilloid
Company, based, as you may know, in the southwestern part of
the United States, and his claim is that the boy child is being
bought for a highly classified defense project. However, we are
not entirely satisfied with the man Wissey Jones's veracity or
credibility; he is a very unusual type of individual.

Senator VOYOLKO. Don't get it. What's this all about?

Senator MANSFIELD. Jack, would you mind translating for
Senator Voyolko?

Senator SKYPACK. Look, Senator, this guy tries to buy this kid. We want to know how come.

Senator VOYOLKO. Why'n't he say so? I wish you'd talk in good plain American, Mr. Broadback. Three quarters what you say, it's Greek.

Senator MANSFIELD. I think it would help not only the Senator from Winfield County but all of us, Mr. Broadbent, if you would try throughout these upcoming hearings to keep things orderly. You've heard me say before, the best way to get to the end in a hurry is to begin at the beginning. If you have a fault—

Mr. BROADBENT. You have to realize, sir, that with people constantly interrupting, bringing in new questions—

Senator MANSFIELD. The word I used was 'try.'

Mr. BROADBENT. Mr. Wissey Jones was first seen entering the town of Pequot on the sixteenth instant on a collapsible motorcycle. He was wearing some golf knickerbockers, or plus fours, of a vintage so old—

Senator SKYPACK. Now just one minute, young fellow. What kind of a motorcycle was that?

Mr. BROADBENT. You see, Mr. Chairman. It's not easy—

Senator MANSFIELD. I was wondering about that motorcycle myself.

Mr. BROADBENT. This is a European-type machine, as I understand it, rather light-weight, which unlocks in the middle, so to speak, in such a way that the two wheels fold against each other. Makes a compact bundle. The wheels are light, the tires scarcely more than bicycle tires, and the motor a tiny one-lunger, so a man can easily lift the whole thing up, especially when it's folded. Then when you want to ride, you unfold it, open it out, and it locks with the two wheels in line the regular way. Several persons in the lobby of the Mulhausen Hotel in Pequot witnessed a sharp altercation, Mr. Wissey Jones's bap-

5

tism of fire in the town, one might say, when after registering he attempted to carry his machine, folded, under his arm into the passenger elevator. As I was trying to tell you, this gentleman had some mighty old-fashioned pants on. Also a pork-pie hat. Turtle-neck sweater, black. His luggage was a haversack, or hiking bag, strapped to his shoulders, and a pair of saddlebags that rode over the rear wheel of this machine. I think you can already see why we've got a little trouble about credibility here. Anyway, he lit into the elevator boy—

Senator SKYPACK. They have elevator girls in the Mulhausen down there. In fact, all the Mulhausen chain, they wear these black satin slacks, or pedal pushers.

Mr. BROADBENT. I'm going on preliminary information the investigator shot up to me last night, Senator. I'm doing the best I can.

Senator MANSFIELD. Lay off, Jack.

Senator SKYPACK. All right. All right.

Mr. BROADBENT. Mr. Jones belabored the elevator boy, or girl, verbally, and was then heard shouting and seen gesticulating with his free hand at the desk. As you may know, the hotel down there, formerly the Depot Hotel, has been modernized— Mulhausenized, I think they call it, and the desk has this long slab of black pink-veined soapstone supported on interlacing aluminum M's, and overhead a neon sign, *Guest Representative*, which is what they call the room clerk, and here's this stranger, with the neon sign throwing a trembling violet light on his pearl-gray pork-pie, and his folded motorcycle under his arm, shouting at the fellow behind the desk that vice-presidents of United Lymphomilloid don't ride in service elevators. Mr. Salamenko, the duty clerk at the desk at that time, informed our investigator that the man Wissey Jones does not look you in the eye, but fixes his stare above your eyes, at about the level of the hairline, and keeps—

Senator SKYPACK. If you're lucky enough to *have* a hairline.

Mr. BROADBENT. Mr. Chairman, I appeal to—

Senator SKYPACK. All right, Broadbent. Can't you take a rib?

Mr. BROADBENT. The man Wissey Jones, if he is what he represents himself to be, is something rather unusual in the line of a businessman—intellectually keen, said to be bright as a new penny. I guess all kinds of people have been going into business since the war.

Senator VOYOLKO. Mr. Broadback, sir, you mind telling me what you're leading up to?

Senator MANSFIELD. I'm afraid I can't see, myself—

Mr. BROADBENT. If the Chairman will indulge me . . . Gentlemen, I'm not a crystal ball on this picture. I'm going along on sparse details, because our investigator has only had a few hours, two working days, to be exact, in Pequot, and I'm trying to pick up the threads.

Senator MANSFIELD. Shouldn't we be a lot clearer on our facts before rocketing along and holding hearings?

Mr. BROADBENT. I'm convinced, sir, that the case deserves the committee's prompt attention.

Senator MANSFIELD. Surely a few days.

Mr. BROADBENT. There has been violence in the town there, stemming straight from these matters. That's why—

Senator SKYPACK. Now you're talking, Broadbent. What sort of trouble?

Mr. BROADBENT. I don't want to go too fast, here. The information—

Senator SKYPACK. Give, Broadbent. Let's not get coy.

Mr. BROADBENT. I've told you I'm hazy on the details. It seems anyway a bomb was thrown.

Senator VOYOLKO. Who at?

Mr. BROADBENT. I really would rather wait for fuller material,

7

Mr. Chairman. . . . I understand this was not the only incident, there was other trouble as well, but I'll have better information by tomorrow. At any rate, what I have in hand is enough, I can assure you, to warrant an urgent inquiry by our committee.

Senator SKYPACK. All this rhubarb, why nothing in the papers?

Mr. BROADBENT. There's only a weekly down there in Pequot, the *Pequot Drummer*, and I guess—

Senator MANSFIELD. Are you absolutely sure, Mr. Broadbent, that you're not indulging your proclivity for building things up? Just a little? You remember the Hendport hearings.

Mr. BROADBENT. On the Bible, Mr. Chairman, you have a duty and a responsibility to get into this situation.

Senator MANSFIELD. Who's going to put us straight on the facts?

Mr. BROADBENT. The main witnesses, as things are shaping up, will be the man Wissey Jones himself, of course; the boy he's trying to purchase, Rudd's the name; and the boy's parents; then there's the Superintendent of Schools and possibly some other school people on the alleged educational angle; a certain young boy who is said to be a close associate or accomplice of the Rudd youngster; and perhaps two or three others.

Senator MANSFIELD. You can produce these witnesses tomorrow morning?

Mr. BROADBENT. Oh, yes, sir, some of them, enough to make a good start.

Senator MANSFIELD. Where will we sit?

Mr. BROADBENT. We better be in Committee Chamber 202, there's liable to be some interest as we go along.

Senator MANSFIELD. I hate that room. Curving row of thrones we have to sit in, and the amphitheater effect for the spectators. Makes me feel like a proconsul at a hand-to-hand between martyrs and lions.

8

Senator SKYPACK. Thin skin, Aaron. Why don't you relax and enjoy it?

Mr. BROADBENT. I've already reserved the room, Mr. Chairman. After tomorrow's papers . . .

Senator MANSFIELD. You mean to say you've given out another of your releases?

Mr. BROADBENT. Senator, a man who goes around buying boys—

Senator MANSFIELD. I hope that for once we can proceed with order and decorum. In an orderly way, Mr. Broadbent. Keep things in order. And I would hope that there would be no browbeating of witnesses.

Senator SKYPACK. All right, Aaron, let's don't forget you can do a lot of harm by being namby-pamby, too. We can see what develops.

Senator MANSFIELD. But I would hope—

Senator SKYPACK. And don't forget, Aaron, those headlines don't do Senator Mansfield any harm back in the hustings.

Senator MANSFIELD. I suppose there's a measure of truth—

Senator VOYOLKO. So what's the picture? Room 202—what time?

Mr. BROADBENT. I have the room for ten.

Senator MANSFIELD. I guess we can recess, gentlemen.

(Whereupon, at 4:50 p.m., Thursday, October 24, the hearing was recessed, subject to the announced recall of the Chair.)

9

FRIDAY, OCTOBER 25

(The committee met, pursuant to call, at 10:10 a.m., in Committee Chamber 202, Capitol Offices, Senator Aaron Mansfield presiding.)

Senator MANSFIELD. The committee will be in session. I will have to remind the spectators that you are guests of the committee, and ask you to remain orderly at all times. We're very crowded in here, and we're going to go along with good order and decorum. Thank you.

Mrs. Rudd, will you stand to be sworn?

Do you solemnly swear the testimony you are about to give in the matter now pending before this committee shall be the truth, the whole truth, and nothing but the truth, so help you God?

Mrs. RUDD. I swear it.

TESTIMONY OF MRS. PAUL RUDD, HOUSEWIFE, TOWN OF PEQUOT

Mr. BROADBENT. Will you kindly identify yourself for the record, Mrs. Rudd?

Mrs. RUDD. I'm Maud Purcells Rudd, and I'm married twelve years to Paul Rudd.

Mr. BROADBENT. Of Pequot? Your address?

10

Mrs. RUDD. We live in the Slatkowski block on River Street.

Mr. BROADBENT. And that's in Pequot?

Mrs. RUDD. That is correct.

Mr. BROADBENT. Please answer fully, Mrs. Rudd. Complete your thought each time.

Senator MANSFIELD. Don't be afraid, ma'am. Speak your mind. We try to be fair and square here.

Mrs. RUDD. Thank you.

Mr. BROADBENT. Your occupation?

Mrs. RUDD. I work in Stillman's.

Senator SKYPACK. Stillman's, Stillman's. It's very difficult, Mrs. Rudd, if witnesses come in here and don't answer fully and honestly. We're not from Pequot, how are we supposed to know what Stillman's is, what you do, all that?

Senator MANSFIELD. I believe she was about to tell her actual work, Jack. Let's not rush the witness.

Senator SKYPACK. All right.

Mrs. RUDD. I sell in the women's underthings.

Mr. BROADBENT. Will you kindly tell us, Mrs. Rudd, in your own way, about the events of the past week in Pequot?

Mrs. RUDD. It's about my boy, my Barry. They want to take him away. This man came to me, he talked so fast I couldn't understand what he was getting at. And Mr. Cleary, at first he was against it, and then he was pushing me to give in. The boy's father wants to sell, he says—

Mr. BROADBENT. One moment, Mrs. Rudd. You say 'this man.' Which man is that?

Mrs. RUDD. The buyer. The child buyer. He came there to the house, after Paul and I were home from work. Mr. Cleary had been to see us first. They talk about the boy's own good! A boy should be with his mother.

Mr. BROADBENT. Please, Mrs. Rudd. Would you, for the record, identify the Mr. Cleary of whom you spoke?

11

Mrs. RUDD. Barry calls him the G-Man. G is for Guidance.

Mr. BROADBENT. He is the Guidance Director of the Pequot public schools, is that right? And he came to you first?

Mrs. RUDD. He was against it, body and soul. Then, after, he tried to sell us like everyone else. When they come at you a mile a minute—

Senator MANSFIELD. Mr. Broadbent, this is the usual muddle.

Mr. BROADBENT. Sir, you'll recognize that this is a highly emotional witness.

Senator MANSFIELD. Elicit information, Mr. Broadbent.

Mr. BROADBENT. I'm trying—

Senator SKYPACK. Excuse me, Mrs., but I wonder if you know what's at stake in this situation. You realize the national defense is involved here.

Mrs. RUDD. This is my boy. This is my beautiful boy they want to take away from me. My home is ruined; the windows are all smashed.

Mr. BROADBENT. Mr. Cleary came to you—

Mrs. RUDD. What are you trying to do to me? Why do you drag me up here? Are you trying to take my boy away from me, like all the rest of them?

Senator SKYPACK. All right, all right, Mrs.

Mr. BROADBENT. —and Mr. Cleary's position was—

Senator MANSFIELD. Could we—

Senator SKYPACK. Let her stand down, Aaron. Let's get her out of here.

Mr. BROADBENT. Please, Mrs. Rudd.

Senator MANSFIELD. You're excused, Mrs. Rudd. Yes. Thank you. Would you help her out to the corridor, Mr. Broadbent?

Senator SKYPACK. I can't stand a woman sobbing like that.

Senator MANSFIELD. Seems to me you took your part in bringing it on, Jack.

Senator SKYPACK. Now come on, Aaron, you're not going to

try to play politics with these hearings, in front of the press, an audience, all that?

Senator VOYOLKO. What was the matter that lady? So upset.

Senator MANSFIELD. Is she all right now, Mr. Broadbent? Whom did you intend to call next?

Mr. BROADBENT. I will ask for Mr. Luke Wairy.

Senator MANSFIELD. Bring in Mr. Wairy. . . . Please be sworn, Mr. Wairy.

Do you solemnly swear that the testimony you are about to give before the Standing Committee on Education, Welfare, and Public Morality of the State Senate will be the truth, the whole truth, and nothing but the truth, so help you God?

Mr. WAIRY. I do.

TESTIMONY OF MR. LUKE S. WAIRY, CHAIRMAN, BOARD OF EDUCATION, TOWN OF PEQUOT

Mr. BROADBENT. Kindly identify yourself, sir, if you please, by name, residence, and occupation.

Mr. WAIRY. Luke S. Wairy, 414 Silver Hill Street, Pequot. I'm in the clock business by trade, but I suppose what is relevant here is that I'm Chairman of our School Board. That's practically an occupation in itself, gentlemen.

Mr. BROADBENT. If our information is correct, Mr. Wairy, you seem to be a man with some half-dozen occupations. Besides your own manufactory—that's the Early Bird Alarm Clock Works of Pequot, isn't it?—

Mr. WAIRY. It is, sir.

Mr. BROADBENT. Besides that concern, and the Board of Education, you may confirm to the committee, if you will, sir, that you are also a member of the vestry of the Silver Hill First Church, chairman of the Helping Hand Committee of the Lions' Club, immediate past chairman of the Red Feather Drive, past chairman of the Town Planning and Zoning Commission—I won't begin to go into the entire record, sir.

Mr. WAIRY. Well, now, that's all right, we're all citizens and Christians.

Senator MANSFIELD. I would like to say, sir, that it's an honor for us representatives of the people to have appear before us a man of such evident probity and public spirit, and such a good sound businessman, sir, as yourself. I gather you are also currently top scorer in the Treehampstead Thursday Duplicate Bridge Club.

Mr. WAIRY. I may say, Senator, that your investigators have some reputation, upstate in our area, for rigorous thoroughness, and I fear they've put their tape on me. I'm impressed.

Mr. BROADBENT. Would you fill the committee in, sir, on the basic facts about the town of Pequot—population, tax capabilities, so on?

Mr. WAIRY. We have—at the last census we had—a population of twenty-seven thousand five hundred. We have two high schools, three junior highs, and eight elementary schools; we run a K-six, seven-nine, ten-twelve school system, if you want to be technical. At the present time our tax rate is thirty-two point six mils. Frankly I believe our assessments are some years behind the times, and by and large the evaluations run only around forty per cent of true value. Personally I am deeply concerned about the trend of the town, because where you used to have a pretty fair balance of industry and real estate for your tax base, you now have these developers going ahead any old way and putting up a lot of cardboard ranchers for the young people, young breeders, and we're getting to be a bedroom town for Treehampstead, rather than keeping the growth of the grand list on an even keel all along the line. I don't like it.

Mr. BROADBENT. Thank you, sir, I believe that will do for now about the community you so ably represent. We were wondering, sir, if you would mind giving us a coherent account of the recent happenings in Pequot.

Mr. WAIRY. I will not burden your record unduly, gentlemen. I am not up on all the details. I'm not a great hand at inventing details.

Mr. BROADBENT. Since the man Wissey Jones has alleged certain so-called educational purposes, among others, for his activities, we thought—

Mr. WAIRY. Sir, we concern ourselves at Board meetings with bursted boilers. Whether the custodian can be asked to use the gang mower on the football field, that kind of thing. We don't get into educational matters near as much as some people think.

Mr. BROADBENT. Who would have the basic facts? Mr. Owing?

Mr. WAIRY. You won't get anything out of the Superintendent. We have the devil's own time at Board meetings getting him to give a dry description of anything, because he changes things around right in front of your eyes while he's picturing them. I have a standing joke about his memos being riddled with what I call his 'nearest exits.'

Senator MANSFIELD. I wonder, Mr. Wairy, if you wouldn't just begin at the beginning, tell us what you know of the events of the past week.

Mr. WAIRY. Know of my own firsthand knowledge?

Senator MANSFIELD. Or what you've heard. It doesn't particularly matter, at this stage, just so as you begin at the beginning.

Mr. WAIRY. As it happens, I did see Mr. Jones arrive in Pequot the other afternoon, let's see, my gracious, has a week flown? I was just coming out of John Ellithorp's drugstore, with John, he's a portly figure, we were chatting there on the sidewalk—you see, Pequot's laid out along the river, the Pohadnock River, which is really only about thirty foot across, though it's capable of a severe rise in the backlash of these autumnal hurricanes we've been getting, recent years; the business street, River Street, with most of the stores and also a number of tenement blocks, backs right onto it. Ellithorp's store is next to the crossing of River Street and the Treehampstead Road Bridge. There's a stop light. First thing I heard was this funny hollow popping, like a baby outboard motor being run inside an oil drum, and I looked over, and there was this Mr. Jones, as I later knew him, on his folding machine with one foot down on the street waiting for the light to change. That's a long light there. We had a bad accident two years ago, this out-of-town Caddy, personally I think intoxication was involved, Mrs. Burritt, seventy-one, gentle as a geranium, she was killed on the spot. The light finally changed, and the popping started up—I had my eyes on him all the way; he pulled up right alongside John Ellithorp and myself, and—

Mr. BROADBENT. We understand he made a very peculiar appearance.

Mr. WAIRY. Young fellow, I come from a long line of men who thought nothing of New England winters—liked 'em. We aren't intimidated by originals. We're used to originals up our way, believe my word. My grandfather was a knife sharpener, six foot nine inches, he could lift a telephone pole, played the flute nice as ever, summer evenings he'd have a big crowd of children in the street in front of his shop, playing tunes. No, sir, don't try to put me off. I like Mr. Jones. I admire him. He came to the plant and paid me a courteous call, and he was dressed like you and me, Mr. Counsel, in a regular store suit, and I commented on his previous costume upon arrival, and he said—he's outspoken, one of the qualities I value in a man— he said he's a corporation vice-president, and he owns thirty-two tailor-made suits, eighteen pairs of shoes, but he has this one moderate-priced ready-made brown suit that he wears to call on school people. Rotary wheel in the lapel buttonhole. The point is, he understands how to sell an idea. The motorcycle clothes —he's not afraid of being spattered by raindrops, that's all. I don't need to be told what I think, Mr. Counsel.

Senator MANSFIELD. You were telling about the street corner.

Mr. WAIRY. Yes. He stopped his machine and tipped this hat he was wearing, to John and myself, and I must admit, Mr. Counsel, it was a funny-looking flattish hat, and he said, 'Day, gentlemen,' he said, and then he looked straight at me, and he said, 'Sir,' he said, 'you look like you might be Chairman of the Board of Education around here.' Well, that hit me right between the lungs, you know. Later turned out it wasn't any guess, he'd done his work in advance, he knew perfectly well who I was. Here's a businessman who isn't afraid to do his homework. I admire this fellow. He's first-rate. Well, we're standing there, he wants to know about the hotel, and he's making an appointment to see me, and here comes Dr. Gozar down the sidewalk.

Mr. BROADBENT. This Dr. Gozar—

Mr. WAIRY. This Dr. Gozar is principal of Lincoln Elementary. A woman.

Mr. BROADBENT. Yes, sir, we have called Dr. Gozar to testify, the Rudd boy being in her school, and I was wondering if, for the committee's benefit, you would give us your assessment of Dr. Gozar. It would be a help.

Mr. WAIRY. Assessment?

Mr. BROADBENT. If you would tell us a bit in confidence about the people we're going to have to question on this case.

Mr. WAIRY. You mean you have the prosecutor's itch, young man, you'd like to know a few weak points you can work on?

Mr. BROADBENT. Not at all, I—

Mr. WAIRY. I don't know whether your investigators happened on *this* fact for my dossier or not, Mr. Counsel, but I once went to law school myself, and we had an expression for

17

the glint I see in your eye—the warmth of your cheeks: 'D.A. fever,' we called it. Right?

Mr. Broadbent. I don't know what you mean, sir. You were about to say, on Dr. Gozar.

Mr. Wairy. She's a great big man of a woman, and I'd say she's contented with her lot. She gives an impression—she has a constant, barking, bass laugh—that she's mighty glad to be so overwhelmingly a doctor. She's a Ph.D., that's where the 'doctor' comes from, and her doctorate is backed up by half a dozen other post-graduate degrees, because, my heavens, she takes a laborer's job in a factory every summer and goes to summer school to boot. When *she* talks about social adjustment, you can take one look at her and see that she doesn't mean the pale, wishy-washy conformism that so often seems to be intended by school psychologists who use that phrase. She's what we call an old-timer; I mean a real New Englander. She's got a traprock forehead and a granite jaw; stone ribs, too—but there's a passionate optimist living behind all that masonry. Let's see, grew up on a farm, a survivor of Elton's Seminary for Women, sixty-seven years old, been principal of Lincoln Elementary for thirty-eight years, and she's grown younger ever since I've known her, which has been most of the time she's had that job. She started out kind of hidebound, but she's wound up wise, freedom-loving, self-reliant, tolerant, and daring. And flexible. For about the last half of her tenure at Lincoln, she's demonstrated that she feels there's not any single mandatory school program for which there could be no substitute. She's a talker: she'll bend your ear! But *verbum sap.*, Mr. Counsel. I would not press her too hard. I wouldn't try to take *her* skin off, because the first thing you know, young man, she'll have broken your whipper off from your snapper.

Senator Skypack. What about the G-man? What's his name? Where does he fit in? What was that name, Broadbent?

Mr. BROADBENT. Cleary.

Mr. WAIRY. Mr. Cleary? He's an ambitious young man. I understand he grew up in Watermont, and that he's descended from an Irish immigrant who came to America in the fourth decade of the nineteenth century and spent the vigorous years of his life laying railroad tracks up the Connecticut Valley and across Massachusetts to Boston; the old boy may well have been in the gang that Thoreau mentions as putting down the road-bed along the far side of Walden Pond from his cabin. In the rare moments when Mr. Cleary alludes to his background, he's inclined to say that he didn't come from the wrong side of the railroad tracks, he came from between them. That picture pleases him, I'd imagine, because it strengthens his idea he's going someplace. The feelings of his immigrant forebears about being Irish in anti-Irish times were evidently handed down to him; I mean he seems to have a firm conviction that the world is hostile. I don't know whether he sets any store by Our Lord, but he surely believes in the Devil, whose big job, Cleary'd say, is to snatch the hindmost. Survival of the fittest, that's him—to be fit and out front is the works with him: 'in shape,' he calls it. Know what he wants? He wants recognition; he thinks mere happiness isn't worth a candle. All this makes him very useful to us as Director of Guidance in Pequot—for the time being—because at the moment we're useful to him. He'll go far—far away from guidance and Pequot, I'd guess.

Mr. BROADBENT. This is all most helpful, sir. Now, there's one other person—I understand this lady has been rather recalcitrant, been fighting the proposition the man Wissey Jones has put forward. I mean the Rudd boy's teacher, Miss Perrin. Could you tell us—

Mr. WAIRY. I know Miss Perrin a bit, I ought to, she's one of the old hands around home. She was teaching when I was in school; she taught me. Right now she's a delicate, white-haired

19

woman in her middle sixties. She's kindhearted, homey, rather old-fashioned; she seems—she's always seemed—tired and puzzled by life. She's docile, on the surface, and she'll appear to follow any policy the Super or the Board puts out, but she holds to the familiar ways of doing things, and she's leery of a lot of the newfangled educational notions. And she's got a steel backbone, believe me, fragile as she looks and acts.

Mr. BROADBENT. We understand she was in some trouble, radical activity—

Mr. WAIRY. That's all gone and forgotten, my boy. Thirty years ago! There was a depression then, people got emotional, and we've discounted what she did. I wouldn't go into that, if I were you.

Senator VOYOLKO. What about this kid? Some guy wants to buy some kid, right? What's with the kid?

Senator SKYPACK. Aaron, sometimes we sit here and we think our distinguished colleague from Winfield County isn't listening to the proceedings, and then he comes up with a question that's right in the bull's-eye. You'd think we'd forgotten what we were here to investigate, but not our enlightened friend from Winfield County!

Senator VOYOLKO. This kid. This guy wants to buy this kid.

Mr. BROADBENT. The boy, sir, Barry Rudd.

Mr. WAIRY. Well, I've heard he was pretty clever. Struck me as a mouth breather the one time I saw him close up. His upper lip is rather short, his large upper teeth are tilted slightly forward, and the mouth tends to sag open. It's a habit that detracts a little from the reputation for quickness. Personally I wouldn't hire—

Mr. BROADBENT. Do you know, then, why Mr. Wissey Jones, whom you have pictured as an outstanding businessman, wanted to buy him?

Mr. WAIRY. We have only Mr. Jones's word—and look here,

young fellow, don't try to sneak thoughts into my head that aren't there.

Senator MANSFIELD. Mr. Broadbent, you're way off the track again. This is extremely frustrating. Mr. Wairy was trying to put together a straight account. We left him on the corner there with Mr. Jones and Dr. Gozar and that druggist, and you come along—

Senator SKYPACK. Wait a minute, Aaron. I'd like to hear some more about the proposition myself; you can't have your ducks in a row for every shot, Aaron. Now, sir, just what was this purchase supposed to be about?

Mr. WAIRY. Well, it was most extraordinary, Senator, a daring innovation in human engineering, as I understand it. I just got a sniff or two of it. I think I should leave the details to the man himself. I really don't know much about it. He's been secretive, you know.

Senator VOYOLKO. About this bomb.

Mr. WAIRY. I beg your pardon?

Senator SKYPACK. We understood there was a bombing down there.

Mr. WAIRY. You must mean the little stink bomb at the lecture.

Senator MANSFIELD. For shame, Mr. Broadbent!

Senator VOYOLKO. Who they fling it at?

Mr. WAIRY. It was at a clarifying lecture by the State Supervisor for—

Senator MANSFIELD. Mr. Broadbent, you really must curb—

Mr. BROADBENT. We'll develop this aspect a little later, Mr. Chairman, and we'll—

Senator SKYPACK. There was mention of other incidents, Broadbent.

Mr. BROADBENT. The compromising situation of the boy, Barry Rudd, with the young lady, the mortician's daughter,

Miss Renzulli, sir, would you tell us—?

Mr. WAIRY. These are ten-year-old children, young fellow. You make it sound . . . You'd better ask Dr. Gozar and Miss Perrin about all that.

Mr. BROADBENT. About the assault on the Rudd home. Here are these decent working people sitting quietly in their home at night, and out of nowhere—

Mr. WAIRY. I'm not the man to ask about such things. Ask the proper authorities. We have law-enforcement officers in Pequot, sir. We may be off the main throughways, but we don't live in the Middle Ages, you know.

Mr. BROADBENT. Sir, I think you rather shrugged off the question of the man Wissey Jones's motive for making this and similar purchases. There's a possibility of a morals line here, and we can't afford to dodge it.

Mr. WAIRY. Morals? I thought it was a matter of dollars and cents.

Senator SKYPACK. Look, Wairy, you heard the committee counsel warn you not to duck this just because it smells bad.

Mr. BROADBENT. Do you seriously and sincerely believe, Mr. Wairy, that the purpose of Mr. Jones's transaction was quote educational unquote? I mean when a man in his late thirties goes around buying ten-year-old boys.

Mr. WAIRY. We have what the man says. I have no reason, in the way of firsthand knowledge, to question his word, nor have I any reason to believe it—of my own sure knowledge, that is.

Mr. BROADBENT. Thank you, Mr. Wairy, you may step aside.

Senator MANSFIELD. The committee wants to express its gratitude for you coming up here, a busy, successful man, and testifying for us, and we assuredly thank you, sir. And I certainly hope you won't have taken any offense over—

Mr. BROADBENT. I will call Mr. Wissey Jones.

Senator MANSFIELD. Please stand for your oath, Mr. Jones.

22

Do you solemnly swear that the testimony you will give here before us will be the truth, the whole truth, and nothing but the truth, so help you God?

Mr. JONES. Yes, I swear it will be so.

TESTIMONY OF MR. WISSEY JONES,
OF UNITED LYMPHOMILLOID CORPORATION

Mr. BROADBENT. Please identify yourself for our record, sir.

Mr. JONES. Wissey Jones. Vice-President, United Lymphomilloid of America, Incorporated, in charge of materials procurement.

Mr. BROADBENT. You regard small boys as 'materials'?

Mr. JONES. Yes, sir. Indeed we do, sir.

Mr. BROADBENT. Sir, I will put it to you directly. Have you ever been booked on a morals charge?

Mr. JONES. I beg your pardon?

Senator SKYPACK. I think you heard him, mister.

Mr. JONES. Mr. Chairman, I think these subordinates of yours ought to know that my duties have an extremely high national-defense rating. I agreed to come up here—

Senator MANSFIELD. What a way to start, Mr. Broadbent! I really would suggest that you begin at the beginning for once.

Mr. BROADBENT. We have a responsibility—

Senator MANSFIELD. You heard Mr. Wairy's endorsement of Mr. Jones as a top businessman in the country, whom he admires. There's such a thing as common courtesy, Mr. Counsel.

Senator SKYPACK. All right, Broadbent, us 'subordinates' can come back to that stuff later.

Senator MANSFIELD. Senator Skypack is no subordinate but a co-equal colleague of mine, Mr. Jones, an able elected State Senator from Sudbury County. Only by virtue of a modicum of seniority—

Mr. Jones. I humbly beg your pardon, Senator.

Senator Skypack. All right.

Mr. Broadbent. Our Chairman, sir, desires that you begin at the beginning. Would you tell us what your first act was on your arrival in Pequot?

Mr. Jones. I requested and obtained an interview with the Superintendent of Schools, Willard Owing.

Mr. Broadbent. You didn't bathe and change first?

Senator Mansfield. Now, Mr. Broadbent.

Mr. Broadbent. Well, Mr. Chairman, you put me on a spot. Exactly where is the beginning of things?

Senator Mansfield. Spare your sarcasm, Mr. Counsel. Please proceed, Mr. Jones, as you were going. We invite as much detail as you care to give.

Mr. Broadbent. Where did this meeting with Mr. Owing take place, sir?

Mr. Jones. The school administration offices in Pequot are in a former private house, or mansion, on, I believe, Second Street, a big Victorian affair with a widow's walk on an octagonal tower above the roof. I am told Mr. Owing can be seen up there on the widow's walk some evenings after closing time, pacing back and forth in the fresh air and trying to think up ways of avoiding decisions. That's his reputation, anyway. In the rooms of the house there are ornate fireplaces of pink Vermont marble, and the floors creak so loudly that I judge very little deep thinking can be done in there. There's a smell all through the house of mimeograph ink, and the rattle of the buzzer and the clicking of the jacks of the telephone switchboard in the foyer can be heard upstairs and down. I want to give you a picture of a school system informed with rectitude, paper progress, safe activity, hesitation. The roofs of all the school buildings in Pequot are pitched; no modernistic chicken coops—

Mr. Broadbent. Your interview with Mr. Owing, when was this?

Mr. JONES. Thursday morning, October seventeenth, of this year, at nine oh four *ante meridian.*

Mr. BROADBENT. I take it the appointment was for nine o'clock.

Mr. JONES. I am always punctual. I may say I have been kept cooling my heels by certain other superintendents for far more than the four minutes Mr. Owing made me wait. I was ushered in by the receptionist-telephonist.

Senator SKYPACK. Listen, Jones, do you always buy ten-year-old boys?

Mr. JONES. Not at all, sir. Within the past month I have bought two excellent female specimens, eleven and thirteen years of age, respectively. It is true that the majority are males.

Senator MANSFIELD. Please, Jack. We were just getting onto a straight line for once. Kindly go on, sir; you were admitted to the Superintendent's office, and—

Mr. BROADBENT. What took place, Mr. Jones?

Mr. JONES. I was led in there, and I would say he looked satisfied. He was sitting behind his desk in a white-paneled room, a cheerful place, with his back to two big French windows, floor-to-ceiling almost, and their metal Venetian blinds sliced the morning sunlight into layers. Did I say he looked satisfied? Seemed he might bust. Everything about him was too tight: his collar, armpits of his coat, his vest—the buttons and buttonholes on it made a trail of parentheses down his chest and belly. Veins stood inflated on the backs of his hands, on his neck, and in the middle of his forehead. He gave an impression of a man containing a superabundance of oxygen, or maybe helium. He wasn't fat; he was just too well filled, and I vouch that what he was stuffed with was uncertainty. He looks like a naturally healthy animal, but I understand that people around town call him a politician. He's elusive, that's the point. Mr. Cleary, the Guidance Director, told me one of his colleagues once complained to him, after an interview with Mr. Owing, that he

25

couldn't make out just what the Superintendent had been driving at, and Mr. Cleary told me he said, 'Nobody ever can. He's never what you think he is. Just when you think you have him pinned down as a worm he flies away as a moth.' It's apparently impossible to hold him to anything he says, because he either denies having said it or declares on a stack of Bibles that that wasn't what he had meant. I don't intend to cast doubt on his integrity. No, I'm told he brings to everything he does a prodigious sincerity and decency which are crippling. A man just can't put that much energy into *wanting* to do the right thing and do it, too. His indecisiveness shows itself not only on school issues but also in trifles. I took him to lunch the other day, and you should have seen him trying to decide what to eat. He wrestled with the menu as if it had been a two-hundred-pound man.

Mr. BROADBENT. On the occasion of your first interview—

Mr. JONES. Yes. I began by asking Mr. Owing what sort of provisions are made in the Pequot schools for children of the particular kind I buy. He was, at first, very cautious. 'I'm afraid of anything too special for these clever children,' he said to me. 'I'm afraid of it for our community. We don't like anything that smacks of privilege. But don't worry,' he said, 'we'll reach these children. We'll take care of 'em with enrichment.' Phooey! Enrichment! He made it sound as if schools were bakeries and children were loaves. I may as well tell you at the outset, gentlemen, I have nothing but contempt for the wordy soft-heartedness, or maybe I should say -headedness, of the educational world, in which a simple spade is commonly called an Instrument for Soil Development. Mr. Owing was leaning back in his swivel chair, and he was toying with a pair of binoculars. Through the venetian blinds behind him I could see, beyond a stretch of lawn, the backs of three white houses, and at first I assumed that Mr. Owing was an office-hour voyeur, but a little later in our conversation I saw in the yard a feeding station around which a number of birds were playing who had a curious way of clinging to the wood, heads downward, looking out nervously at the dangerous world. He was a Watcher. I asked him what the birds were. 'Nuthatches,' he said. 'White-breasted. I think so anyway. I'm not positive. We have a child,' he said, 'of the kind that interests you. He can tell you the family, genus, species, and subspecies of every bird—every living thing you could imagine. In Latin.' And that was the first I heard of the Rudd boy. But of course the moment I expressed interest in him, Mr. Owing backed off. Began giving me the on-the-other-hand treatment. Afraid he'd gone too far. Mr. Owing never asked why I was interested, or what my errand was. I guess he assumed I was just another teacher working on a doctoral thesis so as to get ahead. He said he thought he'd better turn me over to the Guidance Director—a likable young man, he said, certainly a useful man, he said, on what he calls, with a characteristic parsimoniousness of imagination, his 'educational team.'

Mr. BROADBENT. You mean to say he at no time asked you the actual purpose of your visit?

Mr. JONES. Not at that interview.

Mr. BROADBENT. And it did not occur to you to force this information on him?

Mr. JONES. Indeed it did. At the end of our talk I expressed interest in buying one or more of a certain category of children. I didn't tell him the whole story then. I had measured Mr. Owing—as a matter of fact, I had had some briefing information beforehand, tabbing him—as a vacillator. He was liable to turn to all sides for help if a difficult problem was thrown at him, and to talk indiscriminately. And what I wanted least of all was talk, until I'd had time to look around and be ready to jump. Later, of course, I gave Mr. Owing the full picture, but by then complications had set in.

Senator MANSFIELD. When you say 'buy,' I suppose you mean that you actually buy the child from its parents?

Mr. JONES. It's not quite that simple, sir. Everyone who has the slightest hold on a child that I begin to dicker for asks—and usually gets—a price.

Mr. BROADBENT. So Mr. Owing sent you down the line to Mr. Cleary.

Mr. JONES. What I needed most at that starting point was an ally, and Mr. Cleary—

Senator SKYPACK. Was willing to do your dirty work for you?

Mr. JONES. At the beginning Mr. Cleary was rather interfering. He took it upon himself, without my knowledge, to meddle with the Rudd family. Later he was more co-operative. Much more.

Mr. BROADBENT. You told Mr. Cleary your whole story?

Mr. JONES. I saw in Mr. Cleary a man more interested in advancement than in ideas. He's the sort of man you can trust.

Mr. BROADBENT. You saw this right away?

Mr. JONES. My business is sizing people up.

Mr. BROADBENT. And Mr. Cleary?

Mr. JONES. Is a realist. He distrusts emotion of any kind. Explains exuberance in himself by the keenness of the weather, the lack of humidity in the air; depression or a feeling of shame he can attribute to a pork chop he ate for lunch. He wants to get ahead—to be boss. Once he got the idea that I, too, am a pretty hardheaded fellow, he opened up to me all the way—told me all about how to 'get along' in Pequot, about his 'system.' He does people great favors; he's solicitous; he helps people plan their futures; he drags confessions out of them; he terrifies them with psychiatric 'insights'; he lends them money, serves them cocktails, tells them secrets, flatters them with intellectual argument. He also knows how to manage people by getting the goods on them.

28

Senator MANSFIELD. Dear me! This was to be your ally, Mr. Jones?

Mr. JONES. Absolutely dependable, Senator. No idealism whatsoever.

Senator SKYPACK. Listen, Jones. We understand you arrived in Pequot on a foreign motorcycle. Is that right?

Mr. JONES. That's correct. Yes, sir. I ride it everywhere.

Senator SKYPACK. Why?

Mr. JONES. Why? Because it gives me extreme pleasure. I have a sensation of flying, skimming along over the highways on those thin whirling wire spokes.

Senator SKYPACK. Sir, Mr. Broadbent tells me that our investigator down in Pequot reports that three motorcycles were involved in the gang attack on the Rudd home. Was yours one of them?

Mr. JONES. I'm afraid I don't know what you're talking about, Senator.

Senator SKYPACK. You say that like somebody who knows exactly what I'm talking about. I want to know—

Senator VOYOLKO. This kid, now. You the guy's buying the kid?

Mr. JONES. I am, sir, if I am successful in—

Senator VOYOLKO. O.K. So you're the guy's buying the kid. Now we're getting someplace. What's with the kid? This boy.

Mr. JONES. What about him, sir?

Senator VOYOLKO. You tell me, mister. How about him?

Mr. JONES. Barry Rudd is fifty-six and three eighths inches tall, medium height for his age. Weighs ninety-eight pounds, nine ounces, compared with a norm for the age of seventy-seven pounds. Twenty-two pounds overweight, other words. Lung capacity one hundred twenty-eight inches, where the standard is one twenty-five. Shoulders twelve and one half inches across, average for the age. Strength of grip thirty-six point four pounds compared with a norm of fifty point four. Right shoulder slightly lower than the left.

Senator MANSFIELD. You make him sound like a cut of veal, Mr. Jones.

Mr. JONES. Not at all. There's a flame. . . . Let me tell you: The face belongs to a beardless old man. It is round, ruddy, and impassive, and when words that stand for strong feelings pass the short, tight lips, only a flicker of expression, like distant heat lightning, can be seen around the eyes, which are startlingly clear, direct, and alert.

Mr. BROADBENT. Is this boy of the kind and caliber that you want?

Mr. JONES. He definitely is.

Mr. BROADBENT. Can you tell us why you want him?

Mr. JONES. One of his former teachers put it better than I could. Or I think perhaps it was Dr. Gozar, his principal, you know. 'Why is he outstanding?' she said. 'Because he has this mood of intensity. That you don't teach. You don't say, "Flex. Tighten your mind. Have desire." Barry,' she said, 'makes this mood about science more than any child I've ever seen. He creates a certain tension out of nothing—a sense of excitement. That comes from within—and the funny thing is, you can't really see it on the surface.' That's what she said, and that's why I want him.

Mr. BROADBENT. What do you think of his misbehavior with the Renzulli girl? Would you—

Mr. JONES. That has nothing to do with me.

Mr. BROADBENT. To the contrary, Mr. Jones. Barry Rudd, when asked by our investigator what had caused him to get in that particular pickle, said, and these were his words, 'I did it on account of Mr. Jones.' And that is all he would say. How do you explain . . . ?

Senator SKYPACK. Broadbent, let's us subordinates hold back on that angle till the proper time.

Mr. BROADBENT. Very good, Senator. I withdraw the question. On another point, Mr. Jones, you think very highly of Miss Perrin, the Rudd boy's teacher, don't you?

Mr. JONES. She's a perfectly adequate old-fashioned teacher; she has the knack to a fair degree. I'd say that.

Mr. BROADBENT. You're sure you wouldn't go farther?

Mr. JONES. Not much. Miss Perrin teaches not by the book but by an instinctive anecdotal method. She's warm and loving, and mostly she's loved by the children, though dark and dangerous images keep creeping into her stories in class. She tends to buck at newfangled pedagoguery, but she's always mild and never sure. She seems to have a lot of the vagueness, the uncertainty as to exactly what's going on around her, of Nikolai Dmitrievitch Levin in *Anna Karenina*. Do you have time to read, Mr. Counsel?

Mr. BROADBENT. In college—

Mr. JONES. She's not hideously ugly, but she's not very good-looking, either. During my visits I noted a number of mistakes, slips, some absent-mindedness. I must say she treats her pupils as adults, though she speaks in a sing-song syllabic voice, as if she's reading out of a primer.

Mr. BROADBENT. You speak of her pretty coolly, sir, but I put it to you, sir, did you not buy her an expensive gift last week?

Mr. JONES. Mr. Chairman, is this sort of question—

Senator MANSFIELD. It may be. It may not be. What are you developing, Mr. Broadbent?

Mr. BROADBENT. I am going to step over there by you, Mr. Jones, and I am going to ask you to identify this booklet. I lay before you now this notebook, or booklet, and ask you to identify it. What is it?

Mr. JONES. Where did you get that?

Mr. BROADBENT. It is a small notebook, of thin blue paper, navy-blue leatherette cover with gold impressed markings. Please simply identify it.

31

Mr. JONES. You know perfectly well what that is: It's my expense-account book. It says *Expense Account* right there on the front, with my initials. When did you steal that off me?

Mr. BROADBENT. I would point out, Mr. Jones, that there is an item entered here—'Gift, Miss Perrin, $125.' That's a substantial gift, sir.

Senator MANSFIELD. What are you trying to suggest, Mr. Counsel? Miss Perrin's getting on. Mr. Wairy pointed that out. She's a gray-haired lady.

Mr. BROADBENT. I'm suggesting that that's a rather large gift, Mr. Jones.

Mr. JONES. I needed her on my side.

Mr. BROADBENT. I see here that on last Friday's date you entered in your expense account an item of six dollars for an office visit to a doctor.

Mr. JONES. I had a headache after my conversation with the Guidance Director. I think you would have, too.

Mr. BROADBENT. What doctor did you visit?

Mr. JONES. I didn't actually see a doctor.

Mr. BROADBENT. But you entered an item in your expense account.

Mr. JONES. As a lawyer, sir, and a rather young one, if I may be forgiven for saying so, you might not realize that with tax laws the way they are, the corporation executive—

Mr. BROADBENT. I get it. Did your headache clear up all right?

Mr. JONES. Thank you, it did. Immediately after making the entry in my expense-account book.

Mr. BROADBENT. Fiscal therapy?

Mr. JONES. Never knew it to do any harm.

Mr. BROADBENT. I see here another item. 'Entertaining parents —$78.93.' Can you spend that much out on the town in Pequot, sir?

Mr. JONES. Again, it was a matter of wanting—

Mr. BROADBENT. Of bribery, sir?

Mr. JONES. Mr. Chairman, I submit to you that this young gentleman—

Senator SKYPACK. Is no gentleman? No, sir, nor is this a tea-and-ladyfingers party, sir. Just what was to be the purpose of your buying this boy, Mr. Jones? I think it's time you came clean.

Mr. BROADBENT. Excuse me, Senator Skypack, before you get into that. I respectfully suggest to the Chairman that this document, or book, which I have laid before Mr. Jones, which he has identified, be admitted into the record.

Senator MANSFIELD. It will be entered into the record.

(The document referred to was marked 'Jones Exhibit No. 1' and filed.)

Senator SKYPACK. And now, Mr. Jones.

Mr. JONES. My purpose? I buy brains. When a commodity that you need falls in short supply, you have to get out and hustle. I buy brains. About eighteen months ago my company, United Lymphomilloid of America, Incorporated, was faced with an extremely difficult problem, a project, a long-range government contract, fifty years, highly specialized and top secret, and we needed some of the best minds in the country, and we looked around, and we found some minds that had certainly been excellent at one time, but they'd been spoiled by education. By what passes for education. Our schools, particularly at the elementary and secondary levels, speak with great confidence of their 'solutions' for what they call the 'gifted'—though there seems to be little or no agreement as to the exact nature of this category. There's a great deal of time spent on these so-called solutions, which are for the most part based on psychological and sociological theories and data between twenty and fifty years old, but no one seems to know what really works. One school says special classes, another says acceleration, an-

33

other says enrichment. No one knows. They argue back and forth. Well, we have the answer at United Lymphomilloid.

Senator SKYPACK. And it is?

Mr. JONES. Do you think I'm insane, Senator? In front of this gallery? And the press?

Senator MANSFIELD. We will go into Executive Session. We will reconvene in my inner office, Room 417A, in five minutes, gentlemen.

(The committee retired to the designated room and came to order, in Executive Session, at 11:18 a.m.)

Senator MANSFIELD. We will be in order. Now, Mr. Jones, perhaps you will feel able—

Mr. JONES. I will say this much. The reason U. Lympho— that's what we who work there call the company for short—the reason U. Lympho wants to get brains early is connected with a basic difficulty a brilliant youngster has in this country. At an astonishingly early age he goes through a quest for meaning, for values, for the significance of life, and this quest turns, also early, into a struggle to make a place in society and to find values in it that will meet his particular needs. I hardly have to tell you that the culture in which we live is riddled with inconsistencies, from the point of view of a child with a quick mind, who sees that he is punished more than he is rewarded for his brilliance. A bitter inner inharmony results. The individual expends so much emotional energy trying to resolve this inharmony that, having started out in primary and elementary school years the most normal and well adjusted of all his peers, he winds up, before very long, the least so. Our system at United Lymphomilloid is to get the brains early and eliminate this conflict altogether.

Senator SKYPACK. And how is that done, sir?

Mr. JONES. I'm sorry, Senator, but this is a matter of security. With a stenographer—

Senator MANSFIELD. Off the record. You may step outside a few minutes, Miss Bean.

(Discussion off the record.)

Senator MANSFIELD. All right, Miss Bean, you may resume. On the record.

Senator SKYPACK. I want, personally and on behalf of my constituents in Sudbury County, to thank you, Mr. Jones. You've been a most co-operative witness. It's a thoroughly patriotic scheme. I'm sure my colleagues—

Senator MANSFIELD. We all understand that this is in confidence. I mean, so much as a whisper outside this room.

Senator SKYPACK. Impressive, Mr. Jones. Great business.

Senator MANSFIELD. Senator Voyolko, you clearly understand—

Senator VOYOLKO. Huh?

Senator SKYPACK. Keep the big mouth shut.

Senator VOYOLKO. Sure, sure, sure.

Senator MANSFIELD. We will stand recessed until after lunch.

(Whereupon, at 12:10 p.m., Friday, October 25, 19—, the hearing was recessed.)

AFTERNOON SESSION

(The hearing was resumed in Committee Chamber 202 at 2:30 p.m.)

Senator MANSFIELD. We will have order now. Proceed, Mr. Broadbent.

Mr. BROADBENT. I will ask for Mr. Willard Owing.

Senator MANSFIELD. Please stand to be sworn, Mr. Owing.

Do you solemnly swear that the testimony you will give in the matter pending before the Standing Committee on Education, Welfare, and Public Morality of the State Senate will be the truth, the whole truth, and nothing but the truth, so help you God?

Mr. OWING. I do.

TESTIMONY OF WILLARD OWING,
SUPERINTENDENT OF SCHOOLS, TOWN OF PEQUOT

Mr. BROADBENT. Please identify yourself, sir.

Mr. OWING. It is a pleasure to be here, gentlemen. It is rare enough for the educator and the legislator to sit face to face.

Mr. BROADBENT. The record will show that you are Mr. Willard Owing, Superintendent of Schools in the township of Pequot, if you have no objection.

Mr. OWING. Glad to be here. Eager to help.

Mr. BROADBENT. We understand that you were the first person the man Wissey Jones came to see in Pequot.

Mr. OWING. Gentlemen, I hope you lawmakers will come down and visit us, come back to school, teach us about democracy.

Mr. BROADBENT. Mr. Jones put his proposition to you?

Mr. OWING. He was most congenial, sir. We had a pleasant talk about provisions for the gifted.

Mr. BROADBENT. He outlined the deal he wanted to make?

Mr. OWING. Under most circumstances, I told him, enrichment in the ordinary classroom, in the heterogeneous group—

Mr. BROADBENT. I put this question to you: Did he tell you what he wanted?

Mr. OWING. He seemed rather ill-informed on our recent thinking about the developmental process. On the other hand, he was friendly, distinctly friendly. A constructive approach.

Mr. BROADBENT. Mr. Chairman, I—

Senator MANSFIELD. Please try to answer the questions, Mr. Owing.

Mr. OWING. Of course. Willingly, Senator. Anything.

Mr. BROADBENT. Did Mr. Wissey Jones tell you he wanted to buy a young boy?

Mr. OWING. I want to help in any way I can.

Mr. BROADBENT. Mr. Owing, sir, would you kindly tell us your understanding of the man Wissey Jones's plan?

Mr. OWING. He seems bitterly opposed to enrichment. I couldn't get at the reason. It seemed to be a matter of emotion, like so many parents we have coming in. Mind you, we have an exceptionally fine type of parent in my little bailiwick.

Mr. BROADBENT. Sir—

Senator SKYPACK. Listen, Owing, answer the man!

Mr. OWING. My dear Senator, I am most eager to help.

Mr. BROADBENT. The man Wissey Jones, under oath before

this committee, testified that you were the first person he saw in Pequot, and that he outlined to you his plan to buy a child, and that you turned him over to Mr. Cleary. Is this—?

Mr. OWING. Mr. Cleary is a strong believer in enrichment, if I'm not mistaken; dead set against acceleration. . . .

Senator SKYPACK. Look here, Owing, we understand Cleary's a schemer.

Mr. OWING. He's a planner, if that's what you mean, sir. No one in the town school system, including me, can take on a complex problem of curriculum or budget or transportation and effect a tidier schedule of operations, combining practical foresight with an unerring avoidance of criticism from tax-payers. He can see pitfalls from a year's distance. Oh, I bank on him.

Mr. BROADBENT. You talked to Cleary shortly after your interview with Mr. Jones? You made a special trip to Lincoln Elementary for this purpose. Is that correct? You hurried over there—

Mr. OWING. I'd like to ask my Board to promote Mr. Cleary to Assistant Superintendent; he has the qualities—agressive, superlative organizer, respected by the teachers. On the other hand, of course, what holds me back is that I sometimes feel a slight undertow there, a troublemaking tendency.

Senator SKYPACK. You mean he's one of the hotheads that are stirring the whole thing up? He might be responsible for the violence?

Mr. OWING. I didn't mean quite that.

Mr. BROADBENT. I think you did. That's what you suggested.

Mr. OWING. No, really, that's your implication. Or do I mean inference? Goodness, sometimes I wonder.

Senator SKYPACK. You called him a troublemaker.

Mr. OWING. Not exactly.

Senator SKYPACK. Did you or didn't you call him a trouble-maker?

38

Mr. Owing. The point is, the violence, as you call it, is quite outside the authority of the school system. If we asked our schools to take on matters that properly belong in the home, the church, the town hall—

Mr. Broadbent. Do you have any idea who was behind the assault on the Rudd home?

Mr. Owing. I will say this to you: I think Mr. Cleary *may* have caused some trouble by short-cutting things, by going directly to the Rudd family after my briefing without waiting to talk with the child buyer. I mean, on the basis of the information I was able to give him—

Mr. Broadbent. And that this may have had some connection with the night attack by a gang of hoodlums on the Rudd family home?

Mr. Owing. No, no, I didn't say that.

Mr. Broadbent. Can you give us an account of the attack?

Mr. Owing. All I meant was that Mr. Cleary was hasty. Or may have been.

Mr. Broadbent. You don't believe he was behind the assault?

Mr. Owing. As I understand it, all or most of the windows were broken. Some sort of ordure or slop was poured down the chimney. I was telephoned by the police at nigh onto midnight, I was dead to the world, I thank God for the talent for sound sleep even after a parlous day. Let's see, it must have taken place at about eight, nine. The police had succeeded in capturing only one person—running away down the street; and you'll never guess who that was.

Mr. Broadbent. We know, sir, who it was.

Mr. Owing. Barry Rudd.

Mr. Broadbent. Yes, we knew that. On another point: We understand that Miss Perrin, the Rudd boy's teacher, has been strongly opposed to Mr. Jones's purchase of this boy. Why would that be, sir?

Mr. Owing. Imagine my astonishment when I heard that that

39

young genius, with his enigmatic face, was in jail like a common criminal! But I thought, you never can tell with these precocious ones—

Mr. BROADBENT. Why are some people fighting this excellent proposition?

Mr. OWING. She's a fine, patriotic lady. She has the Declaration of Independence and the Bill of Rights tacked on the underside of every desk top in her room.

Senator SKYPACK. That second thing you mentioned there, Bill of Rights, isn't that where they have all those amendments? The Fifth Amendment's in that, isn't it, Broadbent?

Mr. BROADBENT. The first ten amendments, I believe—

Senator SKYPACK. You call that patriotic, Owing? Holding up the Fifth Amendment to every kid?

Mr. BROADBENT. Mr. Owing, do you call what she is alleged to have done in fomenting and leading a teachers' strike, some years back—a strike, in effect, against taxpayers and little children—you call that patriotic, sir? But on another point, Mr. Owing, about this bomb that was thrown—

Senator MANSFIELD. Mr. Broadbent!

Mr. BROADBENT. About this stink bomb that was thrown, could you tell us—

Mr. OWING. Miss Perrin has always—

Senator MANSFIELD. I must say, Mr. Owing—

Mr. OWING. It came in a window. As near as we can make out, it was lobbed in one of the auditorium windows from the asphalt playground outside. It landed about four feet in front of the apron of the stage, and it made a yellow cloud. Phui! I never!

Mr. BROADBENT. Have you any theory as to who might have—

Mr. OWING. You were asking about Mr. Wissey Jones and enrichment—

40

Mr. BROADBENT. Mr. Chairman, I give up. Uncle.

Senator MANSFIELD. Thank you, Mr. Owing, you may be excused. We appreciate your coming up here to testify.

Mr. OWING. Enrichment—

Senator SKYPACK. Is there a bailiff? Could we have a bailiff?

Senator MANSFIELD. Mr. Broadbent, kindly escort Mr. Owing . . . Yes. That's it. Thank you.

Senator VOYOLKO. Who was that fella?

Senator MANSFIELD. Thank you, Mr. Broadbent. And now.

Mr. BROADBENT. We will hear Mr. Sean Cleary.

Senator MANSFIELD. Please be sworn, Mr. Cleary.

Do you solemnly swear that the testimony you will offer will be the truth, the whole truth, and nothing but the truth, so help you God?

Mr. CLEARY. Yes, I do.

TESTIMONY OF MR. SEAN CLEARY,
DIRECTOR OF GUIDANCE, TOWN OF PEQUOT

Mr. BROADBENT. Please identify yourself for the record as to name, residence, and occupation, sir.

Mr. CLEARY. I'm Sean Cleary, 221 Second Street, Pequot, and I'm Director of Guidance for the public schools of that community.

Mr. BROADBENT. You call yourself Director of Guidance. Exactly what does that mean, sir?

Mr. CLEARY. Well, I was trained as a vocational-guidance counsellor, I got my M.A. in education at Perkins State Teachers, studied under Professor Sender, head of the vocational-guidance department, and I met the State requirements in vocational guidance by holding a job as a stamp-press operator in the Northeastern States Bottle Cap Corporation in

41

Treehampstead for six months. In other words, I was an expert in how to help high-school students decide what career to follow, how to train for it, how to get a job. So then I was hired into the Pequot system, and I was assigned not only vocational guidance but also psychological guidance for the high school, as well as psychological guidance at Lincoln Elementary, where my office is situated, in a former coat closet. I have seven hundred twenty students. I am also in charge of audio-visual and driver training. I coach basketball. I monitor the library study hall. I—

Mr. BROADBENT. What exactly do you do in what you call psychological guidance?

Mr. CLEARY. I give psychological tests, I.Q. tests, so on. Then I also have to do a great deal of nursemaiding of both children and mothers, and I give parents what we call parent-teacher therapy. Among students I am supposed to solve and cure insubordination, gold-bricking, dullness of mind, smoking, drinking, sexual promiscuity, law fracture, money madness, suicidal selfishness, aggression, contempt for property, want of moral anchorage, fear of failure and of fear.

Mr. BROADBENT. Have you had psychological training?

Mr. CLEARY. There hasn't been time for that as yet. Or money—the taxpayers are rather hostile to the *idea* of guidance.
. . . I hope to get an in-service credit in play therapy this next semester, and after that, who knows? Of course I have tried to read whatever I could. I have had to become an unwilling student of abnormal psychology, and I may say, Mr. Chairman, I am constantly on the alert for signs of lunacy in everyone with whom I come into contact. This very minute . . .

Senator MANSFIELD. I see. Yes. Very interesting. Are you—

Mr. CLEARY. Sometimes, I must confess, I feel a sort of whirl of vertigo, and I have a thrust of suspicion that I myself am bats and that what seems to be madness in the people with whom I am conversing—

Senator MANSFIELD. Yes, yes, fascinating, yes.

Mr. CLEARY. —is only my own insanity which I project onto them.

Senator MANSFIELD. I see. Yes. Surely. Dear me. Senator Voyolko, do you have any questions?

Senator VOYOLKO. Huh?

Mr. BROADBENT. Now, Mr. Cleary.

Senator MANSFIELD. There was something I wanted to say. . . . Oh, yes. Mr. Broadbent, I suppose that after our last witness even you will welcome some consecutive testimony. I mean, something in a straight line.

Mr. BROADBENT. I was just going . . . Now, Mr. Cleary, would you search your memory and begin with the very first thing that happened on the morning of the day you met the man Wissey Jones?

Mr. CLEARY. Hmm. Dr. Gozar. Yes. Before school I had a talk with Dr. Gozar, our principal at Lincoln. We were standing out on the grounds, waiting for the first bell. It was one of those October days we have around here when the sky's like a thin plastic balloon; the maple trees were turning to gold and the dogwoods were already bronze. We were lounging against the jungle gym on the playlot, and we had to speak up to hear each other, because some of the older boys' voices over next the blank auditorium wall were like bugles. Dr. Gozar stood with her back to the steel-pipe frame, her arms raised and spread, gripping two high pipes with her hands. She's in her late sixties, but she made a picture of health and confidence, I tell you. She has the shape of a thirty-year-old woman, and with her arms pulled back that way . . . She has an oval head set on a strong neck. White teeth—her own, I believe.

Mr. BROADBENT. And you and she were having a discussion.

Mr. CLEARY. We were talking about the talent search I had been conducting, which had in fact been my idea to begin with. Now, to give you the background on my own point of view, I think I should tell you I flatter myself that I'm a realist. I think the worst I can call anyone is 'naïve' or 'emotional.' This is a tough world, and I've come to regard all gentle and soft feelings, my own more than anyone else's, as slop, bushwa, naïveté, sentimentality, and what confounds people who don't agree with me, like Dr. Gozar, is that I'm so often right. I won't say always. It's a jungle world, and I'm dedicated to being as tough as I can, or seeming so, anyway. I'm not afraid of anything except blushing. Quite frankly, the decisive things in this world are position and money, and of these two the former is by far the more important, because money, though it may help with appearances, can never buy prestige or a real power to manipulate. Money power is bogus; that's why so many rich people are unhappy. Command is the only really satisfying wealth.

Mr. BROADBENT. You mentioned that you were discussing the talent search with Dr. Gozar.

Mr. CLEARY. I assume that you want me to be frank with you, so I'll simply say that Dr. Gozar was getting nosey about it. She wanted to know how I ever got the School Board to fall for it, and I explained that I had, on my own initiative, dug up support for the project from a foundation, so it wouldn't cost the taxpayers a cent; that appealed to Mr. Wairy, the chairman of our Board, in a big way. My original idea was to identify the neurotic youngsters, so we could open a parent-child clinic, but the Foundation for National Superiority in Education, which sponsors the project, felt that there should be a slightly different emphasis, and since it was providing the cash—

Mr. BROADBENT. How do you actually carry out the talent search?

Mr. CLEARY. Well, the Pequot Talent Search is hunting for

the top one per cent of the gifted and the bottom twenty per cent of the retarded in our community.

Senator MANSFIELD. And you still call it a *talent* search?

Mr. CLEARY. Mr. Owing persuaded the Foundation to include the retarded because he knew we'd never get it by the School Board and the community if we didn't take the hardship cases into account. Undemocratic.

Mr. BROADBENT. How are you finding your talented children?

Mr. CLEARY. We have tests for intellectual gifts, as well as subjective screening for talents in music, painting, dramatics, dance, pottery—

Senator SKYPACK. Pottery!

Mr. CLEARY. We have a Talent Commission of leading citizens. Mrs. Ferrenhigh happens to have a pottery wheel. She—

Mr. BROADBENT. Go on, please.

Mr. CLEARY. We also have tests for creativity, leadership, aggressive maladjustment, and potential alcoholism. The Foundation left these last two in, from my original apparatus, as recognition of my contribution.

Mr. BROADBENT. What was your disagreement with Dr. Gozar?

Mr. CLEARY. We had several differences, but mainly she objected to one of the tests in the battery we use to ferret out intellectual abilities.

Mr. BROADBENT. What was that?

Mr. CLEARY. It's something called the Olmstead-Diffendorff Game.

Senator SKYPACK. Game?

Mr. CLEARY. It's called that in order to decrease the subject's tension. The Olmstead-Diffendorff Game, called by its authors 'A Test of General Intelligence,' was designed to answer a criticism frequently made of the Stanford-Binet, Wechsler, and

45

other intelligence scales—that, stressing verbal skills, they are loaded in favor of children from upper-class social and economic backgrounds, where books and word facility have tenaciously hung on from nineteenth-century mores. The Game, consisting entirely of problems developed by cartoons in comic-book style, and drawing heavily for content on the child's world of television, sports, toys, and gadgets, is culture-free and without social bias. It's fun, too.

Mr. BROADBENT. And you—

Mr. CLEARY. I pointed out to Dr. Gozar that we are living in the Space Age, and—and just then the first bell rang.

Mr. BROADBENT. What happened?

Mr. CLEARY. We went toward the main entrance, where we encountered Miss Charity Perrin. She addressed me in a quite unfriendly and critical fashion.

Mr. BROADBENT. She is Barry Rudd's teacher, right? Is she a good teacher?

Mr. CLEARY. Her pedagogical methodology is unorthodox. Her techniques of encouraging wholesome motivation for mastery of critical skills, habits, understandings, knowledges, and attitudes, and of achieving dynamic personality adjustment of the whole child to both the learning situation and the life situation are, though soundly rooted in the developmental tradition, rather eccentric, and indeed they defy exact categorization.

Senator MANSFIELD. But can she teach, Mr. Cleary?

Mr. CLEARY. We don't know. The children won't tell us.

Mr. BROADBENT. You said she criticized you. What for?

Mr. CLEARY. She said my talent search was a phony because teacher's pet, Barry Rudd, wasn't on it—not for intellectual gifts, anyway. He is on it in another category.

Mr. BROADBENT. But I thought he was the brightest child in the history of the Pequot system.

Mr. CLEARY. He was only in the sixty-fourth percentile in the Olmstead-Diffendorff Game.

Senator SKYPACK. Why won't the children tell you? About that teacher, I mean.

Mr. CLEARY. I have a theory, and it runs this way: Miss Perrin manifests a curious combination of maternal and infantile drives, so that the children love her on two levels, as if she were both a mother figure and a peer. Loving and being loved—that's all she lives for. You see, she's one of your kind that believes everyone is nice. She loves the world. 'People can see something good in people if people look for it in people.' She gives more than lip service to bromides like that; she lives them —and the result is that admiration and pity are often synonymous for her, and when she feels repugnance for another person she turns it against herself. Evidence that people are not invariably nice, of which there seems to be plenty in Pequot, she uses as occasion for forgiveness, and this gives her a comforting feeling that *she's* nice. We psychologists have a term for her difficulties: she suffers from the Nice Mouse Syndrome.

Senator VOYOLKO. Jeest, Mr. Broadback, the minute you get talking about the boy you have to go off on a long tackle about some old maid.

Senator MANSFIELD. I agree, Mr. Broadbent. Let's hew—

Mr. BROADBENT. And after you talked with Miss Perrin, sir?

Mr. CLEARY. I entered the school and walked quickly across the dark front hall, which reverberated with children's shouts and struck my nostrils, as it always does, with the smells of floor oil, chalk, hanging clothes, and the queer, pungent dust that seems to lurk wherever knowledge is. Do you know what I mean?

Mr. BROADBENT. Please carry on.

Mr. CLEARY. You're interested in the Rudd boy, so I'll tell you that I saw him in the hall as I passed. I don't mind telling you I have a negative reaction to that boy. He stood woodenly, his legs slightly parted, arms stiff at his sides, and he gave a whole effect of having been pampered by his mother. His clothes, and the boy himself, seemed to have just come out of the washing machine. Out from the starched tubes of the shirt sleeves came soft, reddish, round, clean arms, with tiny veins mottling the surface; his flesh looked like a certain kind of pink tourmaline. The torso was chunky and waistless; the hips ran straight up to the shoulders. I wondered: Could the boy have combed his hair that fussy way himself?

Mr. BROADBENT. And then?

Mr. CLEARY. I sat down to some case-history work in my cubbyhole, and before long Dr. Gozar came in, saying that Mr. Owing was in her office, he'd walked—she said he was puffing like a choo-choo—all the way from the administration building to see me. I'm not in the habit of getting social calls from the Super every day, so I presented myself toot sweet. Dr. Gozar left us alone. I managed to get Dr. Gozar's desk chair, so I had an odd feeling—it almost made me chuckle out loud—that *I* was the Superintendent and *he* was the Guidance Director; and this feeling was reinforced by the fact that Mr. Owing had begun to perspire. He blurted right out that he was in a quandary. Mr. Owing saying he's in a quandary is like anybody else saying good-morning-how-are-you. You just come to expect it. But this time, I must say, the fix was an interesting one. He said he'd just talked with a man who wanted to buy a brilliant child —if we could provide just the right one.

Mr. BROADBENT. And he wanted you to name the right one?

Mr. CLEARY. It's never quite that direct with the Super. You have to wait him out, till he asks your advice.

Mr. BROADBENT. How do you mean?

Mr. CLEARY. He said it was sort of hard to know what to do, and I said we really didn't know enough, and he agreed with

48

me, but I didn't quite catch what he said so I begged his pardon, and he said he was thinking, so I offered him a penny for his thoughts, and he said he wasn't really thinking, he was just wondering, and I said sometimes I wondered myself, and he seemed relieved to hear that, and I said that, oh, yes, sometimes I lay awake nights, and he said he was a good sleeper, he thanked God, but it was the daytime that bothered him, and I asked what he meant by 'bothered,' and he said, 'Well, you know,' and I said, 'Yes, I know,' and he said he often had to stop and then start all over again, and I said the same went for me, and he asked me if I really felt that way, too, and I said some of the time, and he asked me when, mostly, and I said it wasn't easy to say exactly, and he said he supposed I was right, and I said I could see his point, though, and he said he was glad of that, and I said, 'I know, but . . . ,' and he said, 'That's the trouble,' and I knew he was about to explode, and I said 'Well?' and he was pretty near the end of his rope, and I said, 'Well?' again, and then it came out. He said, 'What do *you* think, Cleary?'

Mr. Broadbent. By that time you'd had plenty of time to make up your mind.

Mr. Cleary. I said that of course the Rudd boy was the only possibility.

Mr. Broadbent. But he wasn't even on your talent-search chart for being brainy.

Mr. Cleary. That's exactly what Mr. Owing pointed out. I said, bushwa, everyone knew Barry Rudd was the brightest boy we'd ever had in Pequot.

Mr. Broadbent. You proposed selling him?

Mr. Cleary. No. I've found it doesn't pay to move that fast with Mr. Owing, because he'll find doubts enough to wipe out a quick move. You let him stew, and stew, and stew, then what you tell him gives him such relief that you're in. Besides,

I saw some advantage at first in playing against a sale, and I went straight to the family to get their backs up—I admit now it was a miscalculation.

Mr. BROADBENT. What made you realize that was a miscalculation?

Mr. CLEARY. The child buyer. Mr. Jones.

Mr. BROADBENT. Please explain.

Mr. CLEARY. I counted at first on strong resistance, both in the community and the school system, to his proposition, and I think it would have developed, but by the end of my first conversation with him I realized that he was the shrewdest thing I'd ever seen on two legs. He's a devil. He's first and foremost a corrupter. His job is to find the irresistible temptation for each person who controls the destiny of the boy, and satisfy it, and, by golly, he's doing it; I believe he's doing it.

Mr. BROADBENT. I take it he found yours, Mr. Cleary.

Mr. CLEARY. You don't corrupt a man like me. It's the idealists—

Mr. BROADBENT. That sounds like an evasion, sir.

Mr. CLEARY. Why should I evade? Haven't I co-operated with you gentlemen? . . . All I can say is, the child buyer has eyes that look right into your brain. He looks at your forehead, and the look goes right through, like an X ray, and he reads what's in there. I swear, I believe he does.

Senator MANSFIELD. Thank you, Mr. Cleary, you may stand down. Thank you. Edifying witness. Thank you. . . . Mr. Broadbent?

Mr. BROADBENT. Dr. Frederika Gozar. Show her in, please.

Senator MANSFIELD. Dr. Gozar, will you rise to be sworn, please?

Do you solemnly swear that your testimony in this matter now before us will be the truth, the whole truth, and nothing but the truth, so help you God?

Dr. GOZAR. I do.

TESTIMONY OF DR. FREDERIKA GOZAR, PRINCIPAL, LINCOLN ELEMENTARY SCHOOL, PEQUOT

Mr. BROADBENT. Your name is Dr. Frederika Gozar, and you hold the post of principal of Lincoln Elementary School in Pequot. Is that correct, madam?

Dr. GOZAR. I'm not married. Just call me 'Doctor.' The answer is yes.

Mr. BROADBENT. Your residential address?

Dr. GOZAR. Number 17 Sycamore Street, Pequot.

Senator VOYOLKO. Mr. Chairman, thirty seconds. All I ask.

Senator MANSFIELD. Proceed, Senator.

Senator VOYOLKO. This kid, Dr. Gozall. What's he look like?

Dr. GOZAR. He's fat.

Senator VOYOLKO. I'm glad somebody told me that. It's time somebody around here told me that. Talk, talk, talk. The kid's fat. I'm glad you come here today, Dr. Gozall. Your floor, Mr. Chairman.

Senator MANSFIELD. I would urge, Mr. Broadbent—

Mr. BROADBENT. I know, sir. . . . Dr. Gozar, we have heard testimony from Mr. Wairy, during the course of which he told us of the first arrival of the child buyer in Pequot, on last Wednesday, October sixteenth. He told us that while he and a certain Mr. Ellithorp were talking with the man Wissey Jones on the corner of River Street and Treehampstead Road, Mr. Jones being on his folding motorcycle—that you approached, Doctor.

Dr. GOZAR. That's right. I did.

Mr. BROADBENT. Could you tell us what took place there?

Dr. GOZAR. The first thing my eye fell on, gentlemen, when Mr. Wairy stopped me on the sidewalk with a greeting, was that motorcycle. It had the look of an everlasting child's toy about it. It sparkled. There was a chrome muffler with red cut-glass studs, like rubies, in a ring around its collar, and there was a black-carded airplane compass on the handlebars, and the speedometer had a blue face with luminescent numbers, and there were English-type bicycle hand brakes whose control wires ran down to the wheels through chrome-plated flexible insulation, and there were squirrel tails on the tips of the handlebars, and a red—

Mr. BROADBENT. Did Mr. Jones speak to you?

Dr. GOZAR. Mr. Jones tipped his hat to me, and it was flat as a pancake, his gesture was like lifting the hinged lid of a tankard. An apt thought, by the way, the tankard. That man looks to me like a drinker, under that lid he's probably full of booze. He's got one of those puffy, spongy noses—looks as if you could squeeze a half-pint of Old Crow out of it.

Mr. BROADBENT. Anything else strike you about Mr. Jones?

Dr. GOZAR. The man's eyes seemed to me odd. Negligible, reddish whites. Large brown irises, small pod-like openings. He aimed them at my forehead, and he said, 'Gozar? That wouldn't be Dr. Frederika Gozar, one of the school principals, would it?' I got my mental dukes up at that. A New Englander born-and-bred doesn't like a stranger coming into the township and knowing too much about its affairs. Mr. Wairy said to me that Mr. Jones was interested in talented youngsters, and he said he'd just been telling Mr. Jones about Pequot's talent search. I groaned inside at *that*.

Mr. BROADBENT. Doctor, Mr. Cleary testified here concerning a conversation with you early on Thursday morning last—the day after the child buyer arrived—about this talent search. He claims it was his idea.

Senator MANSFIELD. There you go again, Mr. Broadbent, suddenly shifting your line of questioning.

Mr. BROADBENT. We have a lot of ground to cover, sir—

Senator MANSFIELD. I don't want to get left on that street corner again. Was there anything else there on the street corner, Doctor?

Dr. GOZAR. Mr. Wairy was ill at ease—I tower over him—and he said the talent-search charts were in my office, and Mr. Jones smiled—it's the first and last time I've seen him smile—the smile was like mud drying up and cracking in the sun—and the child buyer (of course I didn't know that that was what he was) said he'd like to visit me, and that displeased me so much that I turned my back and strode away. In a full skirt I can make forty-five inches to the stride.

Senator MANSFIELD. Thank you. Carry along, Mr. Broadbent.

Mr. BROADBENT. Concerning your conversation with Mr. Cleary on the talent search—

Dr. GOZAR. This boy Cleary is a shifty one; I'll bet he spun you a yarn. We were there by the jungle gym—he told you?—and I ragged him on his silly tests, and he agreed that some of them were meaningless, so I asked him why he gave them. He said because people want talent searches; the public wants them. 'It comes down to a question of what your aim is in life,' he said. 'You have to be a realist. The only way to get ahead is to operate. A man can't get to be Superintendent of Schools who doesn't politick and look at the angles.' I said I didn't want to be Superintendent: Who wants to be Willard Owing? I said, 'I just want to stir some of these kids up. I believe in the infinite potentiality of young people, and I think I can do something about it. Maybe I'm dreaming—but if I am, let's not wake me up.' 'That's all slop and sentiment,' he said. He half lifted himself on the bars of the jungle gym, stretching and tensing as if limbering up his powers. 'You've got to face facts,' he said; 'look at things as they are.' I said I thought there was such a thing as being too practical. He swung down off the frame like a chim-

53

panzee and pushed his face right into mine and said, 'You'll pay for that belief someday'—as if he meant that he personally was going to get even with me for being idealistic. Pah! He's no match for a battle-scarred old bitch like me! I tell you, furthermore, I looked right back at him, and his big hypnotic stare sort of wavered and turned aside, and he changed the subject. 'Gad, what lovely weather,' he said, or shouted, letting go the bars, extending his arms overhead, and filling his lungs with the dry air that was already, so early in the morning, scented with leaf smoke. 'Don't these autumn days make you feel twice man-size?' He asked me that. Why, the little snot! He knew I could wrestle him to a fall without being an inch bigger than I am. So I said, 'What do *you* want in life, Cleary?' And he said, 'I want to get out of this dump. I want to get to a nice rich suburban community—station wagons and swimming pools. Some place alive. This place . . . That dingy Intervale section!' I said, 'No, seriously: What do you really want? What keeps you going?' 'What do I want?' he said. 'I want a high salary, and a wife and house and kids, and a Mercedes 190SL, and—' I said, 'Hell, that's anybody. I mean you.' Then he said, 'I want to help people,' and I said, 'Don't make me laugh.' He got red and said, 'I want to be the best damn guidance man in the State.' 'That's more like it,' I said, 'but is that all?' He took one look at me, and then he had the sense to grin, which was a way of saying O.K., I give up. 'You're so full of questions,' he said, 'what makes *you* tick?' And I told him: 'Curiosity.'

Mr. Broadbent. What happened then, Doctor?

Dr. Gozar. We looked up at a high tower of the schoolhouse, because up there the alarm bell fastened against the bricks had started a loud clatter. On the playground the noise of the bell ran through the shouting of the children like a cold blast of wind, and the crowd of pupils swayed and moved toward the building, and Cleary and I strolled toward the front entrance.

The school is an old, dark, brick, two-story contraption, a Norman fortress, built as if learning and virtue need a stronghold, one defended by old-fashioned weapons, a place of turrets and parapets, with narrow slits in the bricks through which scholars with crossbows can peep out at an atomic world. The building makes education itself seem archaic, monastic—shabby, too. The paint on its blinds and trim is cracking; its double front door, with its rattling push bars, is of a dirty tawny color. Above the entranceway, over an arch in relief that doesn't bear any structural weight, our State motto's written in parched and spalled cement letters, 'Land of Steady Habits.' The children hustled past us. A few ran, but the crowd as a whole didn't press, because this was the daily moment of anticipation—of excitement, regret, and fear in the face of another day in school.

Senator MANSFIELD. I remember that feeling. I used to get the shivers.

Dr. GOZAR. On the sidewalk by the street some distance behind us there was a cracking sound of high heels, and I heard a voice call Cleary, and I turned and saw Charity Perrin running along the concrete walkway trying to catch up to us. She's a woman past sixty, you know, very shy in her demeanor, a narrow person, having hardly more beam than one span of my hand—of course, my hand's as big as a big man's hand—and tiny shoulders, and pelvic bones no heavier, I'd guess, than the outspread wings of a sparrow; a delicate, homely woman, but that morning she was wearing the bold colors of autumn, and as she ran the colors turned and flew, so she was like a flurry of October leaves blown along the ground.

Mr. BROADBENT. And she spoke to Mr. Cleary about his talent search?

Dr. GOZAR. I'll say she did! She gave him what-for because Barry Rudd's name wasn't on the talent charts. He said it was so. She asked where. He said on the chart for leadership.

55

'Pah!' she said. 'Leadership, my foot.'

Mr. Broadbent. We thought she was more of a timid person.

Dr. Gozar. It's true, this was a surprisingly spirited retort for her. She's usually much more humble than that. She's so modest that sometimes, I swear, she herself must see the absurdity of her protestations of inferiority. But now and then she'll amaze you. She'll stand up and fight like a cat.

Mr. Broadbent. After this conversation?

Dr. Gozar. I was doing some work in my office, when in comes the Super, puffing like a steam engine, wanting to talk with Cleary. So I went to fetch him. Cleary's office is a dark narrow cavity with a high slit of a window, formerly a coat closet that had a long rack down the middle; you can still see the rack's screw-holed round footprints marching down the center of the floor. Cleary's desk, at the window end, is a still-life portrait of an overburdened man with a procrastinating nature: it's a heap: things have been thrown on it not so much in disorder as in despair. I told him Mr. Owing was in my office and wanted to talk with him. Cleary was reading in some child's folder, and he carefully closed it, tossed it onto the mess on his desk, and stood up, brushing the front of his suit with his hands, as if he'd been having a little feast out of that folder and some gobbets and crumbs had fallen on his lap and chest.

Mr. Broadbent. And did you sit in on this conference between the Superintendent and Mr. Cleary?

Dr. Gozar. Certainly not. I can't stand the Super when he has a head of steam. Quandaries! I vacated.

Mr. Broadbent. So you didn't know that Mr. Jones was trying to purchase a child until later?

Dr. Gozar. That's right, but it wasn't much later. The Super hadn't been out of my office five minutes when this Mr. Jones came to call on me in person.

Mr. Broadbent. What was your impression of him at the time of this visit?

Dr. Gozar. High and mighty! The way he stares at the wrinkles on your forehead, as if your eyes are beneath him. He thinks he's a brave hunter. *Soldat manqué*, that's my estimate.

Senator Voyolko. What kind of monkey you call him, miss?

Senator Mansfield. That was French. She was using French, Peter.

Senator Voyolko. See what I mean? It's getting like the United Nations around here. Some people don't even know what country they live in.

Mr. Broadbent. This conversation was in your office?

Dr. Gozar. Excuse me. You asked my impression of the child buyer, and I want to say just one more thing about him. The man has a terrifying ruthlessness. That bourbon-soaked nose is misleading, the child's-toy motorbike is misleading, the stuff he wears, the fake patience. Even what I was saying about him—the brave front. It doesn't hide what you'd expect. Underneath there's just one slogan: We Must All Obey! He's the devil himself.

Senator Skypack. I don't think I have to sit here and listen to that kind of libelous criticism of an outstanding businessman. Wissey Jones, the concern he represents is making a contribution to the defense—I mean, you just don't know what you're talking about, Doctor.

Dr. Gozar. This young man of yours asked me a question—

Senator Mansfield. That's all right now, Doctor. Mr. Broadbent, go on with your interrogation.

Mr. Broadbent. Mr. Jones came to talk with you in your school.

Dr. Gozar. You remember my saying that Mr. Wairy told the child buyer about the talent-search charts in my office?

Mr. Broadbent. That's right.

Dr. GOZAR. He said he'd come to see them. My office is a big, square, dark room, with mahogany-stained wainscoting as high as your shoulder, and half a dozen bookcases with glass fronts, leather chairs, map globe—and Cleary's crazy charts plastered all over one wall. I said to him, 'Mister, I'm going to be blunt. I've made a lecture on the usefulness of literature, I've appeared at several English groups and reading circles giving that. On the nice way of saying things as opposed to the blunt way. For example, Victor Hugo said, "No army is as powerful as an idea whose time has come." Billy Whizbang said, "Cain't oppose bullplop with buckshot." ' You'll have to excuse me, gentlemen. This is a man's world, and I've gotten used to talking like a man to make my way in it. So I said to Jones, 'To be blunt: Phooey on the talent search.' I told him there was only one child in Pequot worth bothering about for brains, that everyone knew who it was but his name wasn't even on the brain end of the talent-search chart. Jones asked who it was, and I told him, and he asked me if this was the boy who knew all the species of birds and animals, and I said that wasn't all he knew by a long shot.

Mr. BROADBENT. And this was the Rudd boy?

Dr. GOZAR. This was the Rudd boy, all right.

Mr. BROADBENT. Did Mr. Jones tell you his proposition?

Dr. GOZAR. Not just then. He asked me if Barry Rudd had a really extraordinary intelligence, and I said, 'I have a kind of contempt for intelligence all by itself. Coupled with energy and willingness, it'll go. Alone it winds up riding the rails.' So Jones got sarcastic on me and asked if I was one of your educators who believes in concentrating on the retarded. 'That's not educators,' I told him, 'that's missionaries. That's the missionary spirit. Leaving the ninety-nine sheep and going out for the lamb that's lost may be good theology, but it's mighty poor sheepery—and mighty poor schoolery, too.'

Mr. BROADBENT. What is it that the Rudd boy has, then?

58

Dr. Gozar. Enthusiasm! Quite early with children you encounter a certain enthusiasm. You work on that, and in some
cases you find there's interest with only a small amount of understanding. You feel badly about that. But I've always found
you can do more with that, you can play on that. I can think of
some very successful professional men, former pupils of mine at
Lincoln, who I don't think are very bright, but they're living up
very close to their capacities. Bright ones sometimes get stuck
along the route in some little byway of research and stay there
all their lives. But when you get the one in a million with both
—mind as clear as a window and incurable enthusiasm, too!
That's Barry. That's Barry.

Mr. Broadbent. Please go back to your talk with Mr. Jones.

Dr. Gozar. He asked me Barry's I.Q. It's the highest I've ever
seen in forty-six years in the school business, and it's the highest
I'll ever see in my whole life. But who cares? Do you know what
an I.Q. is, my boy?

Mr. Broadbent. Why it . . . it tells how bright a person is.

Dr. Gozar. It does? Are you sure?

Mr. Broadbent. Intelligence Quotient. I once sneaked a look
in my high-school data folder in the principal's office and saw
that I have an I.Q. of one hundred twenty-six. Is that—

Dr. Gozar. Meaningless. Means nothing, unless you can tell
me more. What test was it based on? There are fifty different
tests, some good, some poor. You don't know. You don't even
know the difference between an individual test and a group test.

Mr. Broadbent. No, Doctor, I—

Dr. Gozar. Yet you talk about I.Q. as if it were *a* thing.

Mr. Broadbent. In school—

Dr. Gozar. Personally, after forty-six years in this racket, I
have more respect for the P.Q. than I have for the I.Q. I mean
the Perspiration Quotient. I told Jones that. I told him that
character is all that really matters. You take and give high in-

telligence to a person with poor character, a person who uses his brains to further, rather than adjust, his natural selfish desires, then you're going to wind up with a dangerous enemy to the security of all of us.

Senator MANSFIELD. Could we get back to your conversation with the child buyer, please, Doctor?

Dr. GOZAR. I haven't gotten away from it. This is all what I told *him*. He began a lot of pompous talk then about *national* security—I guess he was leading up to his proposition—about a crisis in national defense. I told him crisis is the essence of democracy. The only way you can get forward motion is crisis. Ideal democracy *is* crisis, individual people gritting their teeth and doing their darnedest to overcome bad situations—cheating, chiseling, unfairness, discrimination, stupidity in high places. So what was he so excited about? Crisis! Well, he said he was worried about what was happening to the younger generation. And I told him, I said, 'I have a firm belief in the infinite potential of people; especially of young people. I suppose you think the younger generation is soft,' I said, 'that it doesn't have spunk, it's made up of loafers and beatniks who can't put their nose to the grindstone the way the older generation did. I belong to the older generation,' I said, 'and I think the younger generation is a distinct notch up. At times these young people don't thrill to the idea of work for work's sake, and in that they're the spit and image of people of our generation. You'll find kids break the law sometimes, but they don't break it anything like as horribly as grown people do. They can act silly in a meeting but not near as silly as some of your grown men in a fraternal-order initiation or even in the august halls of this State Capitol, Senators, excuse me. I've seen a high-school boy whooping with a couple of beers under his belt, but there's a dive called The Beach down our way, and it's so-called grownups who go *there*. For every juvenile delinquent, for every Sonny Wisecarver and

Alfred E. Newman, you have half a dozen Al Capones and Lucky Lucianos and Tommy Manvilles. Sure there's a lot of leeway in the ideals of the younger generation, but I'll stake my career on the fact that idealism is on a higher plane among school kids than it is among their parents. Right today, if it was up to me to sell a program of idealism, hard work, and sacrifice for the sake of a distant goal, and if I had to choose between selling this program to youngsters or middle-aged people, I wouldn't hesitate a minute to pick on the young ones. All right, people can say I'm a starry-eyed visionary, an ivory-tower character, who doesn't know what life really is. I doubt that. I was born on a Western Connecticut milk farm that went broke when I was ten years of age. I missed a few meals from time to time. After high school I attended college through various means, chiefly by working at night in a cotton mill. I've worked summers and spare times, in shops, in cotton mills, as a dishwasher, in dairies, driving trucks, and even, once, in a foundry. I've run crews for the State agriculture service. I've worked as a member of C.I.O. unions, and I've been out on strike. And I've slaved at the books. Oh, yes, I've worked. I've got a B.A. and a B.S. and four master's degrees and a Ph.D. During the Depression I couldn't get summer jobs, so I took nine straight summer quarters at Silverbury College; everything they offered came up on rotation, and I took it all, not for degrees but to learn it, to know it. And listen, I've been a teacher for nearly half a century: that's where if you've been in an ivory tower, you *come out*. I don't think I qualify as an ivory-tower person. I've seen characters that would make your hair stand on end. I reject any ivory-tower classification for myself. If I'm an educational visionary it's not from having been shut in an ivory tower but from rubbing elbows with people who've succeeded through educational endeavor. I'm not soft. Don't think I'm a softy, just because I believe in people. I can be rough and tough when it's needed:

listen: I'm not at all averse to having a little humor going in my school, but I don't have the slightest intention of having a *noisy* school, and one tap of my pencil on my desk in my office will bring a hush to the whole building.'

Mr. BROADBENT. You told Mr. Jones all this?

Dr. GOZAR. I did!

Senator VOYOLKO. What about the kid?

Dr. GOZAR. Yes, I talked to the child buyer about Barry, too. I asked him, did he want to know how I got interested in Barry Rudd? Well, here's how. I work in the biology lab at Wairy High two hours before breakfast every morning. You see, when I first got to college, at Silverbury, I got the idea of being a biologist, to work for the U.S. conservation service. I took two bachelor's degrees, one in biology and one in history, because I figured I wanted to know what I was conserving—a B.S. and a B.A. I worked extra on it and got both degrees in one year; not combined but double. All the time I worked nights in a cotton mill. My shift got off at two in the morning, so I could do some studying before I turned in. I only had eight a.m. classes three times a week. I could get a solid four hours' sleep and be blessed with ordinary good health, and I have maintained that average ever since, to the present time. Four hours of sleep a night. This means I save four hours per night over the usual individual, and when you calculate that I've been doing that for half a century, it works out that I've enjoyed some seventy-five thousand hours of life most people miss. I could sleep longer quite readily, but I've set myself. And I thrive on it. I've been out from work exactly six days in all these years—I had an operation for piles in my late forties.

Senator MANSFIELD. About the child, if you please, Doctor.

Dr. GOZAR. Yes. I've kept up the habit of doing research work in biology. I like the search in research; a research person is a person looking for something intelligently—but it's fun, too.

Did you know, my dear Mr. Chairman, that 'research' and 'circus' are related etymologically? Know who told me that? Barry! Words are his daily bread. Anyway, one morning two years ago, it'll be two years ago in February, I was working at five a.m. in the biology lab at Wairy High, on a project on the caste system of termites—how a soldier termite can develop from a nymph that wouldn't normally become a soldier; in other words, the caste system isn't hereditary. Very instructive for us mortals. I usually work under a single hooded lamp in that big room, with slate tops on the big lab tables, and a sink at each end, and I concentrate pretty hard. It's as silent as King Tut's tomb in there; you could practically hear the queen termites laying their eggs. Well, that morning I heard a gentle stirring, and the edge of my mind thought, 'My God, I'm going to have to set me a mouse trap in here,' and a couple minutes later I looked up, and here was this pale circle of paste at the edge of the light with two of the most beautiful eyes I've ever seen in it, not looking at me but staring at my termites. I don't know to this day how that boy knew about my early-morning work, or how he contrived to get away from home at that hour. His home is in a tenement block on River Street, a quarter-mile from the school, and it was dead-o'-winter, and five in the morning. Anyway, he was just there, and he said, 'Mind if I watch, Dr. Gozar?' He came the next morning, and he had a piece of paper with a list of questions he wanted to ask me. Mind you, the child was only eight—fourth grade. He's been coming ever since. How I love that boy!

Mr. BROADBENT. You think the man Wissey Jones was right, then, in selecting him for purchase?

Dr. GOZAR. There's no child better. Barry combines drive and a keen, keen mind. He calls me Dr. Gozar, and I call him Mr. Rudd. I always call my high-school students 'Mr.' and 'Miss'— you see, besides being principal at Lincoln, I teach biology courses in both of the Pequot high schools—and so I call Barry 'Mr.,' too. He learns from me, and I learn from him. He doesn't mind showing his ignorance to me—why should I mind showing mine to him?

Mr. BROADBENT. What else did you tell Mr. Jones?

Dr. GOZAR. I told him the real reason Barry had been passed over in Cleary's stupid wizard hunt was that Barry isn't a stereotypic Brain. He's fat—

Senator VOYOLKO. You told me that. The kid's fat.

Dr. GOZAR. —but he doesn't have an enlarged head, or a pigeon chest, or spindly legs and floppy wrists, or crybaby eyes. He doesn't even wear horn-rimmed glasses, or any glasses at all.

Senator SKYPACK. You mean this little twerp is a boy's boy?

Dr. GOZAR. Are you a man's man, Senator?

Senator SKYPACK. You damn right.

Dr. GOZAR. Well, these categories are beyond me, sir. All I'm saying is that Barry isn't the commonplace bespectacled Brain. He has a marvelous diffidence about him:

'Knowledge is proud that he has learned so much;
Wisdom is humble that he knows no more.'

Mr. BROADBENT. And did Mr. Jones get around to his proposition?

Dr. GOZAR. Yes, he came to it, sir. Roundabout.

Mr. BROADBENT. How do you mean, roundabout?

Dr. GOZAR. He began by saying that what we need to relieve our talent shortage in this country is a crash program, and I told him I thought that was the worst possible thing you could do. The way they spent hundreds of millions of dollars on the Manhattan Project to work up the atom bomb has a lot of people thinking that all you need to do to unlock supreme mysteries is to have an act of Congress, and empty Fort Knox, and start up a vast Federal agency—that money solves everything. We'll be having a crash program to locate God one of these days, pin

down a definite location for His throne. But I told Jones you
can't free talent with dollars. You can't package talent, you
can't put it in uniform bottles and boxes with labels. Ability
slips through the cogs of a machine; machines are only as bright
as the men who feed them data. I don't want an IBM machine
telling me which of my kids'll be a doctor, which a lawyer, which
a beggarman, which a thief. I don't want these government and
industry scholarships for my youngsters, because a scholarship
is a moral loan; there's *quid pro quo* in scholarships handed
out under something called a National Defense Education Act.
The only real defense for a democracy is improvement. Crisis
and triumph over crisis. It's a failure of national vision when
you regard children as weapons, and talents as materials you can
mine, assay, and fabricate for profit and defense. I tell you, I
can sound off on that subject! And you should have seen friend
Jones when I got going that way. He got red as a McIntosh
apple. The red spread from his nose outward. He began to
sputter and wheeze. So I asked him, straight out, what he
wanted of me, and he told me about wanting to buy a youngster. Perhaps Barry Rudd, if the boy lived up to his billing.

Mr. BROADBENT. And?

Dr. GOZAR. I threw him out.

Senator MANSFIELD. With your bare hands, Doctor? Nape of
the neck and seat of the pants?

Dr. GOZAR. No, sir. My tongue's my bouncer.

Senator SKYPACK. Did he tell you what he has told this committee in confidence, in Executive Session, about what his company does with these brains he buys?

Dr. GOZAR. No, thank you, Senator, I wouldn't be interested
in any of that. The idea of the purchase of talent was enough
for me.

Senator SKYPACK. Mr. Chairman, I submit that if the public
knew about the fine patriotic work that company is doing down
there, a witness like this—

Senator MANSFIELD. Mr. Jones has put us on our honor, Jack. I don't see how we can change that without his permission.

Dr. GOZAR. 'We Must All Obey!'

Senator MANSFIELD. That's not fair, Doctor. There's such a thing as honor, you know.

Dr. GOZAR. I believe in it, but I see very little of it as I wander around.

Senator MANSFIELD. Did you have any further questions, Mr. Broadbent?

Mr. BROADBENT. That's all, sir. You may be excused, Doctor. I will call Miss Charity Perrin.

Senator MANSFIELD. Thank you, Dr. Gozar. . . . Please stand —right there, miss—and we'll swear you in.

Do you solemnly swear that the testimony you are about to give this committee will be the truth, the whole truth, and nothing but the truth, so help you God?

Miss PERRIN. I do.

TESTIMONY OF MISS CHARITY M. PERRIN,
SCHOOLTEACHER, TOWN OF PEQUOT

Mr. BROADBENT. Kindly identify yourself for the record, miss, as to name, address, occupation.

Miss PERRIN. The record?

Senator MANSFIELD. Matter of form, Miss Perrin. We're only trying to do our duty.

Miss PERRIN. Charity M. Perrin. 94 Second Street, Pequot. Teacher.

Mr. BROADBENT. Miss Perrin, were you present, either in the auditorium of Lincoln School in Pequot, or immediately outside the auditorium windows on the black-top playground, at the instant on Tuesday afternoon last when a bomb—a stink bomb —was exploded in front of the stage of the—

Miss PERRIN. I . . . Gracious, I . . .

Senator MANSFIELD. No need to be agitated, my dear Miss Perrin. Don't be fearful.

Mr. BROADBENT. Exactly where were you during the lecture—

Miss PERRIN. If . . . I wasn't . . .

Senator MANSFIELD. Please, Mr. Broadbent, you are aware—

Mr. BROADBENT. Very well, miss, let's go back to the beginning.

Miss PERRIN. The beginning! Oh, dear . . . What do you want me to say?

Mr. BROADBENT. Begin at the beginning. How you were hired, and all that.

Miss PERRIN. Sir, I was hired into the Pequot system as a sixth-grade teacher, let me see, it was January, 19—. That was a queer time of year to be hired; you'll say it was a suspicious time of year to be taken on. Here's how it happened. . . . But let me say, first off, you have to remember that those were different times. We teachers were poor. I mean, there was a depression, hot-lunch money was not provided for teachers unless they were extreme hardship cases, multiple dependency—

Senator MANSFIELD. Broadbent, I don't see why we have to go back *that* far.

Mr. BROADBENT. If you wouldn't mind holding your horses just a moment, Senator, I think we've just had a rather remarkable statement from this lady. Do you mean to suggest, miss, that a teacher ought to be supplied, gratis, with all the amenities—hot soup, medical insurance, fringe benefits of all kinds? Is that what you mean?

Miss PERRIN. Oh no, sir, I didn't mean . . . I don't hold with . . .

Mr. BROADBENT. Do you mean to suggest that teaching is not a service career, a calling—I mean, that people go into teaching for the material ends of life? Do you mean that, Miss Perrin?

Miss PERRIN. Oh, no, sir. I believe a teacher is a servant of society. I have a real sense of vocation about my teaching. I like to take second place.

Mr. BROADBENT. That's more like it, ma'am.

Miss PERRIN. The only thing is—

Mr. BROADBENT. Don't forget you're under oath, miss.

Miss PERRIN. When it comes to being *treated* like a servant— well, I get uncomfortable under the collar. I hasten to tell you, sir, it's very hard for me to be angry at anyone: I usually just get hives or the sniffles or a bad case of the scares. But all the same, for a teacher—

Senator SKYPACK. I assume, miss, since they've kept you on in Pequot all these years—

Miss PERRIN. I was born a few blocks east of Lincoln School. I never taught west of it. I've been twenty-four years in the one classroom. I guess I'm sort of provincial, sir, you'd have to call me that.

Senator MANSFIELD. That's neither here nor there, Miss Perrin. Mr. Broadbent, *please*.

Mr. BROADBENT. The day you first were contacted by the child buyer, ma'am. Tell us.

Miss PERRIN. Actually, Mr. Jones visited my class last Friday, but he came in after the second bell and left before the morning was over, and no one ever told me who he was; he didn't even speak to me himself. I assumed he was some professor of education or State evaluator or I-don't-know-what. They're always barging in.

Mr. BROADBENT. So when did you find out what he wanted?

Miss PERRIN. The first approach was by Mr. Cleary, in the form of a sort of pitchman's talk.

Mr. BROADBENT. Where was this, please?

Miss PERRIN. He came to my classroom, during the Show-and-Tell Period. He just sneaked into the room and sat down at the back and observed for the longest time—made me very nervous. A man from your own school administration snooping in your room is different from an outsider. Do you know in the old days on streetcars they used to have these company inspectors, in ordinary clothes, would just ride as passengers and watch the conductor to see he wasn't slipping any pennies in his own pocket? That's what Mr. Cleary made me feel like *he* was.

Mr. BROADBENT. When did he speak to you?

Miss PERRIN. He couldn't break right into the class.

Mr. BROADBENT. Was the class busy when he came in?

Miss PERRIN. I have thirty-nine children, and you have to keep that big a room busy every minute. I have four with very low I.Q.'s; one of them can't read yet, and he's thirteen. I'm trying to bring him along, but it's like molasses in January. Another one who's shrewd as a crow came to me last month fresh from the detention home. We call him Flattop from his haircut. His mother doesn't care where he is as long as he's not at home. The boy feels the prejudice of the other children—you can smell it in the room, it's strong as store cheese. He uses filthy language, and he refuses to do anything I ask, and he's aggressive, but he's unabusive to Barry. It's strange. They're bosom friends. Barry's the only one can manage him.

Mr. BROADBENT. What was the class doing when Mr. Cleary came in?

Miss PERRIN. It was supposed to be the Show-and-Tell Period, but in actual fact we were rearranging one corner of the room. We were dismantling the Humor Nook. You see, our whole room is built around Barry. He brings these interests in, and he's so forceful about them, so irresistible—I don't mean to suggest he's a forceful person, as let's say Flattop is. Barry's more on the gentle side, but he can be extremely infectious. I remember back: before Barry came in, my room was unappetizing in the

69

extreme. There are these forty old hinge-top desks, with lots of initials and designs carved in them, and their steel bases bolted to the floor. We're on a corner of the building, and in the very tall sash windows on the two sides there are these frayed and worn black roller shades; a globe on a bookcase; pictures on the wall of Sir Galahad in black armor staring at the glow of the Grail as if it were the Firestone Hour, and Balboa looking at the Pacific for the first time, and President William Howard Taft in a chair that's a squeeze for him. That was all we had till Barry came in. Since then we've had a geology museum full of quartzes and micas and schists, and a tank of guppies—they carry their eggs within and seem to give birth as mammals do, pushing out these tiny folded-up babies; the children loved that—and a bench of cacti, and a display of bugs and beetles with their scientific names, and pressed leaves, and a word-game bank, and—

Mr. BROADBENT. How do you handle a boy like this Rudd boy, ma'am? Do you give him what you people call enrichment?

Miss PERRIN. Oh, yes, with a boy like that you have to. For example, the other day the health officer was coming to the school, and I sent Barry down to the office to straighten out the dentistry record before the health man came, and Barry did a good job, these cards had to be arranged in alphabetical order, a better job than us grownups would do, orderly and neat and accurate, and I asked him afterward if he'd want to be a doctor or dentist, but no; he was definite about that.

Senator MANSFIELD. You're wandering again, Mr. Broadbent. Could we get back on the subject? About Mr. Cleary. About the child buyer.

Mr. BROADBENT. Yes, sir. Miss Perrin, about Mr. Cleary?

Miss PERRIN. As I say, Mr. Cleary was sitting in the back of the room, and we were taking down the Humor Nook. The thing is, last summer Barry's mother thought he was too serious, and Barry, he adores his mother, and he sensed she thought he should be more humorous. So he went in the humor business. He got these anthologies of wit, these Bennett Cerf books, and joke, joke, joke! It was such a silly mistake. How could he do that? Well, it was easy for him, and the next thing, John Sano, he's a doctor's son, a very able sober boy, he caught the humor bug from Barry, and the first you know we had a Humor Nook on popular demand. It got too much, and I realized I was going to have to stop it. The last thing to do with a joke is put it on display, because it's like hanging a side of beef: it gets high pretty fast. So we agreed to dismantle the Humor Nook, and in its place we were going to set up a Word Market.

Mr. BROADBENT. Exactly what is that?

Miss PERRIN. Barry and his friends have been swapping long words lately, like stamps.

Mr. BROADBENT. Antidisestablishmentarianism?

Miss PERRIN. Oh, that's old hat in the long-word trade, and its meaning is fairly obvious on the surface. John Sano brings in these medical words, like haematospectrophotometer. Barry's found the longest one so far—pneumonoultromicroscopicsilicovolcanokoniosis. It's uncanny the way Barry can decipher these marathon words. John Sano brought one in the other day and asked Barry what it meant—eccentroösteochondrodysplasia, and Barry didn't bat an eye. 'Let's see,' he says. '*Eccentro-* means off center, out of line; *-osteo-*, bone; *-chondro-*, cartilage; *-dys-*, wrong or bad; *-plasia*, connection. Guess that gives you the main idea, John,' he says. He's very offhand but not at all superior about it.

Mr. BROADBENT. And you were setting up a market for these words.

Miss PERRIN. Some people *do* think he acts superior. Several of the teachers. I think it's because he's expressionless. When he gets excited there's only a flicker of facial expression. Some of the teachers ask me about him physically. 'He walks funny. Does he have club feet?' 'Isn't that a strange thick waist for a ten-year-old?' It's curious how jealous teachers can be.

Senator MANSFIELD. About your 'market,' Miss Perrin. And Mr. Cleary.

Miss PERRIN. At the end of the period Mr. Cleary came up to me, and he told me Barry was being considered for sale, and all about it.

Mr. BROADBENT. Was he for it, or against it?

Miss PERRIN. He was strong for it, he was pushing me to the wall about it. Let's see, this was on the Monday. I heard later that on the previous Thursday he'd been running around to the family and all, arguing against it. But the child buyer must have done a selling job on him before the Monday.

Mr. BROADBENT. And what was your reaction?

Miss PERRIN. Mr. Cleary rubs me the wrong way: I don't believe in all that newfangled psychiatry and mental curing in schoolrooms. Sociometrics! Social adjustment—like it was a cream that you applied it thickly morning and evening, then massage it gently till it's penetrated deeply into the pores, wipe it off with tissue. I told him I didn't want any part of it.

Senator SKYPACK. I trust Mr. Cleary explained to you this is part of a national-defense project.

Miss PERRIN. How can you defend a country by taking a boy out of school and away from his mother?

Senator SKYPACK. Are you to judge your nation's defense, miss?

Miss PERRIN. I just feel in my bones it's wrong.

Senator SKYPACK. *As a citizen you have certain—*

Miss PERRIN. Sometimes when people in authority shout at a teacher, she begins to feel like a second-class citizen.

Senator SKYPACK. I WASN'T SHOUTING! . . . Are we going to have to go into the trouble this person got herself into—when was that strike—twenty, twenty-five years ago?

Miss PERRIN. I'm sorry, sir. I . . . I lost my head. I know I shouldn't talk that way. The trouble with being a teacher is that people expect you to be more than human. I think I know what a teacher ought to be like, and I try to be like that, but a hundred times a day I feel I'm falling short. I try to be sensitive to other people's feelings, and I'm willing to give sympathy even where it isn't needed. I want to help. I defer to you, sir; you surely know more than I do about these things. But as a teacher I can't help resenting being stepped on, yet it makes me feel dizzy and sick when I think about getting back at the people who step on me. I'm *determined* to be a good person.

Senator SKYPACK. Mr. Chairman, we're being treated to a disgusting display of self-pity here. I submit—

Senator MANSFIELD. Thank you, Miss Perrin. That will do for now. You may step down.

Mr. BROADBENT. I will call Barry Rudd. Bring him in, please.

Senator MANSFIELD. Present yourself to take your oath, sonny.

Do you solemnly swear that the testimony you will give before the Standing Committee on Education, Welfare, and Public Morality of the State Senate will be the truth, the whole truth, and nothing but the truth, so help you God?

BARRY RUDD. I'm not sure I believe in God. Can He help a skeptic to tell the truth?

Senator MANSFIELD. If you want my advice, sonny, you'd better swear this oath.

BARRY RUDD. O.K. I do. I just wanted to make sure.

TESTIMONY OF BARRY RUDD, MINOR,
TOWN OF PEQUOT

Mr. BROADBENT. Your name?

BARRY RUDD. Barry Rudd.

Mr. BROADBENT. And you are?

BARRY RUDD. Ten years of age. Is that what you meant?

73

Senator VOYOLKO. So you're the kid.

Mr. BROADBENT. I put it to you directly, Master Rudd. Where were you at approximately three o'clock last Tuesday afternoon?

BARRY RUDD. Three o'clock, Tuesday. I was in the biology lab of Wairy High School.

Mr. BROADBENT. Wouldn't that be an ideal place to make a contrivance which, upon being burst, would produce a very bad smell? Commonly called a stink bomb?

BARRY RUDD. A chem lab would be a better place than a biology lab.

Mr. BROADBENT. Does Wairy High School have separate chemistry and biology laboratories?

BARRY RUDD. No, sir. The same room is used for both.

Mr. BROADBENT. I warn you, young man, not to be slippery here.

BARRY RUDD. I didn't mean to be. . . . I was doing a biology experiment.

Mr. BROADBENT. Who was with you?

BARRY RUDD. A friend of mine, Charles Perkonian.

Mr. BROADBENT. Isn't he the one you call Flattop?

BARRY RUDD. Yes, we call him that.

Mr. BROADBENT. A juvenile delinquent, recently returned from Clarkdale Reformatory? Isn't that right?

BARRY RUDD. He's gone square. He really has.

Mr. BROADBENT. Tell me, Master Rudd, do you know the State Supervisor for Exceptional Children, who was lecturing in Lincoln School auditorium at that hour? Do you have anything against that lady?

BARRY RUDD. I know her. Miss Millicent P. Henley. I seem to be one of her wards, as Flattop is one of Clarkdale's—though I realize the analogy isn't too tidy. Miss Henley reminds me of the word 'bipinnatifid.' I'm not sure exactly why, unless it's that Miss Henley uses the first-personal singular pronoun so much, and

74

there are four i's in bipinnatifid. By the way, do you know a common eight-letter word, we all use it every day, with only one vowel in it?

Senator MANSFIELD. We better not take time now—

BARRY RUDD. It's an easy word. Anyway, to get back to 'bipinnatifid.' When I was in second grade, I saw a brown thrasher for the first time, *Toxostoma rufum*, and heard it sing its mocking song, like a mockingbird's, only funnier, truly humorous, and I didn't know what it was, so I described it to Miss Songevine, my teacher at that time, and she showed me the color plate, Common Birds of America, in the big Webster, and I remember that 'bipinnatifid' was at the top of the opposing page, and I looked up its meaning, and that got me interested in leaves and their comparative forms. I pressed them for a while.

Mr. BROADBENT. Wairy High School is only one block and a half from Lincoln Elementary, where the State Supervisor was lecturing last Tuesday afternoon, isn't that so?

BARRY RUDD. Yes, sir, that is so.

Senator MANSFIELD. Mr. Broadbent, I should think with this witness of all witnesses! . . . Begin at the beginning, sonny.

BARRY RUDD. I suppose you mean the beginning of . . . of this. For me it began on Thursday—a week ago yesterday.

Senator MANSFIELD. Very good. Start right in. Tell us everything. Don't leave anything out.

BARRY RUDD. When school let out, I walked with my social-studies textbook in my hand up away from the Flats, where Lincoln is, into the hills on the west side of the river.

Mr. BROADBENT. Were you going home?

BARRY RUDD. No, my house is right in the town, in the Intervale section, the poorer part of Pequot, we have the ground floor of the Slatkowski tenement block on River Street; no, I was just going for what I call a field ramble, a zoological hobby of mine, observation—but I'll get to that. For a while I followed the Treehampstead Road; it climbs in a series of curves onto the ridge where the woods are, and I wasn't long getting out of the town. The town is narrow because it clings to the river; if Pequot were a strip of adhesive plaster you could yank it up off the ground and nothing would be left but the river, no dams or anything, just the river and its valley. As you know, the first part of October this year was mild, almost shy, what I'd call frugal, and then we had that tail end of Hurricane Ella, and then that was followed, remember, by two clear nights with north winds and frosts, light, nibbling frosts, you know, and that sequence had brought the explosive change that every leaf on every tree had been waiting for. The hills beyond the first step of the ridge are round, and they're easy, not too steep, so they'd had farms on them in former years, and I went along their shoulders and eventually left the tarred road and walked down the unmaintained dirt track that leads to the abandoned knife-and-scissors works on Chestnut Burr Creek—through patches of woods of various stages of growth, depending on when the farmers who'd been there had given up and quit, past newly grown-up sprout land of sumacs and hardhack and meadow cedars and young wild cherries, and past other sections—of course you had stone walls dividing these growths, right through the woods—other sections with middle-sized popples and sapling elms and dirty birches, and then past adult forests, great maples, hickories, ashes, oaks, and I tell you, all these woods were dressed in colors you simply couldn't imagine. That afternoon was a climax. I don't know if there'll be but two or three more such days this year, and maybe none that bright, and I guess there won't ever be another one in my whole lifetime exactly like that one, because October around here, as you know, is just a mass of colors in constant motion; the colors are fugitive, you can't stop them from changing and running away. Even every minute that afternoon they changed. There was a blue haze hanging on the hills, and above that there were some small soft gray clouds, and when one of them blew across the sun, all the colors in the woods changed their tones, and the yellows took charge over the softer reds which, just a few seconds before, in the full sunlight, had had the intensity of the center of fireplace flames. I've read in books about the sadness of autumn, the way time turns down toward death in the fall, but I was happy through and through; I saw the colors, and they made me happy. I don't know what's happened these last few days; I'm utterly bewildered. I only know I'll never be as happy again as I was the other afternoon in the woods. The white oaks made a kind of backdrop, because, you know, they hold their leaves the longest, like small leather gloves, still solid green; while the elms and hickories had gone brown early in the dry August we had this year, and in the wind on Ella's train the week before they'd been almost stripped, and their skeletons made a blackish mesh, so the displays of the other trees seemed even more prodigal: deep coppers of the sumac and dogwood, pure yellow of birches and, here and there, ironwood and sassafras, and, best of all, the incredible orange glow of hard maples—like the inside of a Halloween pumpkin when the candle's lit. There was a dry breeze blowing, and leaves of all colors were falling slantwise across the old track where I was walking. On the stone walls there were some white lichens that stood out sharply because of all the color around. Once in a while I passed an old cellar hole, with a big lilac bush or overgrown privet bush standing in front of it, incongruous in the woods, remnants of civilization —you know? I came to the ruin of the knife works and walked along the bank of the millpond, and there it was as if I saw two autumns—one real and the other reflected, until for a second a breeze sort of stepped on the water and moved both the mirrored and the floating leaves on the surface a little. I walked to a big dead trunk of a fallen tree lying on the ground at the upper end of the pond, and I put my social-studies book down on it, and it seems as if putting my book down was the beginning of my troubles. Anyway I just sat on the log and watched and waited.

Mr. BROADBENT. What were you waiting for?

BARRY RUDD. There's a weasel, a long-tailed weasel, *Mustela frenata*, that has a burrow through a hole in the stonework of the old mill. I've wanted to see if it would be gathering new dry leaves for its nest. . . .

Mr. BROADBENT. What happened?

BARRY RUDD. Nothing. There were some *Penthestes atricapillus atricapillus* flitting from branch to branch.

Senator VOYOLKO. Some who?

BARRY RUDD. Some chickadees. That's a curious name, matter of fact. One of those annoying mixed names, the first past Greek, the rest Latin. I hate mixtures. Ouija. Taurosaurus. Macaronic double-talk gives me the heebie-jeebies. Anyway, this cheerful little bird is 'the black-haired black-haired mourner'— *Penthestes*, from the Greek, *pentheesin*, to mourn, and *esthes*, garment, while *atricapillus* is from the Latin, *ater*, black, and *capillus*, hair.

Senator MANSFIELD. Why do you have to have that black-haired part twice?

BARRY RUDD. That takes you down through genus, species, and sub-species.

Senator SKYPACK. By Christopher, if the taxpayers of this State knew what was going on here!

Senator MANSFIELD. Now, Jack, in fairness, we've got to find out all we can about—

Senator VOYOLKO. That's right, Senator, we got to take this kid *apart*.

Senator MANSFIELD. Now, sonny, let's get back on the track.

Senator SKYPACK. If it was my taxes, by gorry.

Senator MANSFIELD. You were waiting for the weasel.

BARRY RUDD. *Mustela frenata.* Besides the chickadees, there was a praying mantis, *Mantis religiosa,* 'the religious prophet,' on a branch of a bush not a foot from my face. Its wings had gone from green to brown with the coming of autumn. It revolved its head to look at me and then took off, like a helicopter, very much like a helicopter.

Mr. BROADBENT. And then?

BARRY RUDD. I got up at last and started off through the woods toward home, and I left the book behind on the trunk of the fallen tree. As I say, I date my troubles from the moment I left my book on that tree trunk.

Mr. BROADBENT. You went home?

BARRY RUDD. I remember I touched every other telephone pole on the way down the Treehampstead Road, because I wanted an A-plus in the oral report I was going to have to give the next morning: I'd chosen the Linnaean System of Binomial Nomenclature as my topic. In town I had to take a detour around off Sycamore Street, because a very unpleasant incident occurred to me last year in front of the shopping center on Sycamore, and I'd rather go out of my way . . .

Mr. BROADBENT. And when you got home?

BARRY RUDD. I didn't go directly home. Along the way I was thinking about nomenclature in general. Names. I once believed the sun, the sky, the mountains, the rivers were all made by hand by the first men. The names of those things sort of radiated from the things themselves, and we knew the names simply by looking at the objects. We needed only to look at a river to know that it was called 'river.' Why? Because it was wet, it ran along between banks. Yes, but how did we know? Because it was a band of water, it was cool; we knew it was called 'river.' But how did we know? Because it was moving water, of course it was a river. How did the first men know it was 'river'? They made it with their hands. But how did they know the name? Well, because it was water, it was dark water, moving along the ground in a regular place. It was a river, and it was called 'river.'

Mr. BROADBENT. What are you trying to tell us?

BARRY RUDD. I'm trying to say . . . I understand about insect processes—how termites digest wood with the help of protozoa that live in their digestive tracts, and how the protozoa themselves digest food in their tiny vacuoles; what effect the gas produced by the flour beetle has on other insects; how many ladybirds it takes to keep the cottony-cushion scale in check in an acre of orange trees. It's easy enough to observe—but to identify, name, classify! To know that termites are of the order *Isoptera*, that the gas-producing flour beetle is *Tribolium confusum*, the cottony-cushion scale is *Iserya purchasi*, and the ladybird that eats it is *Novius cardinalis*, sometimes called *V edalia*—to bring order out of chaos! Senator Mansfield, I noticed early in our talk that you love order—you like to have things begin at the beginning and take their courses, as rivers do.

Senator MANSFIELD. I do, sonny, I do.

BARRY RUDD. I do, too. Most of what we encounter is so sloppy. I've just finished reading *Twenty Thousand Leagues under the Sea*, by Jules Verne. It was wonderful, having all kinds of scientific names—*exempla gratia: Clupanodon, Stenorynchus*, et cetera. It was almost entirely different, from the movie, comic-book, and other versions. For instance, in the movie, 20,000 *Leagues*, the crew fought a giant squid (genus *Loligo*), in the View-Master Slides version it was a giant octopus (genus *Octopus*), but in the book it was a different cephalopod, the cuttlefish (genus *Sepia*). Throughout the chapter, with two or three exceptions, Verne kept calling them *poulps*, which in my French-English Dictionary is French for 'octopus,' though Verne seems to use it for 'any cephalopod.' In those two or three exceptions, however, he did call them cuttlefishes. I say them, because Verne said there were seven.

80

Senator MANSFIELD. Do you mean to say you read this book in French?

BARRY RUDD. Not really. I read the original and a translation side by side. I like to compare.

Senator MANSFIELD. What languages do you speak?

BARRY RUDD. I don't really speak any but ours. I just collect words. My address on my French notebook is in Chinese characters. The Chinese for America, *mei kuo*, means 'beautiful country.'

Senator SKYPACK. Can you speak Russian, young fellow?

BARRY RUDD. A little. Управлеме Квас и Водка Дел!

Senator SKYPACK. I thought so! What the hell does that mean? Damn communist slogan?

BARRY RUDD. It means: 'Administration of Beer and Vodka Production.'

Senator MANSFIELD. In other words, sonny, you pick up your languages where you can.

BARRY RUDD. I do, sir. My own keeps me busy enough. I love anomalies, exceptions. *Vein, vane, vain. Through, dough, bough, rough, cough.* Senator Skypack, do you know how to spell 'fish'?

Senator SKYPACK. What, what, what? What *is* this? I got out of school second year high school. I don't have to be taught lessons by a doggone little fairy like this. . . . *F-i-s-h.*

BARRY RUDD. Wrong, Senator. You spell it *g-h-o-t-i.* You take the *gh* as pronounced in 'rough,' the *o* as pronounced in 'women,' and the *ti* as pronounced in 'nation,' and *g-h-o-t-i* spells 'fish.' I think it was G. B. Shaw who first pointed that out. He wanted to simplify our absurd spelling.

Senator MANSFIELD. You really love words, don't you?

BARRY RUDD. Oh, yes! Kismet, hieratic, mellific, nuncupative, sempiternal, mansuetude, jeremiad, austral, diaphanous, hegemony, exculpatory, homunculus, melanistic, cenobite, prolepsis, platykurtic, mephitic, ceraceous, inspissation, lanate—

Senator MANSFIELD. By the way, what was that common

eight-letter word you were talking about that only has one vowel?

BARRY RUDD. Do you give up? Do you all give up, Senators? Do you give up, Senator Voyolko?

Senator VOYOLKO. Me? Huh? Yeah, I give up.

BARRY RUDD. Strength.

Mr. BROADBENT. Senator Mansfield, sir, if you'll forgive my saying so, it was *you* who wanted things kept in a straight line.

Senator MANSFIELD. You're quite right, Mr. Broadbent. I forgot myself. Please carry on. . . . Strength. One, two, three—

Mr. BROADBENT. You were on your way home, Master Rudd.

BARRY RUDD. Yes, but I stopped off at the Perkonians' on the way to see if Flattop was there, but he's never home. His mother's a laundress, she spends every day of the week in somebody's dark creepy cellar, doing the wash, and she has a morbid dread of rodents, and she drinks. She avoids Flattop and he avoids her; there's a mutual repulsion. But I knew where to find him—at the bowling alleys. We have this twelve-lane bowling center on River Street, with automatic pin spotters, and Flattop hangs around there quite a lot, picks up some change running the house balls through the ball cleaner, sweeping the approaches, so on. I told you he's gone all the way square—even to earning money!

Mr. BROADBENT. He's a pretty tough little character, is he?

BARRY RUDD. Not at all. His haircut sets him apart, and sometimes his behavior does, too. That's all he wants—to be set apart.

Mr. BROADBENT. This haircut.

BARRY RUDD. His head is round, he has a moon face. The hair's blond. The upper surface has been leveled off absolutely flat, a bristling squared-off effect. The hair at the sides has been left rather long, and with the help of some gelatinous hair tonic most of this is combed straight upward and it swoops inward a half-inch or so over the flat area from either side. Then there's a kind of part on each side, just above the ears between the up-swept longer hair and the rest that's just combed downwards. There's more to it than that, but that gives you the general impression.

Mr. BROADBENT. What did you two do?

BARRY RUDD. We sat in the spectators' seats and discussed the stickleback.

Senator SYKPACK. My God! Taxpayers' good money.

BARRY RUDD. *Gasterosteus aculeatus*, the three-spined stickle-back. It has a most interesting reproductive ritual.

Senator SKYPACK. In other words, you boys were discussing smut. Right?

BARRY RUDD. After a few minutes I went home and looked—

Senator SKYPACK. Answer my question.

BARRY RUDD. I don't regard sex play as dirty, Senator. It's a natural reproductive drive. . . .

Senator SKYPACK. By God, now he's going to give a lecture on—

Mr. BROADBENT. Go on, Master Rudd. You went home.

BARRY RUDD. And right away I broke Mother's hand mirror. I looked in it, in a purely speculative way, to see what I'd look like with a flattop haircut, and I dropped it, and it smashed, and I was horror-struck, because I have a strong superstitious bent. A mirror looks beyond you—to your background and into your future. If one breaks, then that means that it doesn't want you to see *beyond*. Once when Napoleon was in the field, the mirror above Josephine's portrait broke, and he couldn't rest until he got home and found that she was all right. . . . In any case, I have reason to dislike mirrors. My physical make-up has been . . . My fatness has been . . . When I was four, I developed a granulated eyelid, and Mother took me to a pediatrician, and in the course of the examination she suggested to the doctor that perhaps the trouble was eyestrain from reading. I was four, you realize. This seemed to the pediatrician a good joke, until he put one of his own office cards in front of me, and I read off the name, office hours, and address. 'I've never seen anything like this in sixteen years of pediatrics,' the doctor said, and he took me down the hall to show me off to a nose-and-throat man. I began to have nosebleeds from my adenoids a few months later, and during a visit this same nose-and-throat man gave me a medical journal to read, and was amazed to hear me deal easily with words like *maxillary*. Of course I was over five by then. I don't mean to be boasting, the point is that two years ago I went back to the pediatrician who had first noticed my reading. My mother took me in for a thing on my face. Well, the doctor —I don't want to name him—stripped me and stood me in a corner. He pointed out to my mother my knock knees, pendant breasts, fat rolls, underdeveloped genitals. He prodded me and kneaded me. 'Look at him!' he said. 'An endocrine case. When he goes to high school and gets in the locker room, the boys'll take one look at him and say, "What's *this?*" ' He said, right in front of me, that he suspected a tumor of the pituitary. He showed my mother some photographs of what I would grow up to be like, and she nearly fainted. He sent me to another doctor who was supposed to be an endocrinologist, and I was in the hospital two days and a night, and five doctors checked all over me and said not a thing was wrong except that I was older than the other boys mentally and this tended to make me sedentary. My father got me a baseball mitt. The hospital bill was a hundred dollars. The same thing happened last year. I had flu, and my mother called in a strange doctor, and he was amazed at the excess fat. I was seventeen pounds overweight. He said I needed hormones. So my mother took me to the top endocrinologist here in the capital and she paid sixty-five dollars to learn that I was still sedentary. My father got me a second-hand bike and shouted at me quite a lot. The doctor said he could make some drastic changes by dosing me up, but that he didn't want to. He said to wait and see if puberty wouldn't iron everything out.

Mr. BROADBENT. After the mirror.

BARRY RUDD. I've always been extremely self-conscious about my physical make-up. Once at the museum I saw the transparent woman, and I offered myself to one of the museum guards as a transparent boy. You see, I have this network of tiny veins on the surface of my skin, so I seem to have waxlike flesh.

Senator MANSFIELD. Now, sonny, after the mirror broke.

BARRY RUDD. Just while I was on my hands and knees picking up the pieces—we only have these two rooms, Mother and Father sleep on a convertible in the main room, my sister and I sleep in the kitchen on a rollaway—this was in the main room by the chiffonier, and, as I say, I was on my hands and knees grubbing around when Susan came in. She's my sister, she's seven. She's known as the beauty of the family: Mother says her hair's like silk, and Momma braids it for her, and then Susan has these enormous black lashes around big pale-blue eyes, so when she looks at you, it's this look of perfect surprise and innocence—completely misleading. She's very shrewd. She took in what happened, and she began to rub one forefinger against the other at me, and teased me, and I called her a brat and got after her, but she's too fast for me.

Mr. BROADBENT. So.

BARRY RUDD. I settled down in the kitchen to a problem I'd been thinking about, and I guess I was there about a half-hour, anyway my mother came in and asked what I was doing there moping. 'Always alone!' she said. I didn't say anything, but I thought of a quotation Dr. Gozar gave me one time. Emerson. 'Solitude, the safeguard of mediocrity, is to genius the stern friend.'

Senator SKYPACK. By God, now he's an all-fired little genius.

BARRY RUDD. Please don't mistake me, I don't think I'm a genius. Only in the sense that I would like to be worthy of Dr. Gozar's . . . that I would like to work as hard as I can. . . . I thought of solitary ones—of the boy Newton playing alone with his machines, Edison with his chemicals. As a child Darwin loved long walks by himself, and once he became so absorbed in thought he walked off the end of a wall. Samuel Johnson, not joining in the sports at school, perhaps because of his defective sight and repulsively large size. Shelley, reading alone. Byron, loving to wander at night in the dark, lonely cloisters of the abbey . . .

Mr. BROADBENT. What was the problem you spoke of?

BARRY RUDD. It was out of my field, which is taxonomy. I was just daydreaming about the possibility of four-dimensional tic-tac-toe. I've played the game in three dimensions. The image I had was of a three-dimensional game moving through space at the speed of light. How would you represent X's and O's and their interplay in the fluid terms of *that* game? You see, I've been able since an early age to think of sizes and shapes and relationships in completely abstract terms, not as concepts related to my body, as is the case with most people. Perhaps I could get away from my body as a basis for size comparisons because it's unsatisfactory to me. I'm plain clumsy. When I try to do something with my hands, I just get mad. My grandfather carved violins; my father can use the tiniest tools. I can't even write: I get so impatient with my fingers when ideas are racing through my head!

Mr. BROADBENT. Master Rudd, how is all this connected—

BARRY RUDD. Senator Mansfield asked me to begin at the beginning and not leave anything out, and I've been trying to tell you everything that happened, everything that went through my mind, on the afternoon when all this began. I suppose the

86

actual *beginning* was what came next, just after Momma bawled me out for being a hermit—a knock on the kitchen door. This is on the street side, and the door's stuck, so I went to the window and saw it was the G-man, and I rapped on the window and pointed to the alleyway alongisde the house, and he went around to the back. I heard Momma open the door there, and I shut the door between the kitchen and the back room, and I began to hear murmuring in there—my name once in a while. I didn't go in, because I assumed the G-man was talking to Momma about my being maladjusted. I'm sort of famous for being what I think is known as one-sided.

Mr. BROADBENT. They were in fact discussing the child buyer?

BARRY RUDD. That's right. But, Mr. Broadbent, I really think Momma ought to be the one to tell you that part. I could give you what she and Father reported to me later about it, but I should think—

Senator MANSFIELD. All right. Let the boy stand down for the time being, and we'll question his mother about this interview. We'll have him back afterward.

Senator SKYPACK. Agreed! We sure better let this freak step down and let another witness take over, Mr. Chairman. My gaskets can only take so much pressure.

Senator MANSFIELD. All right, sonny. Thank you. You wait out there. . . . Call Mrs. Rudd.

You've been sworn, Mrs. Rudd, just take your seat there, please.

TESTIMONY OF MRS. PAUL RUDD, HOUSEWIFE,
TOWN OF PEQUOT

Mr. BROADBENT. We've called you back, Mrs. Rudd, to tell us about Mr. Cleary's visit to your home last Thursday.

Mrs. RUDD. I'm sorry about this morning. It's very hard, when they want to take your boy away, and when you get a lot of officials . . . swearing your word of honor . . .

Senator MANSFIELD. We understand, ma'am.

Mrs. RUDD. When they've ruined your house and home. They came there, it was after dark, only Barry and Sue and I were home, my husband was off bowling, and we knew they were coming, because Barry had had a warning from his friend, that naughty boy, the Perkonian boy knew all about it, so we managed to barricade the doors, and we were waiting—it was like a bad dream—and first we heard some motorcycles—

Senator MANSFIELD. If you don't mind, ma'am, we'll come to that incident a little later. Right now we'd like to hear about Mr. Cleary.

Mrs. RUDD. It's nothing to *you* when a person's home—

Senator MANSFIELD. Yes, ma'am, we're very interested in your home, and we want to ask you all about it, but right now . . . Mr. Broadbent, would you—?

Mr. BROADBENT. If you please, Mrs. Rudd, take your mind back to last Thursday afternoon. You had come home from work and found Barry woolgathering at the kitchen table. Mr. Cleary came to call. Please tell us all about that visit.

Mrs. RUDD. It was a kind of warning. He said he wanted to warn us.

Mr. BROADBENT. Please try to remember everything that was said. Exactly what did Mr. Cleary tell you?

Mrs. RUDD. He told me this man, this big businessman, had come to Pequot, and he wanted to buy Barry.

Mr. BROADBENT. Did he say why?

Mrs. RUDD. He said this man—the child buyer—was buying kids for a defense project, that was all he knew. It was a science project of some kind.

Mr. BROADBENT. Did Mr. Cleary say how much the buyer would pay for Barry?

Mrs. RUDD. No, he only said it would be a terrible temptation, a terrible lot of money. You see, on that occasion he was trying to warn us, he was against the deal.

Mr. BROADBENT. Why was he against it?

Mrs. RUDD. He said Barry was too young. 'Too young to be nailed to science,' the way he put it. I asked what would happen to Barry if we sold him, and the G-man said he didn't know exactly, he said there was going to be some kind of experiment on him. The G-man was kind and sympathetic that day, he was like a doctor or minister at a sickbed, and I opened up to him, I told him how my whole life was poured into Barry. The girl's a sweet thing, but she's just a dividend. Barry's everything —everything I wanted to overcome and accomplish. I grew up in rural villages, I told Mr. Cleary, in Sparta and Hastings Center, and the thing I had to fight against was coarseness. It wasn't just the pigs wallowing in the mud and pushing each other aside in the trough; it was in *me* . . . my family. Coarseness, ignorance. And on top of that there was boredom—nothing to do but work. So I took up reading, both in magazines they had at the community center, *Farmer's Journal, Country Gentleman, Wallace's*, and these novels—I remember them so clear! *Cranford. The Vicar of Wakefield. Our Village. Mary Barton. Old Christmas. Northanger Abbey.* The opposite of pig shove pig, the very opposite. I made myself into the brightest one in my class, I happen to have a fantastic memory, so I could get high marks easily, and I was going to be a surgeon—you see, I even wanted to use knives to cut out the crudity, filth, sickness—and I got as far as an osteopathy course at Budkin State, but that was all. My father was taken with a shock, and he couldn't farm any more, and the Depression came, and with financial worries I never even finished up on osteopathy preparation. Later on I married Paul Rudd. He'd graduated from high school, and his four sisters were all on their way to becoming nurses; I liked that. And we settled in Treehampstead, where Paul took work as a machinest for Trucco, and we had the two children, Barry and Sue. When Barry was five Trucco moved us to their branch plant in Pequot. We didn't prosper, so after a while I took the job in Stillman's—but that was later. All this time Barry was my whole life. *He* was going to be my victory over coarseness. Before he went to school, way back when he was two or three years old, in the afternoons trying to settle him down for his naps I'd read to him—*The Three Bears, Raggedy Ann, Sixty-five Bedtime Stories, Black Beauty, Hans Brinker and the Silver Skates,* and some of the books were way too old for him, but it was so surprising, he'd pay close mind, and the second time I'd read a book, if I skipped any, he'd make a fuss and wouldn't allow it. And there was once, long before that, Barry was still creeping, he walked alone at thirteen months, so it was before that (we could tell from the beginning he was marked to be special: he was born with a caul), anyway, one day we had a visit from Mr. Szerenyi, he lived upstairs from us, a Hungarian, very popular, he was president of the Rakosi Society because Treehampstead has a substantial Hungarian population, but he's crazy on the subject of diets. He had this book, its thesis was that the way to eternal life was through eating seafood and vegetables grown within fifty miles of the sea, and Barry was crawling on the floor, and Mr. Szerenyi started reading in a kind of fierce singsong, right from his breastbone and out through his nose, very emotional. I remember it so well! 'Ingestion of these phlogisticated fibers causes a knotting action of the stomach muscles. . . .'

Senator MANSFIELD. It seems that you, madam, like your son, are blessed with total recall. You surprise a person.

Mrs. RUDD. Blessed? It's a curse, Senator, a curse, when you can't forget any of it! You try to shake it out of your mind, and it sticks there like damp salt. Anyway, he was reading, '. . . This irritation spreads in time through the peritoneal cavities and invests in particular the gastrohepatic omentum with . . .' And then was when it happened. Barry crept to me, and pulled himself up at my knee, and I lifted him in my lap, and where he'd been crashing around with this violent energy, now he suddenly went limp on his back, with an ecstatic expression, watching Mr. Szerenyi's face as he read. Do you see? I mean, *words*.

Mr. BROADBENT. You told Mr. Cleary all this?

Mrs. RUDD. Yes, sir. Am I saying too much?

Mr. BROADBENT. No, please go on. What else?

Mrs. RUDD. About when Barry began to read. I was lying on my bed in my slip reading a magazine, it was hot summer, and the people in the next building, the Lutri block, they lived by screaming, and I *had* to rest.

Mr. BROADBENT. This was before you worked at Stillman's?

Mrs. RUDD. Yes, sir, it was. It was before we even moved to Pequot. Barry was four. Four years, one month, eighteen days, and six hours of age. You'll see in a minute why I figured that out. I was lying in my slip reading a news magazine, Barry was beside me, I remember it was about Lord Mountbatten giving freedom to Pakistan, to Mohammed Ali Jinnah—as if you could give it, from one man's hand into another's. I was reading, almost dozing, and Barry said, 'O.K. I'm ready,' and I said what for, and he said for me to turn the page, he'd finished. I laughed because he was always playing tricks on me, but he said no fooling, he'd finished reading the bottom of the page. So I made him read out loud, and he could. He did. '. . . autonomous nation within the British commonwealth.' Hard words. I've sworn an oath, I wouldn't lie to you. He really did.

Mr. BROADBENT. How had he accomplished this?

Mrs. RUDD. The nearest I can figure it, he'd always watched the page when I read aloud to him, and he was always telling me to go slow. Slower! Slower! And I admit I'd dinned the sounds of letters into him for a long time. And he just put it all together, I guess. It scared me. I thought I'd done something wrong. Then I told Mr. Cleary about another scare—how something you're proud about can scare you. There was this Martha Massiello, lived in the Buffum block, she's a bad drinker, she used to call around at everyone's house every morning, she looked like a tire that was due for recapping, she'd visit hoping you'd pour her a shot, and her main way of keeping contact with humanity was to tell you bad news. So that morning, a few weeks after that first time Barry read to me, she came in and she said, 'Julia burnt her hand,' and I said I hoped it wasn't serious, and she said Julia was 'gonta live.' Martha was already wobbly, and we looked around, there was Barry sitting on the floor with his legs spread and a book between them and he was reading out loud. I guess I looked proud, and I looked at Martha's face, and there was a look of horror, as if the monster Godzilla had come up at her out of the Bay of Tokyo, and she said, 'Holy God, look at little Einstein!' and she coughed and had a hard time breathing, like she had asthma. And I could tell. That was a warning. It was like a finger pointing at what's happened this week.

Mr. BROADBENT. You say that was a warning, and you were scared—did you do anything about it?

Mrs. RUDD. No, on the contrary, I kept right on the same way. I couldn't help myself. I'm still a reader myself, and I guess I pushed Barry hard as I could. I told Mr. Cleary to look around— he could see the mess, and one of the reasons our rooms are so disorderly is that I read when I ought to be cleaning. I don't have a very broad back for housework, I get up at five thirty in the morning, I get my husband's and children's breakfasts, and then I sit down and read till it's time for me to go to Stillman's. I used to read nothing but good books, but now it's *McCall's*, the *Companion*, the *Post*, *Ladies' Home Journal*, *Reader's Digest*—cover to cover. When I was a girl I never could get enough maple syrup. It's the same thing in my reading.

Mr. BROADBENT. And Barry?

Mrs. RUDD. Every time I go to the supermarket I drop him off at the library. I want him to read. I want him to work. I want him to be what I wanted to be.

Senator MANSFIELD. With any luck he'll be that, ma'am, and much more.

Mrs. RUDD. If there's one thing I've done for Barry, it's to make him know that luck doesn't help you, you can't count on luck. The only things that help are to plan and to work.

Senator MANSFIELD. You've certainly given him every opportunity, ma'am.

Mrs. RUDD. I've always immersed myself in what Barry was doing and thinking—but you know something? I feel he lacks a natural affection, filial affection, a son for his mother.

Senator MANSFIELD. We received testimony that he dotes on you, ma'am.

Mrs. RUDD. Appearances aren't always what they seem. It's hard for him to show any feelings; sometimes I wonder if he has any. Except he shows them to Sue: that's one place where he's natural, all right. Brat! Crybaby! Stinker! I hate you! All day long.

Mr. BROADBENT. From what you've said, it sounds as if you got along very well with Mr. Cleary that afternoon. Had you liked him in the past?

Mrs. RUDD. I don't like any school people.

Senator MANSFIELD. That's a rather extreme statement, Mrs. Rudd. What do you mean?

Mrs. RUDD. The things they've done to Barry.

Senator MANSFIELD. Such as.

Mrs. RUDD. You want a 'such as'? I'll give you one! I told you we lived in Treehampstead first, Barry was in kindergarten there. All right, we move to Pequot, and in the fall I call up the principal at Lincoln, Dr. Gozar, and I say, hello, I want to enter my boy, but she tells me the legal age for entering first grade is different in Pequot than in Treehampstead—a child has to be six before the following New Year's Day, and Barry's sixth birthday isn't till January nineteenth. He misses by three weeks—nineteen days. So I tell her Barry's already had a year in kindergarten. He can read. That's too bad, Dr. Gozar says, makes no difference; Lincoln doesn't have a kindergarten. No, she says, no exceptions can be made.

Senator MANSFIELD. What happened?

Mrs. RUDD. I got mad, you can imagine. I said I wanted to talk to somebody higher up. She said I could go see Mr. Owing for all the good it would do me. I did; I made an appointment, and I took Barry, and Dr. Gozar was sitting there, with her arms folded and her jaw sticking out like a snow plow. I guess she'd jacked Mr. Owing up with gumption, and he started in about the way children develop—well-rounded—impossible to make special provisions because of lack of funds—overcrowded conditions—child who's younger than the peer group. . . . 'Give him exercise,' he said. 'Get him outdoors.' I asked if there was anyone else I could see, and Mr. Owing, he went the color of bacon grease, nearly passed out, but Dr. Gozar growled at me: I could see the State Supervisor for *Exceptional* Children, Miss Henley. She put a heavy emphasis, sarcastic, of course, on 'exceptional.' She must have figured I had the usual exaggerated maternal pride. I came up here to the capital to see Miss Henley, and she lectured me for an hour and a half about what happens when you push a child—I couldn't understand one word in ten. But I've always thought that teachers know everything, so I swallowed it all. No school for Barry; we waited out the year. Barry's father got him a basketball and nailed up a backboard and net out on the porch roof; it's still there, the string's all rotted. Barry never touched the ball. All he wanted was to stay in the house, pencil and paper, a book. He spent half his time with Miss Cloud in the library, she's the librarian, she's a hunchback.

Senator MANSFIELD. So he was six and a half when he finally entered first grade?

Mrs. RUDD. Six years, eight months. With a twelve-year-old mind, they tell me. Turned out he had a good year. Miss Bagas was his teacher; at home nights Barry used to write Miss Bagas love notes. I didn't mind that, I was actually glad. One time Miss Bagas had a nice talk with me about Barry's excellent followership. Specially fine, she said, considering he was so much more intelligent than the other kids that it would have been easy for him to be overbearing. She said he was popular; she said good followers are always loved.

Senator MANSFIELD. So things came out all right after all.

Mrs. RUDD. Wait a minute, I haven't told you the end of the story yet. Listen. In June of his first-grade year, Barry was double-promoted. It wasn't at my request, you understand. They skipped him over second grade and put him in the third—just where he'd have been if they'd let him in a year early, only now he'd missed the experiences of second grade and he had to make a whole new set of friends. At that time Dr. Gozar begged me not to talk to other mothers about Barry's good fortune—it would cause envy and dissatisfaction.

Mr. BROADBENT. How were things left with Mr. Cleary the other day when he came to warn you?

Mrs. RUDD. He said not to decide anything without talking to him, as if he was our lawyer, or like that. I was all mixed up, nervy, the way I get if something new happens. All I wanted was what would be good for Barry. Paul came in from work a few minutes after the G-man left, and he was hungry and kind of edgy, wanted to know why supper wasn't ready. So I told him about the visit, the G-man, the child buyer. Right off the bat

Paul was crazy to sell, he wanted to go right out and find the buyer and close the deal. He saw all this big money, saw how we could start and do favors for people. Said we wouldn't ever have to crawl again. I had an awful heavy feeling, as if some force I could dimly remember was going to interfere again in my life. I wanted to go slow. But then Barry came in the room while we were talking, and we told him. We told him exactly what was what.

Mr. BROADBENT. How did he take it?

Mrs. RUDD. As I say, it isn't easy to tell with him. But if anything, I would've said he was delighted. It gave me the shivers, and that heavy feeling got worse.

Senator MANSFIELD. Mr. Broadbent, have you brought Mr. Rudd up here today?

Mr. BROADBENT. Yes, sir, he's available, sir.

Senator MANSFIELD. I'd like to question him.

Mr. BROADBENT. Call Mr. Paul Rudd.

Senator MANSFIELD. Thank you, Mrs. Rudd, we'll excuse you for now. Very helpful . . . Mr. Rudd? Please stand to be sworn.

Do you solemnly swear that you will tell this committee on its present business the truth, the whole truth, and nothing but the truth, so help you God?

Mr. RUDD. I do.

TESTIMONY OF MR. PAUL RUDD, MACHINIST, TOWN OF PEQUOT

Senator MANSFIELD. Mr. Rudd, we've taken testimony from your wife about Mr. Cleary coming to your home, last Thursday, and how he broke the news to her about the child buyer, and she informed us under oath that on being told about this visit, you were eager to take up the deal. What I want to know, sir, is, what possessed you? How would a father want to sell his son?

96

Senator SKYPACK. Don't you suppose it's possible, Mr. Chairman, that this gentleman was influenced by patriotic motives? Just the way, in time of war, a man is proud to see his son sign up with the service, the colors? The nature of this deal was such—

Mr. RUDD. Yes, sir, that's the way I felt. I felt that way. Proud. I did.

Senator MANSFIELD. But, Mr. Rudd, your wife said you wanted the money.

Mr. RUDD. A son's supposed to earn his keep, he takes over and supports the parents. Is that unnatural? I mean on the other side, my father came from Czechoslovakia, and the thing you tried to do was to give birth to sons, so as they would grow up and support you. Girl children weren't worth anything, except *they* could have sons. You put in your sweat and earnings for a boy, food, schooling, getting him ready, and then the time comes, and it's his turn. Is that so unnatural?

Senator MANSFIELD. At ten years of age?

Mr. RUDD. They keep telling me he's got the mind of a eighteen-, twenty-year-old. A young fellow works with his body when he's grown into it, the same should go for working with his head. I don't see that that's so unnatural. My father went to work when he was eleven, in a tannery, he put me to work when I was thirteen. I send him money, room-and-board money, right today. Here's this boy, he's got a perfectly tremendious working capacity with his brain. I can't see it's so unnatural to want to make some use of it. Except the schools of today, they say nobody should work, just be happy, just goldbrick along and the world owes you a living. The older generation owes you the works, that's the attitude. My father, after he came to this country, he got to be a butcher, worked in this chain store, and he was a pretty good butcher, but what he liked to do, he liked to cruise around out-of-the-way lumberyards, and find these pieces of strange wood, fancy-grained, that would have a sounding-board quality, resonance, he could tell by just looking at them, and he would carve violins. In the cellar. A fiddler in his village on the other side taught him, and he made creditable instruments, I mean this big instrument company would buy them off my father, a hundred bucks, two hundred a throw. He has this knack with his hands, and he always liked it better than the butchering. So now he's retired, and his wife's with him, and right today I send half the money, my brother sends half, and it eats into my own living. This last summer Fred Zimmer and I, he lives across the street, we decided to make this skiff and buy us an outboard for picnics down the Pehadnock, at Sandy Point and above the light-company dam, and I tell you, I had to scrimp and dig up the cash from nowheres, and yet I'm still sending my old man fancy-wood money even though he can't really woodwork worth a darn any more, it's just to keep him from getting ill-tempered. We built the skiff all right, and got the outboard but it was darn hard. So why shouldn't I want my son to bring something in? Here's this offer, a tremendious sum of money right on a silver platter.

Senator MANSFIELD. Then you put your son's talents in a class with a knack for repairing machinery or trimming cuts of meat or so on?

Mr. RUDD. I've been rougher on the boy than his mother, I'll have to admit it. I spent years trying to make a regular kid of him, didn't realize how hopeless it was. I'm mechanical-minded, I like to tinker, and I never read a thing unless if it's the sports news in the papers. I don't understand a boy like Barry, I never have. I like to go bowling, I'm in the Tuesday-night league, and I take the whole family to the lanes Tuesday nights, and the boy sits there either reading a book or lately he's taken up writing mystery stories, then he tears them up afterwards, it's only for his own amusement. I've always tried to get him outdoors, catch a ball, get tousled and dirty, but it's just made him keep away from me. He hasn't got enough spunk to show resentment, he just keeps his distance, slinks off. He prefers his grandfather— my old man—to his own father. Oh, he dotes on Grandfather Rudd. It's because the old man tells him these legends, folk tales, from the other side. But *I* show up—the tail between the legs and out of sight.

Senator Mansfield. Then it's your view you have a perfect right to exploit this boy's talents in any way you want?

Mr. Rudd. Why not? I slaved for him for years. I been sitting at a machine over at Trucco eight hours, seven hours a day for years. I fed him, put shoes on him. Why shouldn't he do something for me? Before this deal came along, I was after his mother to put him on TV, get him on a quiz program, exhibit the master mind. Bring in some dough. God knows I tried first to make him regular. I spent months at a time balancing him on a two-wheeler, but the minute I let go, whammo! Off he falls. I'm good with my hands, I'm keeping a one-seventy-two average in my league in the bowling, it gives me the creeps to see him take aholt of a piece of bread at the table.

Senator Skypack. I just wanted to say, Mr. Rudd, you've been taking some rather hostile questioning here, but I feel you should know that some of us applaud your position, your patriotism. I mean, a decent father's instincts . . . I'm just surprised how lenient—

Senator Mansfield. All right, Mr. Broadbent, I've asked all I want to ask. Have you any questions?

Mr. Broadbent. Nothing at present, sir.

Senator Mansfield. Then I think we should pick up with the boy. Thank you, Mr. Rudd.

Mr. Broadbent. Please fetch Master Rudd.

Senator Skypack. Brother, I hope my blood vessels don't rupture on me.

Senator MANSFIELD. All right, sonny, you're sworn. Please just take your seat.

TESTIMONY OF BARRY RUDD, MINOR, TOWN OF PEQUOT

Senator MANSFIELD. Just pick up where we broke off, Mr. Broadbent.

Mr. BROADBENT. So after Mr. Cleary left, your parents told you the situation. What was your reaction?

BARRY RUDD. At first I had a feeling of elation, a sudden lift, because somebody important was interested in me. But I've learned to distrust euphoria. I once thought it was a priceless state of ecstasy, a rapture, like a moment when Blake had one of his visions, say, or when Archimedes in his bath realized he could find out whether the tyrant Hieron's crown was pure gold or alloyed, by a simple displacement test. But I've come to understand that it's not a time of revelation—not for me. My moments of inspiration come when I least expect them, when I'm abstracted, walking up the public-library steps, playing gin rummy with Flattop. It seems as if it's the absent mind that solves the problems of this world—for me, anyway.

Mr. BROADBENT. What did you do?

BARRY RUDD. My homework.

Mr. BROADBENT. Where?

BARRY RUDD. No, we had supper first, then Momma and Father and the Monster stayed in the kitchen and I went in the other room to do my homework. I turned the main-room light on by a Rube Goldberg device I'd made. A string is attached to the doorknob, a system of pulleys and weights, and—

Senator MANSFIELD. I think we can picture it, sonny.

BARRY RUDD. There were two problems in connection with

the device. First, the lamp has a revolving switch rather than a chain pull. Second, turning the light on and off every other time, to allow for departures from the room, presented—

Senator MANSFIELD. Yes, sonny, go on.

BARRY RUDD. I went under the lamp, still burning (I was burning, I mean, not the lamp—though *it* was, too, in its way) with this euphoria—somebody powerful wanted to buy me!—and I began a childish game, very regressed, of playing with my shadow under the lamplight. I'd make my shadow, my other self, first bigger, then smaller; try to jump away from it, disconnect it; try to stamp on it, scare it away. I had thought of my shadow, when I was small, as a gauze thing that could be folded and put in a bureau drawer. Of course you know where that fantasy came from?

Mr. BROADBENT. Then?

BARRY RUDD. I suddenly needed advice, needed to talk with someone I trusted. I saw Grandpa Rudd's picture on the bureau. For years I believed that I could make pictures of people, snapshots, come to life if I could only find the key. I wanted to have a small man, about three inches high, to keep my desk neat at school, tell me stories; he would ride in my book bag. For a long time I thought the key might be to hold my breath and count, forwards or maybe backwards. I realize that this, too, was babyish, but I've clung to a feeling that the pictures, even if they couldn't come all the way to life, could think and see. So I took the picture of Grandpa in my hands, and I asked him what I should do, and something made me drop him, and I had a moment of unrealistic fear that I'd hurt him.

Mr. BROADBENT. What happened then?

BARRY RUDD. As I put my grandfather's picture back, there came over me a feeling of inadequacy—the thought that my heredity was deficient, that I came from a thin line. I thought of some verses of Horace that Dr. Gozar reeled off once when she was showing me a few basic facts of heredity through fruit-fly demonstrations: 'In steers, in steeds, appear the merits of their sires; nor do fierce eagles beget timid doves.' My euphoria drained away as I thought of familial talents: how Adams, the son of a president, became president; how vivid the two cousin Roosevelts were; that the Bachs were musical for three generations; that Addison was the son of a Royal Chaplain, Bulwer of an ambitious army general, Hugo of a king's aide, Boyle of a Lord High Treasurer of Ireland. And I remembered: 'Training increases inborn worth,' Horace went on to say; and I thought of the good fortunes of Mill, Pitt, Mozart, Michelangelo. Then I had to struggle to jack up my spirits, and I thought of unexpected greatness: of Lincoln; of Bunyan, the son of a tinker, Carlyle of a mason, Winckelmann of a cobbler, Canova of a stonecutter, Jansen of a peasant, Kant of a strapmaker. And I thought of *my* father, who'd said he wanted to let me go if he could get a good enough price, in the next room, watching *Maverick* on television.

Senator VOYOLKO. Great program.

BARRY RUDD. I finally got down to work. In order to ensure the success of my report on nomenclature, I first followed a ceremony that had helped me a great deal in the past: I sharpened my pencil, pointed the sharp end successively toward the north, east, south, and west, and then, holding it upright, tapped its eraser end repeatedly on the table while, with the fingers of my left hand, starting with the pinky and moving toward the thumb, I flipped the lobe of my left ear. The pencil, incidentally, was John Sano's. He got an A on his last research report, on bread mold, and I'd borrowed it from him, because a pencil that had written so well for him was bound to write well for me.

Senator SKYPACK. Pinky! My God!

BARRY RUDD. My tapping got out of phase with my earlobe flicking, and I began the whole deal over again, even to sharpening the pencil, to make sure. I know, Senator Skypack, you think this is foolish, you think reliance on this sort of thing—

Senator SYKPACK. You're damn tootin'.

BARRY RUDD. Momma has always dinned into me that leaning on luck, magic, is foolish, and I *know*, in the higher associational and reasoning centers of my cortex, that she's right. Still, just in *case*. Deep down. But don't get me wrong. I work. I work long sessions. I've observed Dr. Gozar—I watch her by the hour, in her natural habitat, the lab, as if I were on a zoological field ramble, *Homo sapiens*, a noble specimen, and I've seen her marked willingness to stay at a task, to withstand discomfort, go without food, disregard fatigue and strain, forget a cold or a headache—above all, to face the possibility of failure, and facing that chance seems to me the first prerequisite of success, or completion. And I've learned concentration. I closed the shouting of Bart Maverick out of my mind. I fought the pencil across the page—how I hate the act of recording! But I'll tell you something: no matter how awkward I may be at stickball or volleyball, no matter how much I'm the butt of the beefers on the playground—and no matter how jaggedly I write, nevertheless when I get in the lab, next to Dr. Gozar, and we're sorting Promethea, Cecropia, and Polyphemus moth larvae, or we're mounting beetles and bugs on pins, I can feel an unusual grace flowing into my fingers, like an electric current. I'm transformed.

Mr. BROADBENT. Is there a connection—

BARRY RUDD. Yes. You asked my reaction to the news about the child buyer. All through my preparation of the report, even thought I was concentrating fiercely, like a horse racing with blinders on, I felt an underlying malaise, but at the same time a remnant of my earlier lift. My unnatural delight was mixed now with a slow sinking feeling. I finished my work and got ready for bed. The Monster was already tucked in: I have to sleep on half the rollaway with her. Momma turned the lights out, and I lay on my back and rubbed my eyes, and I saw a sort of glowing head, a ghost head. I knew it was a mere phosphene, from the rubbing, but I connected it with the child buyer; it seemed threatening. I read for a while with a flashlight under the covers and ate some dried apricots. I've been hit by science fiction lately. My favorite at the moment is James Mull's *The Moon-Skaters,* and somehow the tartness and roughness of the apricots is just right for science fiction. And—Mr. Broadbent, I know you're worrying about the relevance—underneath I had this growing feeling of opposites, joy and fear, partly stemming from the reading but partly not.

Mr. BROADBENT. I see.

BARRY RUDD. When I had grown tired of reading I cut off the flashlight and I lay on my back thinking about a girl in my class, about her thigh area just above her kneecap.

Mr. BROADBENT. Florence Renzulli?

BARRY RUDD. No, Mr. Broadbent. You're strict about relevance; she wasn't in any part of this. I don't like to give names here, so I'll just say it was another girl in my class. You see, Flattop and I had been talking about the stickleback, and I was wondering about applying certain elements of the ritual—something in the book I'd been reading triggered—

Senator SKYPACK. Smut, I knew it was smut. These paperbacks . . .

BARRY RUDD. —but then I got thinking about moving her skirt up, centimeter by centimeter, just to the top of her stocking—picturing Sunday clothes, I mean. Excuse centimeters; from the lab I carry the metric system over into much of my thinking.

Senator SKYPACK. Scandalous.

BARRY RUDD. Then suddenly I was thinking about the child buyer's proposition. The G-man had told Momma that the child buyer was hunting for geniuses. I thought of the refrain Dr. Gozar had put in my head: work! work! She was forever quoting the authorities. Flaubert: 'Genius, in the phrase of Buffon, is only long patience. Work.' Buffon's sentence actually was: '*La génie n'est autre chose qu'une grande aptitude à la patience.*' Carlyle: 'Genius is an infinite capacity for taking pains.' Michelangelo: 'If people knew how hard I work to get my mastery it would not seem so wonderful after all.' Paderewski: 'Before I was a genius I was a drudge.' I thought of going, being bought and going away to Arizona for the vague unclear experiment *on me*. I thought hard about it, because I habitually think the opposite of what I want in order to get my way. Then for some reason I thought about my grandfather; I wanted to make a dream about him.

Senator MANSFIELD. You wanted to *make* a dream?

BARRY RUDD. I have long believed I could make myself dream about the last person I thought about before falling off to sleep. I think of dreams as substances of light that are out in the room around me at night. The room is full of dreams, which possibly are tiny lights that come from the moon or stars. They come from the sky, the night makes them, and they get in the room, crowding around, and they sort of look at you, watching for an opening, and if you think about one of them, it can get in. I think of light as looking at you. A street lamp can see everything that passes; a candle sees the flickering room; a match sees the end of a cigarette. I think of human eyes as giving light. Did you ever see a cat's eyes beside the road?

Mr. BROADBENT. For a boy with a scientific bent of mind—

BARRY RUDD. I know, I know. The cat's eyes reflect your headlights. A street lamp has no optic nerve. I *know* all that, but these are holdovers from a very early age. Sometimes I have a strange feeling, almost a sensation of being on an escalator or perhaps a treadmill, or of slipping or gliding—from one age level to another. An adult thought one moment, a babyish thought the next.

Mr. BROADBENT. And did you dream about your grandfather?

BARRY RUDD. No, I'm often disappointed. I fell into a deep sleep, and the next thing, I woke up with a start—saw the light going across the ceiling when a car passed outside. I knew which way it was going. I figured that out by logic one night a couple of years ago, and then to verify my conclusion I propped a mirror in the window sill and saw that I'd been right. The opposite way. As I lay there I was hit, as if by a blow, by the thought of my father's wanting to sell me. Suddenly I had the feeling that he was the most august yet compassionate creature on earth—a gentle king. I loved him. I wanted him to *teach* me. I thought of Montaigne's father, educating his son with utmost delicacy and consideration, even going so far as to waken the boy each morning with instrumental music. I thought of Jeremy Bentham learning Latin at three and the Greek of Lily's *Grammar* at four and five on his father's knee. Coleridge, Schelling, Pascal, Goethe, Leibnitz—all systematically taught by their fathers. Then my thoughts began subtly to shift toward the notion of fathers' exploiting their sons to gratify ambition or avarice: Robert Peel's father consciously determining that he would mold his son into another Pitt; Mozart's father putting his son's absolute pitch and extraordinary powers of improvisation on display as if the child were a puppet. I thought of Samuel Johnson saying that in order to avoid being put on show as a prodigy he used sometimes to 'run up a tree.' Don't mistake me. I don't put myself in a class with . . . I aspire but I don't arrogate. . . . It only helps to make my own feelings clear if I . . .

Mr. BROADBENT. But I gather that on the whole you and your father—

BARRY RUDD. At that particular moment I had a feeling of intense yearning for his love. I wanted his strong arms around me.

106

Then all at once the full horror of the child buyer's proposal came over me.

Senator SKYPACK. Horror? You don't seem to realize what kind of a deal this is. In a class with getting an appointment to West Point. Better even. Horror!

BARRY RUDD. At first the feeling wasn't explicit. I remembered a little girl in a Sunday-school class I was in several years ago who had a shriveled hand. Then I remembered being chased through the parking lot of the shopping center on Sycamore Street, last year, on my bike, by these big boys, and they kept calling me a queer. 'You know you're a queer, don't you?' I didn't want to fight. I thought that sticks and stones couldn't possibly hurt my bones as much as those taunts did, though I had no idea what they meant. I thought of my childhood fears: When I was three I was afraid of what I called 'polo'—infantile paralysis. Then I was terrified that the Russians would drop a 'hydrant bomb.' Being bitten by a big dog. Being run over. Fire. Spiders. I lay in my bed and wondered if I was going crazy. It had been drummed into me—I remember Miss Songevine used to din this into me—that precocious children grow up abnormal, neurotic, headed for imbecility or insanity. Early ripe, early rot. The Bible says, 'Much learning doth make thee mad.' Seneca: 'There is no great genius without some touch of madness.' Burton, in *The Anatomy of Melancholy*, speaking of men 'out of too much learning become mad.' Moreau de Tours, Lombroso, Lange-Eichbaum—'scientists' who 'proved' the relationship between brilliance and madness; Miss Songevine threw them at me. I felt doomed. Doomed. And in a minute I was overwhelmed by the Great Fear. I was terrified that if I went to sleep again I wouldn't wake up in the morning. I put my hand on my chest to feel my heartbeat—was it steady? I turned my head on my pillow to listen for the rush of blood pumping in my ear. I heard a dog howling in the distance—telling me of death, death.

Then I desperately tried to save myself by classifying the creatures of this earth. Phylum One: Protozoa, the unicellular animals. Classes: Sarcodina, Mastigophora, Sporozoa, Infusoria. Phylum Two: Porifera, the sponges . . . And eventually I fell asleep. I waked up early, by habit, alive. I'd been getting up with Venus—usually to get a couple of hours of work with Dr. Gozar in the lab before breakfast. No Venus that morning, though: it was raining. Upon wakening I found the grip of my hand very weak. I felt as if I'd been running all night.

Senator MANSFIELD. All right. Thank you, sonny. Now, I think that's about all we have time for today, and we have the weekend coming up ahead of us. Is there anything farther you want to ask or add this afternoon, Mr. Broadbent?

Mr. BROADBENT. No, sir, as far as I'm concerned we could call it a day.

Senator MANSFIELD. We will stand in recess then, until ten o'clock Monday morning.

(Whereupon, at 5:10 p.m., Friday, October 25, the hearing was recessed, subject to the announced recall of the Chair.)

(The Committee met, pursuant to call, at 10:05 a.m. in Executive Session, in Room 429, Capitol Offices, Senator Aaron Mansfield presiding. Committee members and counsel present.)

Senator MANSFIELD. Senator Skypack asked for this Executive Session before we go down to the big room. So we'll be in order. Senator?

Senator SKYPACK. I just wanted to tell you people I did some thinking over the weekend about the kind of stuff we had to sit here and listen to in our hearing on Friday, and I just want to serve notice, and I wanted this on the record, serve notice that I'm going to do everything I can to get that arrogant little twerp before we drop these hearings.

Senator MANSFIELD. 'Get'? Just what do you mean?

Senator SYPACK. Show him up. Make him go, for one thing. Him sitting there and saying he doesn't choose to go along with the child buyer, with his plan!

Senator MANSFIELD. I'm rather surprised, Jack, I was very impressed with the boy. Charming. You mean you want to try to force his parents' hand? Make them sell?

Senator SKYPACK. You damn tootin'. I mean, you heard what the buyer told us, what they're doing down there. If this country's going to sit back and let the enemy outthink us, outrocket us, outeducate us. I'll tell you, I'm going to get him.

Senator MANSFIELD. What do you think, Peter?

Senator VOYOLKO. Huh? Me?

Senator MANSFIELD. How did the boy strike you?

Senator VOYOLKO. Fat. He's too fat. He eat too much.

Senator SKYPACK. You can't tell me that boy doesn't know all about the bombing—

Senator MANSFIELD. Stink bombing. You and Mr. Broadbent seem to insist—

Senator SKYPACK. Bomb, stink bomb—what's the difference? What's it matter what's inside—gunpowder or that sulphur-and-acid mixture or whatever they use these days?

Senator MANSFIELD. Seems to me there's quite a difference. Boys make stink bombs. Seems you're familiar with the materials yourself, Jack.

Senator SKYPACK. That's beside the point. The point is, by his own admission he was in the lab there with that goon just before the bomb was tossed. The cops nabbed him red-handed when his own house and home was being shmeared. In trouble with that girl. Broadbent hints around about the *child buyer* and a morals rap—my God, what about this precocious little fiend? I think we got to think about stiffening up the state J.D. laws, you take a case like this.

Senator MANSFIELD. May I ask what you intend to do, Jack?

Senator SKYPACK. I don't know yet. I'm just going to sit back and mull for now—But I don't think we ought to fool around. I think we ought to get that delinquent punk in, for one thing.

Mr. BROADBENT. He's here. He's right downstairs. I intend to call him, second witness this morning.

Senator SKYPACK. All right. Who's first?

Mr. BROADBENT. The buyer.

Senator SKYPACK. All right. I want you to take a good strong line now.

Senator MANSFIELD. Perhaps I ought to remind you, Jack, that I'm still Chairman of this Committee. . . . I mean, we ought at least to work out our tactics *together*. I'm inclined to give the kid a little leeway—

Mr. Broadbent. I think I should tell you, Mr. Chairman, I hold with Senator Skypack on this. I mean this country . . . we can't afford . . .

Senator Skypack. You bet your life we can't afford it.

Senator Mansfield. Peter, I wish I could get you to express—

Senator Voyolko. You take and put the kid on a diet. Then sell him. Get a better price, I bet you get a better price.

Senator Skypack. I told you I wanted to serve notice, and I've served it. So let's get down there and get to work.

Senator Mansfield. Very well. I just want to say, though, Jack, I hope and trust we won't rush things. Keep an even keel. I'm not at all convinced—

Senator Skypack. You haul your keel, Aaron, and I'll haul mine.

Senator Mansfield. I guess we can adjourn to Room 202, five or ten minutes.

(The committee moved to the designated room and came to order, in Ordinary Session, at 10:19 a.m.)

Senator Mansfield. We will be in order. I must give a strict warning to our visitors this morning, we've never been this jammed in here, and we want quiet and orderly behavior so we can conduct our business without interruption. Now, Mr. Broadbent, you tell us you're calling Mr. Jones first off.

Mr. Broadbent. Please bring in Mr. Wissey Jones.

Senator Mansfield. Sir, you have been sworn, so please just take your place over there. Thank you.

Testimony of Mr. Wissey Jones, of United Lymphomilloid Corporation

Mr. Broadbent. This morning, Mr. Jones, the Committee would like to hear about certain events that took place on Friday, the eighteenth—your visit to Miss Perrin's classroom at Lincoln Elementary, where, as we understand it, you first observed the boy Barry Rudd, and your interview later with the boy's parents, and with him, at his home. And I would like to add, sir, before starting the questioning, that we are anxious to help in any way we can to bring this matter to its desired conclusion. We—

Senator MANSFIELD. Mr. Broadbent, I don't believe you're authorized—

Senator SKYPACK. We think if the general public had any idea of the patriotic and beneficial nature of the experiment your company is conducting, that the sympathy that has been drummed up in the press for this boy, largely because you happen to come from out of State—

Senator MANSFIELD. Senator Skypack, we'll follow good order here, please. You may take up the questioning, Mr. Broadbent.

Mr. JONES. I wonder if I could make a modest suggestion before you kick off, gentlemen?

Senator MANSFIELD. Please.

Mr. JONES. I always make it a habit, when I become interested in purchasing a specimen, to visit the public library patronized by the child. You'd be amazed at what turns up in a library. I have done so in Pequot, and the suggestion I would make is that you invite Miss Elizabeth Cloud, the librarian, to testify here in these matters. Miss Cloud is a hunchback; she has a sufferer's face and a most intriguing forehead. I'm inclined to be attentive to foreheads, and hers is truly a collector's item. Lines that seem to have been cut by a sensitive etcher's acid run every which way on it, and each one seems to express a feeling or a fate: one might almost read her fortune in those lines, the way a gypsy can read a hand. At any rate, I doubt if anyone in Pequot knows Barry Rudd better than she does, and she can give you insights through his choice of reading—

112

Senator SKYPACK. She dig out the pornography for him to read? Paperbacks?

Mr. JONES. I think you should talk with her, gentlemen.

Senator MANSFIELD. Mr. Broadbent, will you follow up on this Miss Cloud?

Mr. BROADBENT. I've already passed a note out, sir. We're phoning our investigator in Pequot, and he may be able to drive her right up this morning.

Senator MANSFIELD. Alert of you, Mr. Broadbent, thank you. Proceed.

Mr. BROADBENT. Now, Mr. Jones, about your visit to Miss Perrin's class. Please just start right in and tell us in your own words.

Mr. JONES. I've done enough visiting to make allowances for the sudden change of atmosphere that took place in Miss Perrin's room on my entrance. It's remarkable what an upheaval will take place in a classroom when a visitor enters. Children the teacher can barely control when she's alone in the room suddenly become goody-goody because they have an outsider to impress, and others who are usually docile sense her nervous abstraction and see a chance to slide out from under her thumb. I spent the first few minutes, before I even began to watch the Rudd specimen, weighing this shifted atmosphere. Miss Perrin has a deep sense of her own unworthiness, and she reacts badly to being watched. I saw her speaking sweetly to a boy named John Sano, a friend of the Rudd specimen, but at the same moment secretively pinching him alongside a shoulder blade.

Mr. BROADBENT. What was the class doing?

Mr. JONES. It being the beginning of the school day, the class had a weather session, and very soon I could see the Rudd specimen's dominance of the classroom. *He's* the teacher there, and it's a sign of a curious combination of broken-spiritedness and magnanimity in Miss Perrin that she doesn't resent him. In the midst of the usual clichés of weather forecasting, with the little girls especially trying to inject a whiff of pre-pubertal sex into their talk of fronts and precipitation, in unconscious imitation of TV weather queens, the Rudd boy, perhaps for my benefit, slipped in radiosonde, hygrothermograph, psychrometer. It was just a lot of talk, excepting his part. Anyone could see that it was raining outside. But your average school, you know, *is* like a daily television program these days, and the children are at once actors and audience. Rudd breaks that pattern, however, from the opening minute in the morning: that's my first impression. He's there not just to imitate and watch, but to learn and teach.

Mr. BROADBENT. Any other impressions?

Mr. JONES. Yes. He's bored within an inch of his life: *this* we'll eliminate at United Lymphomilloid, believe me. . . . Miss Perrin droned along with a standard brand of old-fashioned mother's-milk classroom courtesy. 'Excuse me, Paul, I didn't see your hand. . . . I'm pleased to see this group working so well —especially pleased to see Molly working so well. . . . Let's see who's wide awake. I know friend Jock isn't wide awake, because he watched *Meet McGraw* and *Divorce Court* again last night, didn't he? What was it, Jock? Ten thirty? Eleven? . . . David didn't hear what I said a minute ago, I guess. He *still— doesn't—hear*. . . .' And the Rudd specimen sitting there obsessed, it seems, with clocks, watches, calendars. Time fleeing from his voraciousness! Once his impatience came vomiting out: Miss Perrin was pressing Jock, a slow one, to connect a word in a reader with the literal-minded family-magazinish illustration above it, and Rudd blurted out, 'For goodness sake, Jock, hurry up! *Ars longa; vita brevis!*' 'My gracious,' Miss Perrin said. 'Want to know what it means?' Rudd asked. The tactlessness of a quick one. He was just trying to push Jock off the can, I think.

Senator SKYPACK. Sounds just like him, pushing normal young men around.

Mr. JONES. I didn't say 'pushing around,' Senator. And I don't think it's necessarily 'normal' to be Jock. I mean the Jock I saw that day.

Senator MANSFIELD. I gather, in fact, sir, that you were favorably impressed by the Rudd youngster.

Mr. JONES. I was, I must say, favorably struck, I mean from a U. Lympho point of view, by his reaction to something that happened during social studies.

Mr. BROADBENT. Would you describe it, please?

Mr. JONES. I don't know whether you gentlemen are aware of the unusual relationship that exists between Rudd and Dr. Gozar, the principal of Lincoln Elementary. . . .

Mr. BROADBENT. Yes, we know about that.

Mr. JONES. About the early-morning lab work?

Mr. BROADBENT. Yes, yes, we've heard.

Mr. JONES. But a really deep attachment, on both sides . . . Well, Miss Perrin's social-studies class was going along in a humdrum way when suddenly Dr. Gozar irrupted into the room, with a wrinkled nose and her leathery lips drawn up with a string. She was holding high in her hands a soaked textbook that had obviously been left out in the rain, and she handled this object as if it were the carcass of a pet, already putrescent yet bitterly mourned, and she delivered a short speech, a sort of funeral oration. Every time she uttered the word 'book' it seemed as if she meant to use another word—'life,' or 'fire,' or 'spirit.' I watched Rudd's face closely. Most of the children, who couldn't be expected to feel anything but joy over the ruination of a textbook, were just made rebellious by the threatening tone of her words. Rudd wore a mask. Only when the word 'book' came again and again out of the old iron jaws did

115

a sign show on it—a sort of pulling. It was his book. He had left it out of doors. I found this out later, but I also found out that Dr. Gozar knew it then. And she was an ogre. Relentless. She wound up her speech saying, 'The pupil who is responsible for this negligent act—he knows who he is—will remain after school today and will write one hundred times the following sentence: "I must learn to respect town property." He will write neatly and legibly, please. Here, I'll put the sentence on the board for all of you to see.' What was most interesting was to see how Rudd performed after Dr. Gozar left.

Mr. BROADBENT. How did Dr. Gozar get ahold of the book? The boy told us about leaving it in the woods, on a log by the millpond of an abandoned knife works.

Mr. JONES. That's right. I got him to tell me about recovering the book in the afternoon, when I called at his home; he told me the story without a hint of emotion. Do you want me to break in with it now?

Mr. BROADBENT. All right with you, Mr. Chairman?

Senator MANSFIELD. Yes. Go ahead.

Mr. JONES. When he first waked up that morning, he told me —he'd had a fearful night, terror-struck, in consequence of Mr. Cleary's taking things into his own hands—he looked out the window of the kitchen, where he and his sister sleep; it's on the street, River Street, and he saw it was raining, and his first thought was that the leaves would no longer be dry for a weasel he'd been observing in the forest to use to reline its nest. That made him think of his book. He wheedled his father into driving him to school early, when his father went off to work at Trucco. At the school he thanked his father for the ride, walked at a leisurely pace to the front door of the school, entered, let the door slam behind him, glanced over his shoulder to make sure his father's car had pulled out of sight, then turned and burst out of the school and went at a run up the hill and out the

Treehampstead Road into the wooded countryside. He got a
stitch in his side—he's candid about his gawkiness and flabbi-
ness—and he had to walk awhile, but when he came to the dirt
track cutting through the forest downward to Chestnut Burr
Creek, he forced himself to run again. Underfoot, he said, there
was a shining wet carpet of leaves of many colors. Here and
there branches whipped their loads of water drops off onto his
chest. He walked past the ruined knife works and along the
edge of the millpond to the log at the upper end. His book lay
just where he had left it. He picked it up. The cover was slimy,
the cloth of the binding had come unstuck and had curled away
from the cardboard underneath, and the cardboard itself was
warped; many whole pages and edges of other pages were wrinkled and soaked. The boy said he stood for a long moment staring at the pond, which was smooth and iron-black, with myriad
tiny circles of raindrops 'like a celebration of water striders danc-
ing on it'; then he ran away back. When he reached the school
the playground was empty. He ran to the front entrance and
opened the door cautiously and turned to ease its closing so it
wouldn't slam. He was panting, and his chest hurt, and his legs
felt, he said, as if they had a deep-sea diver's boots on. He turned
away from the door. Dr. Gozar was blocking his way. She stood
looking down at him. He said her hips were wide, her shoulders
looked narrow, her head seemed very small; she had a towering,
trompe-l'oeil perspective; she seemed to him enormous, looking
down at him from a great height, her neck bent so her head
wouldn't press against the ceiling. But her face was not so far
away that he could lose sight of its icy sternness. Mind you,
these two people are in love. Passionately. 'What is that you
have in your hand?' Dr. Gozar asked in a horrified whisper.

Mr. BROADBENT. You spoke of Barry's behavior in the classroom after Dr. Gozar left.

Mr. JONES. Yes. It was remarkable. As if nothing had hap-

pened. As if that sentence, that crazy nineteenth-century punishment, weren't scrawled reproachfully across the blackboard.
I think he was showing off for me in a curious way, and at the
same time scrutinizing me—though I never actually caught his
eyes on me. His eyes never seemed to rest on *anything*; they
seemed to be looking inward at the shelves of the busy supermarket inside his head. Yet he was right there every second.
'Homer's father earns two hundred fifty dollars a month,' Miss
Perrin said once. 'How much does Homer's father earn in a
year?' Three or four hands went up, including Rudd's. Fact is
he keeps his hand up most of the time: holds up the elbow of
his right arm with his left hand and just keeps it there because
he knows all the answers. Miss Perrin called on Jock. 'Twelve
months times two fifty dollars,' he said. 'Two times zero equals
zero. Two times five equals ten. Carry one . . .' And so on,
crunching along, step by step. The answer finally came out at
three thousand. Then Rudd spoke out. 'There's an easier way,'
he said. 'What's that?' Miss Perrin said. 'Four times two hundred fifty is one thousand. Three times a thousand is three thousand.'

Senator SKYPACK. Wait a minute, now.

Mr. JONES. He broke the twelve into two elements.

Senator MANSFIELD. Yes, I see that. Four times the two hundred fifty and then—

Mr. JONES. Wouldn't have been too remarkable, except I had
the feeling he *discovered* the short cut just then, on his own.
Washington was mentioned at one point, George Washington
as a youth. Like an electronic scanner, Rudd riffled off contemporaries of young Washington: Johann Bach, famous or-
ganist in Leipzig; Vitus Bering, sailing all the way from the
Baltic to the strait that has his name; Ch'ien Lung, poet-warrior
emperor of China; Voltaire producing *Mérope*; Watt working
in his father's shop . . . and so on. Rapid-fire. He certainly did

dominate the room, in spite of Miss Perrin's efforts to hold him back. It was evident to me, after some time in the class, that the boy had met and fallen under the influence of a first-class mind, which had dealt with him as if he were an adult. His fantastic inner powers are leashed, disciplined. I felt from the way he opened up each thought and even each rote memory for use that he was always reorganizing, that he has at base one of those minds that can never be satisfied with things as they are. That's the kind we want at United Lymphomilloid. Of course the top-notch mind that had influenced this specimen belonged to Dr. Gozar—the old crank who'd ordered him to write a stupid sentence a hundred times.

Mr. BROADBENT. Anything else of interest in the classroom?

Mr. JONES. One thing. They had a recess, and after the recess Rudd gave a so-called research report on the system of binomial nomenclature for plants and animals devised by Carl von Linné. It was synthetic on the whole, tailored, I would judge, rather to get a good mark than to please himself. One touch, though. You remember a few minutes ago I spoke of schools nowadays copying television? I may have had this notion for some time, or I may have gotten it from Rudd, who not only senses it but plays on it to the hilt, though he himself, as I said earlier, is in school to be schooled. He was using an opaque projector, and at one point, being clumsy, he got his thumb caught in the reflector and it showed on the screen. In a pompous network voice he said, 'One moment, please. The picture will be off the air for a few seconds because of technical difficulties. The audio portion of the program will continue. . . .'

Mr. BROADBENT. Now would you tell us, sir, about your visit to the Rudd home?

Mr. JONES. I should say, first, that most of the homes I've visited making purchases of specimens for United Lymphomilloid have been in suburban areas and have been 'nice' houses—natural habitat of the handsome I.Q. High incidence of baby-grand pianos. Hi-fi. Books. Standard-package cultural values. Many foreign cars. Ambitious mothers and ulcerated fathers. But listen: let me tell you about the Rudds' heap. It's down at the tail end of River Street in Pequot, the end that looks like a crushed cigarette butt. The house is one of a series of tenement blocks—frame buildings, tinder boxes. The Slatkowski block, where the Rudds have two ground-floor rooms, is a rickety four-story pile on the end of a row of cheek-by-jowl buildings, separated on the other side from a dingy grocery store by a narrow dirt-paved alleyway. The house is covered with tar paper that has bricks printed on it. There's no entrance to the apartment, if you can call it that, from the front hallway with its creaking stairway leading to the other flats upstairs. There's a heavy door from the Rudds' kitchen, right out to the street, but this is apparently swollen and warped out of all use, and you have to enter by going through the alleyway to the back, where a yard about twenty feet deep separates the house from the retaining wall of the Pohadnock River. There's a sagging lean-to porch roof against the house back there, but no porch; on the bare earth under the roof is a mare's nest of rubbish—I noticed broken dishes, a rusted toaster, old milk cartons, a disemboweled alarm clock with a bell on top like a bicycle bell, a burst bag of hickory nuts. This open-pit garbage mine is only a hint of the slovenliness inside.

Mr. BROADBENT. Mrs. Rudd told us she wasn't too strong on housework.

Mr. JONES. She certainly isn't. That's an understatement. There are just the two rooms, a living room and a kitchen, both of which double as bedrooms. There's a dirty, broken-down couch in the living room that's simply smothered with clothes that need mending, limp magazines, the kids' wet-weather togs, every which thing. There's a don't-care atmosphere. The linoleum on the floor is worn through to the fabric and even to the underlying wood in places, and the plaster on the walls is cracked and falling, so the place looks like Liberty Hall for mice. No pictures, limp gray muslin curtains. The kids' rollaway bed in the kitchen doesn't get rolled away—doesn't even get made. The whole flat is warmed by a cheap kitchen stove on which was balanced, the afternoon I called, a spoked laundry rack draped with mildewy bras and other unspeakables. The tin chimney of the stove goes out the side wall over the alley walkway. Bundles of lint stir in the drafts like the tumbleweed on the desert down in our part of the world. But if you look closely, you see the surprise of this filthy nest.

Mr. BROADBENT. Which is?

Mr. JONES. Here and there, tucked under beds and seats, in corners, wedged under the sink, wherever they can be scuffed away from the pattern of traffic of the four Rudds, are cardboard cartons, containing treasures that belong to the boy.

Mr. BROADBENT. Treasures?

Mr. JONES. Books. Scores on scores of books. God knows how he's scrounged and scraped to get them.

Mr. BROADBENT. So. When you called, who was home?

Mr. JONES. At first the mother and father but neither child.

Mr. BROADBENT. What transpired?

Mr. JONES. The first thing I discovered, of course, was that Cleary had beat me to it. He had the mother so nervous she could scarcely waggle her tongue.

Mr. BROADBENT. You outlined your proposition?

Mr. JONES. You have to slide sideways into my sort of proposition. I got Mrs. Rudd loosened up about the boy. Among other things, she recalled a newspaper article that labeled Barry, when he was nine, a genius. She got it out and made me read it. It was pretty bad—written by an untalented reporter in unconsciously mocking tones. She spoke of her son's careful and painful reactions to that publicity—his trying to find out what genius is. Mrs. Rudd showed me some typewritten notices tacked to the wall above the boy's work table in the living room. William James to the effect that genius is the faculty of perceiving in a new way, or 'unhabitual way,' I think it was. Things like that.

Senator SKYPACK. He was spouting that genius stuff to us, like his personal preserve.

Mr. JONES. I think you get him wrong, Senator. I don't believe he's conceited. He has an almost frightening humility. Dr. Gozar fed him most of that material. Mrs. Rudd told me that after the third-grade year Dr. Gozar was wonderful to the boy; the lab work began when he was in fourth.

Mr. BROADBENT. Did you finally put your proposition to the parents?

Mr. JONES. I did. I explained the entire business to them.

Mr. BROADBENT. Including the facts you gave us off the record on Friday?

Mr. JONES. Everything.

Mr. BROADBENT. Weren't you afraid of leakage?

Mr. JONES. Not at all. Parents of this kind of child have learned, the hard way, to play their cards close to the chest.

Mr. BROADBENT. Even a man like Mr. Rudd, who wanted to sell?

Mr. JONES. Especially a man like him. The very fact that his son seems alien to him makes him excruciatingly sensitive to slurs and innuendoes about the boy from other people like himself.

Senator SKYPACK. You say you told them everything.

Mr. JONES. Every last word.

Senator SKYPACK. Sir, I want to ask you to release for the record the material, the remarkable pioneering your company's doing, that you entrusted to us, off the record, on Friday. I want you to let us put that on the record.

Mr. JONES. Out of the question, Senator—

Senator SKYPACK. Whén the public sees the patriotic . . .
That precocious little J.D. wouldn't have a prayer. . . .

Mr. JONES. You have to realize, Senator, we're living in a free-
enterprise system. If other companies, with which we at United
Lymphomilloid have to compete—

Senator SKYPACK. All the same, mister, if the public could just
know how one little self-appointed genius is trying to sabotage
this country's—

Mr. JONES. I don't feel free at this time. You'll just have to
accept that.

Mr. BROADBENT. What was the price tag, sir? What did you
offer the parents?

Mr. JONES. First of all, cash. My starting offer was twelve thousand five hundred ninety-three dollars.

Senator MANSFIELD. For a human life?

Mr. JONES. I was careful to say that was my starting offer. Besides, the cash was only part of it. You see, people in this country are so adjusted to the TV quiz and give-away mechanism,
as well as to the whole tax-dodge-payola-material-gift-bonus
ritual, that money has become, not entirely meaningless, not by
a good bit meaningless, don't misunderstand me—but the *image*
of reward, you see, has a much more complex texture.

Mr. BROADBENT. So what did you offer?

Mr. JONES. You must remember this was my *starting* position.
A matched set of Brigham metal-linen flax-weight troposphere-
blue airplane luggage—

Senator MANSFIELD. For the *Rudds?*

Mr. JONES. It's basic, Senator: the more inappropriate the
'gift' or 'prize,' the more comfortable the image seems to the
receiver. I mean, you could see that what was called for in that
home was some new furniture, a vacuum cleaner, a *rag mop*.
But those wouldn't tempt. Repulsively necessary. I offered a
Bonson-Telldorf nates-length gossamer-coal-fiber-lined mink-

dyed natural stone-marten bed jacket. A Potença-Borg two-hundred-liter after-drive piston-silver-colored sports-racer convertible. For Mr. Rudd a pair of matched monogrammed ivory-backed military hairbrushes with built-in Swiss nineteen-jewel gravity-wind clockwork razor and music box. These, plus perhaps one or two other small items, to make the list sound a little longer, constituted my starting offer.

Senator Voyolko. Nice stuff.

Mr. Broadbent. Did the Rudds bargain?

Mr. Jones. When they learned that it would be necessary for them to sign away all rights to the specimen, including the right of visitation, and to sign an authorization for experimentation, up to and including major surgery, you could sense a stiffening.

Mr. Broadbent. So you went up?

Mr. Jones. I first increased the cash offer. To sixteen thousand seven hundred thirty-four dollars.

Senator Mansfield. Why these odd numbers?

Mr. Jones. The 'bargain myth.' We've had it thoroughly researched, sir. The buying public is so conditioned to getting a bargain at ninety-nine dollars and ninety-nine cents that our research people tell us these same people don't think they get a good value when they sell something if the figure's round. The prices I mentioned have more 'specie-weight' to them, in the bargain-myth terminology, than a much higher round number, say twenty thousand dollars.

Senator Mansfield. Still seems low. For a human being.

Mr. Jones. Value in commerce, sir, is an illusion. What matters is that the price seems right to the purchaser, or seller, not to an outsider, who may be a Polynesian barterer or an Eastern European communist or—I have you in mind, Senator—a clear-minded realist who sees interlocking relationships of values not apparent to the partners in the transaction. In any case, our negotiations were cut off because the boy came in.

Mr. BROADBENT. What happened then?

Mr. JONES. The parents and I—together with the girl, who arrived home shortly thereafter—moved into the kitchen so the boy could work at the small table in the living room that has been set aside for him. After a few minutes I asked if I could talk alone with him. The father—and by then it was clear that he was itching to make a move—said he'd like to tackle the boy first. I was afraid of his approach, but he was, after all, the father, and he was insistent. He went in. From my seat in the kitchen, when Mrs. Rudd swung the door between the rooms open a few minutes later on some bogus errand she invented to settle her curiosity, I caught a glimpse of the two of them: the porcine limited man standing under the edge of a cone of light, the boy sitting with his elbows on his precious papers looking up into his father's eyes. The two faces were almost opposites— the father's face, though chubby, was mobile and expressive, every passing thought and feeling reflected in a pull and ripple of flesh around the organs of sense, so that an intelligent person like the boy could almost have added a silent sum in the man's mind just by watching the legible face, or, in this case, have read the unspoken underlying thought, 'I want to sell you, son'; while the boy's face, to the contrary, was a soft, round, flaccid, unmoving mystery, only the vivid eyes leaping ahead of the father's words from problem to answer to implication.

Mr. BROADBENT. Did Mr. Rudd have any success with the boy?

Mr. JONES. He returned to the kitchen after a few minutes and shrugged heavily, as if to say, 'I've *never* understood that boy.' So then I had my shot at him.

Mr. BROADBENT. How did you go about it?

Mr. JONES. Realizing that the father—and Cleary before him —might already have soured the boy, I had to adopt a gingerly approach. I started by asking him what had happened to the wet book Dr. Gozar had brought in, and he told me the story. Then I congratulated him on the research report I'd heard him give that morning, and he said, 'I'm going to give a report on superstition next time. It sure is lucky for the kids that I've decided that.' I asked him why lucky. 'I don't mean because it's going to be so good,' he said. 'What I mean is, most of my reports are so dull. "The Linnaean System of Binomial Nomenclature!" On superstition I'll give them some fun. Why thirteen's unlucky. Do you know why thirteen's unlucky?' I said I didn't. 'Probably because primitive man, in his cave-dwelling stage, learned to count by using his ten fingers and two feet. Anything beyond twelve was mysterious, fearful, unlucky. Later man found that twelve was divisible by two, three, four, and six, while thirteen was indivisible, like a big ugly boulder. You know, the duodecimal system makes better sense in a lot of ways than the decimal system, for instance as a basis for money. . . . There were thirteen at the Last Supper. In Scandinavian mythology there were twelve demigods, until Loki, the evil one, came along to make the thirteenth. But, speaking of money, do you know something? I've seen a man turn down a two-dollar bill because it was unlucky, but never a one-dollar bill, yet the one has thirteen letters on it in *E Pluribus Unum,* thirteen letters in *Annuit Coeptis,* thirteen stripes in the shield, thirteen leaves, thirteen berries, thirteen stars, thirteen arrows. Enough bad luck to queer any deal that was based on the buck.' I didn't know whether he was slyly alluding to *my* deal—you know, subtly putting the whammy on me. Anyway, he went on, 'I sure am sorry for the class for time *after* next. I'm afraid I have an irresistible impulse to report to them on the saurians and sphenedons—the lizards and tuataras.' He sighed. 'I guess I just have a soft spot in my thalamus for those creatures.' 'In your *what?*' I said. 'It's inaccurate,' he said, 'to speak of having a soft spot in your heart for something, because the thalamus, in the between-brain, is more properly the seat of the emotions.'

Senator SKYPACK. Ye gods and little fishes! How much of this—?

Mr. JONES. I asked him what he wanted to be. A taxonomist, he said.

Senator SKYPACK. And what the hell might that be?

Mr. JONES. A biologist who classifies animals and plants according to their natural kinships. For some time he's been working up a complete classification of the animal kingdom, according to phyla, classes, orders, families, genera, species, and subspecies. It's all written on a scroll of shelf paper fourteen feet long. He remembers every item on the scroll. He said to me as he was showing it to me, 'I wish I could track down the orders of the *Holothurioidea*, the sea cucumbers, for sure. I know three orders, but I don't know if they have any more.'

Senator MANSFIELD. He spoke to us of wanting to bring order out of chaos.

Mr. JONES. Yes, it's a creative urge—too powerful, I'd say, for old-fashioned taxonomy. He'd wind up in biophysics, I imagine. But of course when we get our hands on him at U. Lympho, there'll be no question of—

Mr. BROADBENT. Please go on, sir, with your interview.

Mr. JONES. The boy showed me what he called his family tree. It was a series of captioned drawings—an amoeba named Amos Rudd; a jellyfish, Medusa Rudd; a fish going ashore, perspiring from the effort, whose name was U. Sthenop Terron Rudd. Then there were dinosaurs named Patrick, Cyril, Wolfgang, and Ludwig Rudd. An anaptomorphus, or lemur, named Actor Louis Phineas Reginald Ignatz Mendel Rudd. A pithecanthropus, a cave man, holding an American flag, named Ebenezer Rudd. Finally he pointed to three snapshots at the bottom and said, 'That's my grandfather, Paul George Rudd, a butcher and violin carver. That's my father, Paul James Rudd, machinist and salesman. And that's me, Barry Rudd—merchandise.' *That* was a sarcastic blow at me—out in the open.

Mr. BROADBENT. How did you counter?

Mr. JONES. I fell back to rally my forces. You couldn't see a trace of anger on the boy's face. He talked on in his gentle expressive voice, about how he *visualizes* taxonomic relationships and the adaptive flow of evolution in his mind. He said his sensations were like those of the dog Buck, in *The Call of the Wild*, who saw the man by the campfire melt, as it were, into a hairy cave man. He could 'melt' the skull of one reptile ('large number of bones—worse than a jigsaw puzzle') into the skull of another. And how he saw evolution as a sort of gliding moving picture—a creature in a setting, then, as a geologic age gives way to its successor, the creature and setting dissolve and change and emerge clearly in new forms. Matter of fact, he led me into a booby trap on all this. Just after we'd talked about these pictures in his mind I asked him if he liked TV. 'Oh, yes,' he said. I asked him what his favorite program was, and he said it was one called *Up from the Mire*. I said I hadn't heard of that one. What sort of program was that? 'About evolution,' he said. 'The gradual changes in the forms of animals. Slight touch of Lysenkianism in the approach but basically mutant genes.' I asked him what channel it was on, what network. 'Oh, no channel,' he said. 'It's *my* program. It's in my head.'

Senator SKYPACK. That little smart aleck *likes* to give people a hard time.

Mr. JONES. I enjoy a specimen that has spunk, but I must admit, he was pressing me a little closely: and he didn't let up either. Next he got in some licks at his father that I think were really aimed at me. 'I distrust television,' he said. 'The trouble with it is that there's too much command, authority. Do this, buy that! I suppose that on the subliminal level, the stove, where warm food comes from, is mother, the TV, with its blustering authority, is father.' And with that he turned a flood of abstraction loose on me; it was like a gas attack. 'During the past year,' he said, 'I've come to the conclusion that a person should never accept any statement, idea, or even any "fact" as being the absolute truth. An important part of this whole idea is the tenet that no statement should be believed merely because it has been made by an authority. There's real danger in the acceptance of the word of an authority without questioning it, because the acceptance may blind us to proof of a more accurate statement. The best example of this danger given to us is the stagnation of thought in the Middle Ages, which resulted from the unquestioning acceptance by most of the time's great thinkers of the utterances of certain ancient authorities. The evidence to disprove some of the old ideas was right before men's eyes, but, blinded by authority, they didn't see it.'

Mr. BROADBENT. What was he getting at?

Mr. JONES. I think he was telling me that he was going to defy his father—and me. I tried changing the subject, but he wouldn't let it stay changed. I asked him how he got along with his contemporaries. And he said, 'Not too badly for an odd ball. Did you know that the schoolboys used to chase Coleridge out of their games and that they baited him all the time? He got to be fretful, scaredy-cat, and tattletale, and stuck up about how bright he was. Once he ran away from home after a squabble with his brother; he was sickly for a long time as a result of the exposure. But, you see, he wasn't as tough as Huckleberry Finn, who ran away because his father wanted to exploit *him*.' . . . The slight stress on that 'him' told me I was up against a pretty tough article myself. I finally decided just to lay my proposition squarely on the table, and I did.

Mr. BROADBENT. What did he answer?

Mr. JONES. One word.

Senator MANSFIELD. Don't tell me, let me guess!

Mr. JONES. You've guessed, all right.

Senator VOYOLKO. Would you spell that out?

Mr. JONES. N. O.

Senator SKYPACK. What the devil, couldn't you go over his head and just buy him?

Mr. JONES. From the father I could have, yes, but the mother said she wouldn't consider it unless the boy agreed.

Senator SKYPACK. By God, we'll change that. Who does she think she is?

Mr. JONES. I'm afraid the mind that'll have to be changed belongs to the boy, Senator.

Senator MANSFIELD. All right, Mr. Jones, we thank you. You may step down now.

Senator SKYPACK. Just want you to know, sir, that some of us here are going to do all we can—

Senator MANSFIELD. Your next witness, Mr. Broadbent.

Mr. BROADBENT. Charles Perkonian.

Senator MANSFIELD. Please just stand up right there, sonny, and be sworn.

Do you solemnly swear that the testimony you are about to give this committee on the matters under consideration will be the truth, the whole truth, and nothing but the truth, so help you God?

CHARLES PERKONIAN. What's all that jazz?

Mr. BROADBENT. Just hold up your hand and say, 'I do.'

CHARLES PERKONIAN. I do.

Mr. BROADBENT. Sit down.

CHARLES PERKONIAN. I do what? Say, what goes on here?

TESTIMONY OF CHARLES PERKONIAN, MINOR, TOWN OF PEQUOT

Mr. BROADBENT. What is your name?

130

CHARLES PERKONIAN. Charley.

Mr. BROADBENT. Full name.

CHARLES PERKONIAN. Charles Aram Perkonian. Junior.

Mr. BROADBENT. You're called Flattop?

CHARLES PERKONIAN. Sometimes Flattop.

Mr. BROADBENT. You're a friend of Barry Rudd?

CHARLES PERKONIAN. Sure.

Mr. BROADBENT. Why do you like Barry Rudd?

CHARLES PERKONIAN. He's cool.

Mr. BROADBENT. What do you mean by that?

CHARLES PERKONIAN. He's *cool.* You stupid or something?

Mr. BROADBENT. Is it true you were released in September from Clarkdale Reformatory?

CHARLES PERKONIAN. What's it to you?

Mr. BROADBENT. On what charge were you sent up there?

CHARLES PERKONIAN. Salt in the battery.

Mr. BROADBENT. Beg pardon?

CHARLES PERKONIAN. Salt in the battery. Stupid. I slugged a stupid driver the school bus.

Mr. BROADBENT. Tell me, Charles, do you know how to make a stink bomb?

CHARLES PERKONIAN. Sure. You take and put some hide-your-color acid and . . . Why'n't you ask Rudd the Crud he's so brainy?

Mr. BROADBENT. Do you think Barry Rudd knows something about the stink bomb that was tossed in the auditorium of Lincoln School while the State Supervisor—

CHARLES PERKONIAN. When that happen?

Mr. BROADBENT. Last Tuesday.

CHARLES PERKONIAN. Tuesday. What's today?

Mr. BROADBENT. Monday the twenty-eighth.

CHARLES PERKONIAN. Monday. Yesterday was Sunday. Right? What'd you say, Tuesday?

131

Mr. BROADBENT. Last Tuesday at three o'clock in the afternoon.

CHARLES PERKONIAN. Tuesday. Today Monday, you say that?

Mr. BROADBENT. That's correct.

CHARLES PERKONIAN. I don't remember.

Mr. BROADBENT. Last Tuesday afternoon you were with Barry Rudd in the biology-chemistry lab of Wairy High School, isn't that right?

CHARLES PERKONIAN. I don't remember nothing.

Mr. BROADBENT. Were you in the lab there with him?

CHARLES PERKONIAN. What day was that again?

Mr. BROADBENT. All right, I'll ask you something else. Do you remember one day after school, about ten days ago, when Barry Rudd came to see you at the bowling alleys?

CHARLES PERKONIAN. The lanes. Sure.

Mr. BROADBENT. You remember that?

CHARLES PERKONIAN. Sure. He come there.

Mr. BROADBENT. You remember discussing a fish known as the stickleback?

CHARLES PERKONIAN. Sure. Sure. That's the one such a sexboat. Sure.

Mr. BROADBENT. You were discussing sex, then.

CHARLES PERKONIAN. All a time.

Mr. BROADBENT. Do you know a girl named Florence Renzulli?

CHARLES PERKONIAN. Sure. She's my class. The one the big bazooms. I mean you take her age.

Mr. BROADBENT. Watch your language, Charles. Everything you say goes into the public record.

CHARLES PERKONIAN. I ain't said nothing.

Mr. BROADBENT. When discussing the stickleback, did he express any special feeling for Florence Renzulli?

CHARLES PERKONIAN. Feeling her? I don't remember.

132

Mr. Broadbent. You have suggested Florence Renzulli is advanced for her age.

Charles Perkonian. I didn't say nothing. I don't remember nothing.

Mr. Broadbent. The other night, when a gang attacked the Rudds' home—

Charles Perkonian. Hey, was that cool!

Mr. Broadbent. You were there?

Charles Perkonian. Why not? It's a free country. Why shouldn't I be there?

Mr. Broadbent. We understand Barry Rudd was picked up by the police. Was he taking part in an assault on his own home?

Charles Perkonian. What you want me to do, finger my pal? I don't remember nothing.

Mr. Broadbent. How many were involved in the attack?

Charles Perkonian. I don't remember.

Mr. Broadbent. Now, look here. You've already said you were there.

Charles Perkonian. I don't remember. I don't remember. I don't remember. A million times if you ask me.

Mr. Broadbent. The windows—

Charles Perkonian. That was cool. Like they had these baseball bats, see. I got me this fungo bat. That was the greatest. They had this signal, see—

Mr. Broadbent. Then you do remember.

Charles Perkonian. Look, stupid, why'n't you pick on somebody your own size? Why'n't you ask the man the funny hat?

Mr. Broadbent. Funny hat?

Charles Perkonian. The flat fedora. You call *me* Flattop!

Mr. Broadbent. You mean a pork-pie hat? You mean Mr. Wissey Jones?

Charles Perkonian. I don't know no names. The guy the

classy motorcycle you can snap it the middle.

Mr. BROADBENT. You must mean Mr. Jones. Why Mr. Jones? What does he know about the assault? What are you trying to say, young man?

CHARLES PERKONIAN. Don't ask me. Ask him. Ask the drugstore guy.

Mr. BROADBENT. The drugstore man?

CHARLES PERKONIAN. The guy a stomach out to here.

Mr. BROADBENT. The druggist? What was the name, Mr. Chairman? Ellithorp?

Senator MANSFIELD. That was the name, yes.

CHARLES PERKONIAN. Ask him.

Mr. BROADBENT. What did he have to do—

CHARLES PERKONIAN. Don't ask me, ask him.

Senator SKYPACK. Now, listen, you little delinquent rat, are you trying to suggest that Mr. Wissey Jones—

CHARLES PERKONIAN. You can call me a rat, I can call you a horse's—

Mr. BROADBENT. Now, Charles.

CHARLES PERKONIAN. What's this stupid jerk think he is, thinks he can call a person anything he wants to call him, thinks he can pick on somebody half his size, quarter his size?

Senator MANSFIELD. Mr. Broadbent, I believe we can dismiss this witness. You'll look into those allegations, of course.

Senator SKYPACK. You mean to say, you're willing to accept the word of a—

Senator MANSFIELD. I said 'look into,' Senator.

Mr. BROADBENT. All right, Charles. That door over there, please.

CHARLES PERKONIAN. Stupid jerk. I'll show that stupid jerk.

Senator MANSFIELD. Let's have our next witness, please, Mr. Broadbent.

Mr. BROADBENT. Miss Millicent P. Henley.

Senator MANSFIELD. Please stand to be sworn, ma'am.

Do you solemnly swear that the testimony you will give here before the Standing Committee on Education, Welfare, and Public Morality will be the truth, the whole truth, and nothing but the truth, so help you God?

Miss HENLEY. I swear it.

TESTIMONY OF MISS MILLICENT P. HENLEY, STATE OFFICE OF EDUCATION

Mr. BROADBENT. Please identify yourself, madam.

Miss HENLEY. My name is Millicent Parmelee Henley, and I am the State Supervisor for Exceptional Children.

Mr. BROADBENT. You operate out of the State Office of Education, here in the capital, is that right? You go all over the State, giving advice, laying down the law to the town school systems, right?

Miss HENLEY. That's correct.

Mr. BROADBENT. What do you understand by the term 'Exceptional Children'?

Miss HENLEY. You have, first of all, the unfortunates: the retarded, the handicapped—deaf, dumb, clubfooted, spastic, so on. Our hearts go out to them. Then you have a smattering of the gifted—many of whom are emotionally disturbed.

Mr. BROADBENT. The gifted and the clubfooted are in the same category?

Miss HENLEY. They are exceptional, yes. Lord Byron, as I remember, was both—but then, we don't run across many Byrons in this State, do we?

Mr. BROADBENT. Would you tell us, please, how you happened to get into this Rudd situation?

Miss HENLEY. Mr. Cleary, the Guidance Director down in Pequot, telephoned me on Monday last to inform me that a

135

controversy was building up among the teaching staff in the town's elementary schools, and particularly at Lincoln Elementary, over the Rudd case, and he asked me to come down and set forth some fundamental doctrine, straighten the teachers out, the misguided ones.

Mr. BROADBENT. So a lecture was set up?

Miss HENLEY. Mr. Cleary assembled all the primary and elementary teachers in the Lincoln auditorium, on orders from Mr. Owing, the Superintendent.

Mr. BROADBENT. Would you describe exactly what happened on that occasion?

Miss HENLEY. It will be important for you gentlemen to understand a little about this boy and his particular problem as a backdrop for what happened. May I—?

Mr. BROADBENT. Please.

Miss HENLEY. I think perhaps I should introduce my remarks to you gentlemen on the subject of this boy's problem exactly as I did in my . . . brahaha . . . unfortunately interrupted lecture of last Tuesday. It's so hard for people with a limited background on educational psychology—

Mr. BROADBENT. Proceed, madam.

Miss HENLEY. I'd like to give you a few insights into the learning process. We have to look for individual differences in terms of the reaction threshold, for the laws of operant behavior are the same for all. Learning depends on the restructuring of the Gestalt field. Learning starts with failure, the first failure is the beginning of education. The essence of learning by repetition is the effort to reduce the tendency to hesitate or fail in relay. The significance of the Pavlovian work is that there is no physiological limit to the power of association, for anything that affects the nervous system can come to 'mean' anything else. The repetition of bonds, according to Thorndyke, strengthens the bonds, *if* the connections are rewarded, and the Gestaltists tell us that repetition has not merely a cumulative effect but brings new insights and the perception of new relationships in the learning situation. In Hull, as in Thorndyke, mere repetition produces only reactive inhibition; improvement depends on reinforcement by reward. *The Forty-first Yearbook* of the N.S.S.E. attempted to bring a rapprochement between the associational and gestaltist theories. Guthrie accepts contiguous conditioning only—similar to Thorndyke's association-shifting and Skinner's S-type conditioning. Hull's reinforcement theory is related to Thorndyke's law of effect and Skinner's R-type conditioning. It is curious, by the bye, that a theory based on observable minutiae—proprioceptive stimuli precisely coincident with specific muscular responses—should gain its support from purely anecdotal observations. At any rate, habit strength—

Senator MANSFIELD. One vowel, Senator!

Miss HENLEY. I beg your pardon?

Senator MANSFIELD. I was just pointing out something about the word 'strength' to Senator Skypack, ma'am. Please excuse the interruption.

Miss HENLEY. Habit strength increases when receptor and effector activities occur in close temporal contiguity with primary reinforcement, that is to say, diminution of need, or with secondary reinforcement, a stimulus or reward associated with need reduction. Kohler's apes could use a means to an end— e.g., moving a packing box in order to reach a banana. Whether they could, in time, use a typewriter to write *War and Peace* is another question, clearly opposed to the bundle hypothesis, that a percept is made up of sensations bound together by association. Am I making myself clear, sir?

Senator VOYOLKO. Huh? You talking to me?

Miss HENLEY. Do you follow me, sir?

Senator VOYOLKO. Yeah, sure. Not real close. Like I'm a few feet back.

Miss HENLEY. All right. Now, when we come to the intra-psychic motive—

Senator MANSFIELD. I think maybe that's enough background, ma'am.

Miss HENLEY. I had only just begun—

Senator MANSFIELD. Do you think that's a sufficient fill-in, Senator?

Senator SKYPACK. Ample. Ample.

Senator MANSFIELD. And you, Senator? You satisfied?

Senator VOYOLKO. Me? I'm up to here in it.

Senator MANSFIELD. Very good. Miss Henley, where did you psychologists learn all this?

Miss HENLEY. From mice. Mostly from mice. We put hungry mice in mazes—

Senator MANSFIELD. I see. So the Rudd boy—

Senator SKYPACK. What I want to know, miss. Just one thing. Are you for this boy or against him?

Miss HENLEY. In cases where the need reduction—

Senator SKYPACK. For or against?

Miss HENLEY. I was getting to that. . . . To oversimplify, the purpose of my lecture was to give a dire warning to all the teachers present on maladjustment on the part of these extreme deviates at the upper end of the bell curve.

Senator SKYPACK. I still want to know—

Mr. BROADBENT. Excuse me, Senator, could I have the witness a minute? Can you tell us quite simply, madam, what happened —how your lecture was interrupted?

Miss HENLEY. I certainly can. I was standing here, behind the lectern. The edge of the stage was here. Mr. Owing and Mr. Cleary were sitting back here. Everything was going along very smoothly when I heard this curious *pop*, I couldn't tell exactly where the sound came from, I was concentrating on my train of thought, and then—here, just in front of the lip of the stage—I

saw billowing up a curious yellow cloud. I thought at first—I
have a thing about electricity, thunderstorms, defective wiring—
I thought at first it was a short circuit of some kind, and I'm
afraid I uttered a rather piercing summons to the fire department. Shortly thereafter a response to an exteroceptive stimulus
on the part of my olfactory apparatus—

Senator MANSFIELD. You mean you smelled the stink bomb.

Miss HENLEY. I certainly did. Putrefaction such as you have
never—like that of one of those horrible ditches in the *Inferno*,
where the sinners lay in a river of excrement: were they the Flat-
terers? If there's anything I hate, it's a saccharine compliment.

Mr. BROADBENT. Have you any theory as to who may have
thrown the bomb? We understand it probably came in one of
the auditorium windows, so that would rule out any of the audience. Have you any theory? Know anyone who might
want—?

Miss HENLEY. I can't imagine that it was anyone but the subject of our meeting. Who else could feel that way about me? It
was obviously a small boy's kind of trick. I feel so badly about
that youngster, because we school people have failed him somehow.

Senator SKYPACK. All *right*. That's all I wanted to know.
Let's have the next witness.

Senator MANSFIELD. Just a minute, Jack. Anything else you'd
like to say, ma'am?

Miss HENLEY. Well, yes. I'd just like to say that where you
run into trouble with these children is in *singling them out*. The
kind of thing Dr. Gozar has done in the lab work with this boy.
I came right out and said this in my lecture. We talk about the
defense of democracy—how undemocratic can you get? Why
shouldn't the next child get the extra help—the slow learner?
The extremely gifted child should not be removed from the
common-learning situation. He's the last one who needs extra

attention. And don't think, just because I'm a specialist on your deviates—

Senator MANSFIELD. I must say, ma'am, you make them sound like little sex fiends.

Miss HENLEY. I may specialize in deviates, but I don't forget the norm. The norm is the bedrock of our society. You can't neglect the median child in favor of the exceptions. You remember F.D.R.'s great declaration: 'This is the era of the common man.' That's democracy, gentlemen! Not a society where you have an elite telling the rest of us how to live.

Senator SKYPACK. I agree with you, miss. We can't have these double-domes getting in there and—

Senator MANSFIELD. All right, ma'am, I think we have the drift of it. Thank you for coming here and helping us out.

Senator SKYPACK. You heard what she said about who threw it, Aaron.

Senator MANSFIELD. Your next witness, please, Mr. Broadbent.

Mr. BROADBENT. Word has just been sent in to me, sir, that the librarian has arrived. I will call Miss Elizabeth Cloud.

Senator MANSFIELD. Well, that was quick. It isn't often that I give myself occasion to congratulate you, Mr. Broadbent. . . . Over there, please, Miss Cloud. Just stand there to be sworn.

Do you solemnly swear that the testimony you are about to give this committee on its present business will be the truth, the whole truth, and nothing but the truth, so help you God?

Miss CLOUD. I do.

TESTIMONY OF MISS ELIZABETH CLOUD, LIBRARIAN,
TOWN OF PEQUOT

Mr. BROADBENT. Please identify yourself for the record, madam, as to name, address, and occupation.

Miss CLOUD. Elizabeth B. Cloud, 27 Maple Street, Pequot, Chief Librarian of the Town Free Library.

Mr. BROADBENT. You are acquainted with a school child named Barry Rudd?

Miss CLOUD. Acquainted! Jehosephat, I should say I *am* acquainted with Barry. I've been nourishing him since he was knee-high to a grasshopper—or, as I guess he'd put it, as tall, or perhaps as short, as the ginglymus joint between the femur and tibia of *Melanoplus spretus*. You may have gathered, Barry's a great one for saying things the accurate way, even if it's the hard way. And so, for that matter, am I. He may have caught a bit of that from me—or I from him. We've been making a game of it together for years.

Mr. BROADBENT. Would you give a little background of your relationship?

Miss CLOUD. There isn't much background. Mrs. Rudd brought Barry all the way over from Treehampstead when he was barely five. Treehampstead is a regular city, but as is so often the case they have a blah library, stacks and stacks of Victorian pablum and rental-library trash; and I guess Mrs. Rudd had heard about me and the child-heaven I keep—my story-telling hours, the space I give the kids' books; they come first with me. I don't have a Children's Corner; I have an Adults' Corner in my library. And besides, my humpback, there's something about the luck of my back: the tykes think of me as a gnome or a magic thing—a living apple stump, something like that. We get along. Anyway, here came Mrs. Rudd shaking and fretting because some school idiot had made her think that Barry's being able to read so early was a form of sickness. So I took him over. We had an afternoon together each week till the Rudds moved to Pequot, and from then on—well, we're just pals.

Mr. BROADBENT. Would you say that your, ahem, misfortune, madam, has made the boy Barry Rudd feel specially close to you, with his, ahem, exaggerated mentality?

Miss CLOUD. Why don't you come out from behind those euphemisms, Mr. District Attorney, or whatever you are? 'Misfortune?' You mean my hunchback? You mean that Barry's brilliant mind is like a crooked back, and that's why we're pals? Deformity is our bond? More like it that *you* have a twisted mind, sir.

Mr. BROADBENT. I was only trying—exceptional—

Miss CLOUD. This is one of the reasons I like children better than adults: they haven't learned yet that honesty between human beings is a form of social blooper, like belching, to be apologized for if it accidentally bursts out.

Senator MANSFIELD. I'm sure he meant no offense, Miss Cloud.

Miss CLOUD. I like it better when the offense *is* intended, sir. I know then where I stand. Perhaps I'm like a child myself in that particular respect.

Senator MANSFIELD. If we could go on with our questioning.

Mr. BROADBENT. Would you tell us, please, madam, about the boy Barry Rudd's reading interests?

Miss CLOUD. Well, like many of my young ones, he started in with Lewis Carroll and Kenneth Grahame and Robert Louis Stevenson—difference being that he read the books himself, memorized them, improvised from them. I'll skip the feeling-out period. Recent years he began to get into geology, zoology. *Before the Dawn of History* by Charles R. Knight. *Monsters of Old Los Angeles* by Charles M. Martin, about the prehistoric creatures of the La Brea tar pits. Then, suddenly, *Moby Dick*, on account of the stuff on whales. Insects, their origin. Then he had a period of Robert Frost—he has a strong lyrical urge, loves to talk about natural things. Thurber by the measured mile. He has a persistent mind. When he gets on a track, he traces it down and gets what he wants—*all* of what he wants.

Mr. BROADBENT. Dr. Gozar told us—

Miss CLOUD. I know: biographies. Dr. Gozar has been a wonderful prod to that boy. She goes along behind him with a pitchfork aimed at his seat—and how he runs! He's read biographies by the dozen. Boswell's *Johnson* twice. He doesn't like the Maurois-type popular biography; he prefers your tartar-steak kind of thing. Facts, original sources, lean meat. He roots around in footnotes like a boar going after truffles. The last year, year and a half, he has been reading the biographies of 'the biggest brains who ever lived'—I've had to send off for a lot of them through our library exchange system. Newton, Goethe, Pascal, Leopardi, Voltaire, Comte, Michelangelo, Arnauld, Wolsey, Laplace, the younger Pitt, Schelling, Grotius.

Senator SKYPACK. I don't see we're getting anyplace. When Mr. Jones told us to talk to this person, Mr. Chairman, he must have . . . Look, miss, this boy been coming to you for sex books?

Miss CLOUD. Matter of fact, he has. Indirectly anyway. Just recently.

Senator SKYPACK. I *thought* so! And you dished them up to him?

Miss CLOUD. I dish up whatever a young mind wants and needs, sir. Barry became interested first in courting rituals between mammals, fishes, birds—you know, the drumming of ruffed grouse, bill-clapping of nesting storks, the throaty chant and spiral climb of the woodcock.

Mr. BROADBENT. A fish called the stickleback?

Miss CLOUD. You know about that? He told you about that? I found him that one!

Senator SKYPACK. So you're the one's been feeding him this stuff. . . . Is that a *public* library down there, miss?

Miss CLOUD. Town Free Library. Supported by local taxes and a State allotment. You're welcome any time, sir. Anyhow, I was telling you. After a certain amount of this courtship material, Barry suddenly wanted some technical stuff on human beings.

Senator Skypack. I knew it. I knew it.

Miss Cloud. He wanted a couple of gynecological texts, and I gave him—

Senator Skypack. By gorry, Aaron, it's time we got after these public libraries. Openly handing out this smut to minors.

Miss Cloud. Senator, if you call *Transactions of the American Gynecological Society* 'smut,' then you've set some kind of record in bibliographic classification. And the basic works by Curtis, Wharton, Novak—they're about as smutty as the Rosetta stone. And about as easy to read.

Senator Skypack. I'm serious, Mr. Chairman. We've got to get in there and root this dirty stuff and filth out of these libraries, if it's getting to the minors.

Senator Mansfield. The boy is a bit young for that sort of book, Miss Cloud. What do you suppose his purpose was in wanting them?

Miss Cloud. I hold back nothing from a child's mind— within reason. I can smell a bad smell as well as the next person, but where there's curiosity, healthy curiosity, I believe in satisfying it. If you thwart and withhold—then's when the prurience and sneaking and perversion begin.

Senator Mansfield. But you haven't answered my question. Why did the boy want those books?

Miss Cloud. At the time I had no idea. It wasn't until the P.-T.A. protest meeting on the Rudd-Renzulli case—

Senator Mansfield. Why did the P.-T.A. hold a—?

Mr. Broadbent. We have Mrs. Sloat, sir, the President of the Lincoln P.-T.A., waiting outside. I intend to call her before long. We'll get the full story.

Senator Mansfield. After that you knew why he had wanted the books?

144

Miss CLOUD. It was only a guess.

Senator SKYPACK. You don't have to do much *guessing,* Mr. Chairman. It's bad enough on the newsstands, but I say that when the librarians of our public libraries start dealing out sex and sadism to our children!

Miss CLOUD. If you come down to the Town Free Library in Pequot with the intent of pulling out books and making a bonfire of them, sir, I'll be there to welcome you—with a fourteen-gauge shotgun. Please be warned.

Senator MANSFIELD. We'll have order, please. Resume your seat, Jack. Miss Cloud! That is the subject for another set of hearings, perhaps—not this one, anyway. I think we can excuse Miss Cloud now. Thank you for coming up here.

Miss CLOUD. Thank me for coming up? I was practically kidnapped!

Senator SKYPACK. Imagine a crippled virgin like that handing out sex and sadism!

Senator VOYOLKO. Before you go, lady.

Miss CLOUD. Yes, sir?

Senator VOYOLKO. Could I touch your hump?

Miss CLOUD. You certainly may, my dear Senator. I hope it brings you great good luck.

Senator VOYOLKO. Thank you, thank you. Real obliging. Skypack, ain't you gonta—?

Senator SKYPACK. Not with a ten-foot pole.

Senator MANSFIELD. All right, Mr. Broadbent, who's next? . . . Thank you, Miss Cloud, very forthright. . . . If I may just . . . No, I can reach right across here. . . . *Thank* you.

Mr. BROADBENT. Mr. Paul Rudd. Please have him brought in.

Senator MANSFIELD. You're already sworn, Mr. Rudd. Take your place.

Testimony of Mr. Paul Rudd, Machinist,
Town of Pequot

Mr. Broadbent. Mr. Rudd, I've asked you to come back here to tell the committee about what happened, the chat you had with Mrs. Sloat and your subsequent futile conversation with your son, that took place on Thursday afternoon, the twenty-fourth. The afternoon before the P.-T.A. meeting took place that night.

Senator Mansfield. Now, just a minute, please, Mr. Broadbent. We'll want to get the timing straight on this. This was after the stink bombing?

Mr. Broadbent. After the stink bombing—that was Tuesday afternoon. After the attack on the Rudds' house—Tuesday evening, or night. After the boy was caught with the Renzulli girl—Wednesday in broad daylight at school. It was after all those things. In fact, the P.-T.A. was going to meet *because* of these happenings, to discuss—

Senator Mansfield. Why do you jump around in this way, Mr. Broadbent?

Mr. Broadbent. I have to catch my witnesses when I can, Mr. Chairman. This Mrs. Sloat is a busy woman. Two, three committee meetings a day, seems to me. This happened to be the only chance I could snag her this whole week, and Mr. Rudd's testimony is germane to hers, and I'm going to ask Miss Perrin some questions, too. . . .

Senator Mansfield. Well, it's very aggravating. For weeks I've been trying to get you to unfold your material for us in a straightforward, orderly way, Mr. Broadbent. All right. Go ahead, now.

Mr. Broadbent. Mr. Rudd, I'll ask you to tell us what you were doing last Thursday afternoon, the twenty-fourth.

Mr. Rudd. In the afternoon I was fixing the windows. That bunch of hoods.

Mr. BROADBENT. You were replacing the glass panes?

Mr. RUDD. Throughout. Every single one.

Mr. BROADBENT. You know the glazing trade?

Mr. RUDD. Learnt it thirty years ago. I picked up carpentering, fancy masonry stonework, I can do surveying, pump out septic tanks, any kind of machine press. Twenty kinds of work. Like I was saying here the other day: Why can't the boy earn his keep? Do you suppose Mr. Brain-child would stoop to learn something useful, something that would maybe bring in a living, part of a living even?

Mr. BROADBENT. You were replacing the windows one by one. Would you tell us what happened, please?

Mr. RUDD. By the way, somebody ought to pay for those windows. Everybody's offered plenty free advice, interference, you people, but I'm the one who's out of pocket on this deal. Here's the buyer with a big fat check in his pocket, all kinds of luxury items Maud and me've been wanting all our lives, and so far I'm the only one that's had to put out. I wonder if you gentlemen realize what a full set of glass costs for a person's home, putty, sprigs, some primer, sash tool, putty knife—it don't come to scratch feed. You people sit up here. Who looks out for the ordinary citizen like me?

Mr. BROADBENT. Please just tell us what was happening.

Mr. RUDD. I come home there the night before and find every blasted window smashed to smithereens. . . .

Senator MANSFIELD. Couldn't Mr. Rudd give us the details of the attack on the house while he's at it? I mean, to clarify—

Mr. BROADBENT. He wasn't there when it happened. You'd want—

Mr. RUDD. I wasn't there. I was down the bowling lanes. . . . So I came home and found all this broken glass, it was kind of a chill in the weather that night, too. So as soon as I could I got them to give me the afternoon off at Trucco, and, like I say,

I was putting in these new panes, I was working on the kitchen, on the front, I was just trimming up and beveling the putty, when this brand-new Buick drives up, and this lady gets out and comes right acrost the sidewalk.

Mr. BROADBENT. Had you known Mrs. Sloat before? Did you recognize her?

Mr. RUDD. I vaguely seen her, they have this covered-dish supper over at the school every year. Maud drags me.

Mr. BROADBENT. And what did Mrs. Sloat want?

Mr. RUDD. All right, see how you'd feel about it. This woman is one of those ones that's into everything. She has this fox thing around her neck, a complete fox head looking at you with these bossy little brown glass eyes, it's like the lady's looking at you like a President, and the fox is looking at you like a Vice-President. The two of them.

Mr. BROADBENT. She has a child in Barry's school?

Mr. RUDD. You see, our school district cuts across the Intervale and runs up onto the west hill, so you have a mixed group, you have the tenement-block people and some of the wealthy two-car-garage split-level people. And I don't know, this lady is one of your up-the-hill heart-bleeders. She's an improver. I say wealthy. I mean, like this new Buick and probably a second-hand Pontiac for the husband.

Mr. BROADBENT. What did she want?

Mr. RUDD. She lit into me. I was working on the windows, I wasn't in a mood for it.

Mr. BROADBENT. What did she say?

Mr. RUDD. She said juvenile delinquency was the parents' fault. The parents ought to go to jail. I hadn't even heard about this Florence Renzulli thing yet. I'm just the handyman around there, general repairman to fix the breakage all about my son that's so advanced. So she demanded I come to the meeting that night, this meeting about what are we going to do with the younger generation? First the stink bomb. Then our house. Then Barry's in this sex trouble. She's counting the disasters on her fingers. Barry in sex trouble? That was news to me. I knew he was advanced for his age *mentally*, but . . .

Mr. BROADBENT. And?

Mr. RUDD. She suddenly started taking off on Miss Perrin. That's Barry's teacher.

Mr. BROADBENT. We know.

Mr. RUDD. She said Miss Perrin was trying to get the meeting called off. She said Miss Perrin wasn't fit to be a teacher, all like that. She really railed along.

Mr. BROADBENT. What did you say?

Mr. RUDD. What did I say! I couldn't have wedged the narrow side of my putty knife in between the words. I didn't have a look-in. First thing I knew, I heard her say I was to be there at eight o'clock sharp and then I'm reading the word ROADMASTER on her rear end going down the street.

Mr. BROADBENT. After that, what happened?

Mr. RUDD. Well, I was just beginning to have my reaction, I'd been too surprised to even get proper mad, but after she left I was building up, I tell you I could've smashed some windows myself—when Mr. Brain-child comes sashaying home. Whistling. 'Surrey with a Fringe on Top'—most cheerful gol-dang song ever written.

Mr. BROADBENT. And you then had a talk with him?

Mr. RUDD. Which didn't exactly give me relief.

Mr. BROADBENT. What do you mean?

Mr. RUDD. I mean I asked him what his objection was to going off with Mr. Jones and saving his country, et cetera. And you know what he said? I remember the words. You want to hear what he said?

Mr. BROADBENT. Yes, we do.

Mr. RUDD. 'I don't give a fig for my country.' Either 'fig' or 'frig,' I'm not sure of anything any more in this world.

Senator SKYPACK. Did you hear that, Mr. Chairman? Do you need more than that? Are you satisfied now?

Mr. BROADBENT. What else, Mr. Rudd?

Mr. RUDD. I asked him what he did give a fig for, or a frig for. Know what he said? 'The future of the animal kingdom.'

Mr. BROADBENT. Thank you, Mr. Rudd. That's all.

Senator SKYPACK. My God! Don't you think it's about time we cracked down, Aaron?

Senator MANSFIELD. All the same, Jack, don't forget that human beings are part of the animal kingdom.

Senator SKYPACK. Now I've heard it all! *You*, Aaron!

Mr. BROADBENT. I will call Miss Charity Perrin.

Senator MANSFIELD. You've already taken your oath, Miss Perrin. Please just be seated.

TESTIMONY OF MISS CHARITY M. PERRIN, SCHOOLTEACHER, TOWN OF PEQUOT

Mr. BROADBENT. We have information, Miss Perrin, that as the boy Barry Rudd's teacher you opposed the holding of the emergency Lincoln P.-T.A. meeting last Thursday evening. Is this correct, and if so, why did you take such a position?

Miss PERRIN. I wouldn't say opposed, sir. It wouldn't be for me to—

Mr. BROADBENT. Did you not solicit the support of Dr. Gozar in trying to prevent the meeting, and did you not telephone Mr. Owing and Mrs. Sloat on the subject?

Miss PERRIN. I did make some calls, and I realize it wasn't for a teacher. . . . The initials P.-T.A.—I realize P. comes before T., I know I don't have any business—

Mr. BROADBENT. Just tell us why, Miss Perrin. What was your angle?

Miss PERRIN. To be perfectly honest, there was one aspect . . .

Mr. BROADBENT. Which was?

Miss PERRIN. But, truly, it's giving me too much *credit*, to say I 'opposed.' I wouldn't have the nerve to—

Senator SKYPACK. All right, all right, miss. Spit it out.

Miss PERRIN. You mean, the aspect—?

Senator SKYPACK. I mean, spit it out.

Miss PERRIN. Well, there was one thing. Mind you, the parents at our school are good people, very kind people, and they put a lot of time and effort into school affairs. But it often seems to me—I'll say it sometimes seems to me—that they—I don't want to be too harsh—they miss the point.

Mr. BROADBENT. Specifically?

Miss PERRIN. This meeting, you see. It was to be a big explosive meeting about the troubles last week—about the decline and decay of the younger generation. About the unfortunate incident at Miss Henley's lecture, and the attack on the Rudds' home, and what someone saw Barry and Florence doing. The meeting was going to be all about those things. What's Wrong With American Youth?—and not a word, either before the meeting or at it, about the real point.

Mr. BROADBENT. The real point?

Miss PERRIN. The child buyer.

Mr. BROADBENT. The proposition wasn't discussed?

Miss PERRIN. Not a whisper. Neither before or during. It was just taken for granted, I guess. Forgive me, I know I have no right to criticize—but what I'd like to say is, if all you look for is delinquency, you're going to find it. There's so much good in young people—sometimes our best parents, I mean a cultured mother like Mrs. Sloat—it sometimes seems to me they're not really interested in good education for their children, they're only interested in getting school people fired.

Senator SKYPACK. You trying to condone these perpetual

sex incidents, Miss Perrin?

Miss PERRIN. No, of course not. I—

Senator SKYPACK. How's your memory, miss?

Miss PERRIN. Oh, I have a very poor memory, sir. I've often wished . . .

Senator SKYPACK. It seems you have, miss. Do you remember a certain teachers' strike in the northeastern part of this State in the year—

Senator MANSFIELD. Let's get back to that meeting, Jack.

Senator SKYPACK. It's perfectly obvious, Aaron. This lady has no respect for the authorities. I mean we've got the facts, here, why don't we use them?

Senator MANSFIELD. Pretty ancient facts, Jack. Mr. Wairy told us that had all been forgotten. Mr. Broadbent, the meeting.

Mr. BROADBENT. Now I want you to confine yourself, Miss Perrin, to the teachers' side of things at the meeting. Mrs. Sloat will give us the parents' slant. What did the teachers have to say?

Miss PERRIN. There was a lot of talk about Barry, of course.

Mr. BROADBENT. What was said—strictly by teachers?

Miss PERRIN. Dr. Gozar said he's a topnotch student who'll make an outstanding research scientist; that his interest is deep, scholarly, tending toward the theoretical . . . Gaining in poise . . .

Mr. BROADBENT. Anyone else?

Miss PERRIN. Miss Bagas, first grade, said she considered him extremely sympathetic—told how once another child had a stopped-up nose while reciting, and Barry blew *his* nose very hard several times, as if that would clear out the other child's nostrils.

Mr. BROADBENT. You trying to say there was nothing but praise?

Miss PERRIN. There were favorable comments. I hate to repeat unkind—

Senator SKYPACK. I'd advise you to be a co-operative witness, miss.

Miss PERRIN. Why should I go against my—?

Senator SKYPACK. The initials U.C.N.T. mean anything to you, miss?

Miss PERRIN. Oh.

Senator SKYPACK. Ever hear of the Union of Clerks, Nurses, and Teachers, miss? Ever hear about the rotten apples in that barrel, miss? Ever hear about the part it played in the upstate teachers' strike, back in the Depression?

Miss PERRIN. I . . . Dear me, I . . .

Senator MANSFIELD. Jack. I really feel—

Senator SKYPACK. All right. Let her answer the questions, then. If she's going to sit there and pass judgment on parents and lawmakers.

Miss PERRIN. Please. I want to do my duty. I know I have a responsibility. . . . Miss Songevine, it's common knowledge the children call her The Knife. She talked about him in the third grade, the beginning of the year they had a reader, *Our Friends Around the Corner*, and she said, 'He'd gone through the whole book the second day and remembered everything in it.' Miss Songevine has this sarcastic edge to her voice. 'He had a good-humored tolerance,' she said. ' "I've come to class; I have to sit here." ' Miss Songevine said she thought she could use him to present some social-studies material on the blackboard 'with a little elegance,' she said, 'but he couldn't read his own writing.' She gave up using him for demonstration work. But I've heard Barry criticize her, too. Says she used double negatives.

Senator SKYPACK. I don't see this is getting us anywhere, Aaron.

Miss PERRIN. I do want to help, Senator. I do. Do you want more adverse comment on Barry? 'His attitude of superiority to the work we're doing'—Miss Trent. Immature. Conceited. Lack of facial reaction. Strange chunky torso. That's what some of them say. Anything else you want? I do realize . . .

Senator SKYPACK. It's this same sniveling attitude as before from this witness, Aaron. Couldn't we move on?

Senator MANSFIELD. Were you finished, Mr. Broadbent?

Mr. BROADBENT. I'm inclined to go along with Senator Skypack, Mr. Chairman. The witness . . .

Senator MANSFIELD. Thank you for testifying, Miss Perrin, that will be all for now.

Mr. BROADBENT. The next witness will be Mrs. William Sloat.

Senator MANSFIELD. If you will just stand—in front of the chair there, please, Mrs. Sloat—and I'll swear you in.

Do you solemnly swear that the testimony you are about to give on the matters now pending before this committee will be the truth, the whole truth, and nothing but the truth, so help you God?

Mrs. SLOAT. I do.

TESTIMONY OF MRS. JEFFERSON SLOAT, PRESIDENT,
LINCOLN P.-T.A., PEQUOT

Mr. BROADBENT. You are Mrs. William L. Sloat?

Mrs. SLOAT. No. Mrs. Jefferson Sloat.

Senator VOYOLKO. Crying out loud, we got the wrong witness?

Mr. BROADBENT. We understood from our investigators that you were a Mrs. Bill Sloat. Bill L. Sloat.

Mrs. SLOAT. I am called Bill.

Mr. BROADBENT. That's *your* name?

Mrs. SLOAT. No, it's my nickname.

Mr. BROADBENT. That's your nickname? Your friends all call you Bill?

Mrs. SLOAT. That's correct.

Mr. BROADBENT. Your real name being?

Mrs. SLOAT. Wilhelmina Langwell Sloat.

Mr. BROADBENT. You are President of the Lincoln School Parent-Teachers' Association?

Mrs. SLOAT. And concurrently President of the Pequot P.-T.A. Council. And President of the Pequot Republican Women's Club, and President—

Mr. BROADBENT. Yes, madam, we understand you're a devoted public servant. As we understand it, madam, you called an emergency meeting of the Lincoln School P.-T.A. last Thursday evening, to discuss—

Mrs. SLOAT. To discuss delinquency. The shocking looseness of our young people. I say 'young.' These things are happening at a younger and younger age; *that's* the disturbing thing.

Mr. BROADBENT. Exactly. And would you mind describing the meeting for our benefit, madam?

Mrs. SLOAT. We started with the usual business meeting, and this took longer than normally because we had a rather heated discussion of our next Get-Acquainted Night. Mrs. Toll wanted the traditional hot covered-dish supper, and Mrs. Bennett, who has only lived in Pequot nine years and, you know, she has the typical newcomer's desire to revolutionize everything, well, she wanted a Mexican-style smorgasbord. Toward the end of the discussion, in walked Mrs. Singerly, right down to a seat in front of the auditorium—she hadn't been invited, I purposely wanted to keep this meeting in the family; she's on the Board of Education, and she has an insufferable attitude and carriage. Walking down the auditorium—as if to say, 'Are you looking at me? Did you notice me yet?' Typical! I remember her when she was just a lowly program chairman at Pohadnock Elementary. She'd heard about our closed-doors meeting—

Mr. BROADBENT. Excuse me, madam.

Mrs. SLOAT. —and she made it her business—

Mr. Broadbent. If I may interrupt.

Mrs. Sloat. —to come uninvited—

Mr. Broadbent. If you *please*, Mrs. Sloat. We are interested in the Rudd case. These Senators are busy men. If you would kindly confine your details.

Mrs. Sloat. Of course. We got to the delinquency problem at about a quarter to nine. I don't know if you've heard of the shocks we've had in our peaceful village the last few days.

Mr. Broadbent. Yes, madam.

Mrs. Sloat. One's at a loss—I think it must've been our young men going overseas, the last couple of wars, mixing with foreign riffraff, geisha girls, existentialists. Our Customs people ought to charge a duty on immorality. It's all imported. You know that.

Mr. Broadbent. Madam, I beseech you. The Rudd case.

Mrs. Sloat. Mrs. Bontecu told us that she remembered traveling on the train, I think it was to Springfield, this was last year, and the Rudd boy was on there, all alone. He was going to visit relatives, Easter-vacation time. Imagine sending a nine-year-old child on a train trip alone! They ought to abolish reformatories like Clarkdale and turn them into penitentiaries for parents. I mean it. Mrs. Bontecu said that boy would talk to *any*one. She overheard him talking to this Jewish man about how the Egyptians buried their dead, the way they used to stiffen up the dead flesh for mummies. Then the thing happened that Mrs. Bontecu wanted to tell us. The boy had a pair of hamsters with him in a box, sort of like guinea pigs, and he took them out, and they were running all over the car, and *then*. One of them, it must have been a female, had a litter of babies right there just off the aisle. The boy gathered a whole crowd around to watch, and as Mrs. Bontecu said, she told this story to illustrate that this boy was already interested in sex in his *ninth year*. You talk about precocious.

Mr. BROADBENT. What else, madam?

Mrs. SLOAT. Here's something I brought along with me. Two years ago Mrs. Parsons had to call on the Rudds in an every-parent membership-drive canvass, their home is a pigsty, anyway Mrs. Rudd was bragging about Barry, and she showed Mrs. Parsons this little sign that was tacked over the boy's work table. Molly Parsons was so scandalized that she asked Mrs. Rudd could she have it, and Mrs. Rudd seemed flattered and gladly gave it to her, and Molly kept it all this time and brought it to our meeting. Here, I'll just turn it over to you.

Mr. BROADBENT. Thank you.

Senator SKYPACK. What does it say, Broadbent?

Mr. BROADBENT. It's a little sign, like an ad. It says, 'Are you getting DUMB? TRY PROFESSOR B. RUDD'S MACHINE THAT WILL MAKE YOU SMART.'

Mrs. SLOAT. To show the *conceit* of that boy.

Mr. BROADBENT. Could we admit this document into the record, Mr. Chairman?

Senator MANSFIELD. It will be admitted.

(The document referred to was marked 'Sloat Exhibit No. 1' and filed.)

Mr. BROADBENT. Please go on about the meeting, madam.

Mrs. SLOAT. Mrs. Singerly—the School Board one—tried to take up for the boy, but I'm glad to say she was hooted down. She tried to say that Barry Rudd has a 'notable dissatisfaction with present explanations of the way the world works,' that he is 'non-Panglossian,' whatever that is, and a lot of other affected statements. But then fortunately we got off on trying to find constructive solutions. Maria Tenn, she's one of the sixth-grade room mothers, she proposed that we set up a committee to look into the Reading Shelf in Miss Perrin's room, see if it's some of this insidious material in the textbooks and outside-reading books that accounts for the promiscuity and lack of respect for property in our youngsters. And Mrs. Toll introduced a resolution of censure of Mr. Sean Cleary, he's our man in charge of what they *call* Guidance, on account of the Tell-Who Test he used in the talent search, because he had questions in there like 'Tell who among your friends cheats a little on tests,' and 'Tell who's a liar in your class.' Any parent with any self-respect has been trying all these years to teach her children not to tattle, and here you have the school system *insisting* on it.

Mr. BROADBENT. We understand you summoned Mr. Rudd to the meeting. What part did he play?

Mrs. SLOAT. We'd intended to call him to task for his son's— I mean, it's up to a father to tighten the cinch, get a stiff curb bit in there, hike up on the reins.

Mr. BROADBENT. What was said to Mr. Rudd?

Mrs. SLOAT. We didn't have time.

Mr. BROADBENT. What about Miss Perrin?

Mrs. SLOAT. Well, I think this business of tenure. Now, she's a perfect example. Your hands are tied, you can't let a teacher like her go if you want to. They get entrenched in there, dug in—automatic raises every year.

Mr. BROADBENT. In another connection, Mrs. Sloat. What do you feel the position of your organization would be with respect to the man Wissey Jones's proposal to buy Barry Rudd and take him—

Mrs. SLOAT. The P.-T.A. couldn't meddle with that kind of thing. That's a business matter, the P.-T.A. has no right to get into questions of private enterprise. Of course, if you want my own *personal* opinion, it would be good riddance. They say the boy's a budding genius, and I say I don't trust geniuses.

Senator SKYPACK. Other words, miss, you think the boy should be sold.

Mrs. SLOAT. Definitely. I speak only for Bill Sloat, you understand. But definitely.

158

Senator SKYPACK. That's enough for me.

Mr. BROADBENT. Thank you, madam. That will be all. Yes, you may step aside. The first door. Mr. Chairman, I'd like to call Master Barry Rudd.

Senator MANSFIELD. O.K., sonny, just take your place again.

TESTIMONY OF BARRY RUDD, MINOR, TOWN OF PEQUOT

Mr. BROADBENT. Now, Master Rudd, we understand that you were present at the second interview in Pequot between the man Wissey Jones and your school Guidance Director, Mr. Cleary—the crucial interview, as we see it, in turning the tide toward the violent events of this past week in Pequot. We want to question you about that conversation.

Senator MANSFIELD. What day was that?

Mr. BROADBENT. That was Saturday, sir, Saturday the nineteenth.

Senator MANSFIELD. Then that was before any of the disturbances we've been talking about? You keep dodging around so.

Mr. BROADBENT. Considerably before. Yes, sir. You'll remember the man Wissey Jones arrived in Pequot on the Wednesday, the sixteenth, and he began digging on Thursday. Thursday was the day Mr. Cleary went to the Rudd family, and Mr. Jones talked with the Rudds on Friday. Then this conversation took place on Saturday. The violence and all didn't begin till the following Tuesday. And, as I've said, I want to bring out that this interview laid the groundwork for those later occurrences. Where was this interview held, Master Rudd?

BARRY RUDD. It was in the hotel, the Mulhausen, in Mr. Jones's suite.

Mr. BROADBENT. How did you happen to be present?

BARRY RUDD. Mr. Cleary stopped by the house—Saturday's

my luxury day, and I was all settled down with Aldington's life of Voltaire—and said he'd been summoned to see the child buyer, and he insisted I go with him.

Mr. BROADBENT. Why did he want you along?

BARRY RUDD. As I think Momma told you, he was against the child buyer's proposition at that time, and I guess he thought I'd take his part—or my own, if you want to look at it that way.

Mr. BROADBENT. And he conducted you to Mr. Jones's room at the Mulhausen?

BARRY RUDD. It was a suite. On the way in, when Mr. Cleary mentioned the name Wissey Jones at the desk, it was like waving a wand. Everyone began to bow and say sir, even to me. Mr. Jones had only been there three days, and it was as if he owned the place.

Mr. BROADBENT. So then Mr. Jones received you.

BARRY RUDD. He was in a dressing gown made out of the silk with a Paisley design—splotches that looked like a bunch of *Paramecia caudata,* a species of unicellular slipper animalcule that is found in abundance in putrefying infusions; with the result that I had at once a reaction of mild nausea. His folding motorcycle was in one corner of the room. This was the living room of what the hotel calls the Uncas Suite, named for *Le Cerf agile,* the nimble deer, as the French called Uncas, with prints of Mohegans and rather cheesy Indian motifs—but the room's on the southeast corner of the building, and it was flooded with cheerful sunlight.

Mr. BROADBENT. How did the conversation begin?

BARRY RUDD. With suspicion and black looks. I guess Mr. Jones felt that the G-man had crossed wires on him, and the G-man must have been afraid that the child buyer was going to queer him with the Superintendent, or something. As they sat glaring at each other I wondered, as I have many times: Why don't looks mix or bump when they meet? Why can't you feel an angry look when it hits your cheek? Sometimes when Momma looks at me I have a sensation of warmth on my skin and it almost seems to me as if it's a kind of ray she emits from her eyes. I know what you're thinking, Senator Skypack: 'Unscientific.' I know. I can almost feel *your* look, Senator. B-r-r-r-r!

Mr. BROADBENT. Please go on, Master Rudd.

BARRY RUDD. Mr. Jones was imperious. How dared Mr. Cleary oppose him? Mr. Cleary stuck his lower lip out and said I was too young at ten to make an irrevocable commitment to science, or to anything else. I hadn't even gone through puberty; wasn't a man yet by a long shot. It was too early to start burning bridges. Mr. Cleary jabbed manfully at a pillow next to him, as if emphasis and punishment were synonymous. 'How does the youngster know at this point that he won't decide in ten years to be not a scientist but, let's say, a baker, or a bricklayer, or a certified public accountant?' He stared at me while he was saying that, I guess to see how I'd respond to those gratuitous downgradings; I didn't care. I've known since I was eight that I'm going to be a scientist. He said, 'What if he's a failure?' That didn't bother me either; being a failure doesn't enter into my plans. You know what I thought? I thought: 'Listen, Mr. G-man, Shubert and Mozart were both *dead* before they reached your age. There isn't all the time in the world. Liebig discovered fulminic acid when he was sixteen. Galileo discovered the isochronism of the pendulum when he was seventeen. Pascal invented a calculating machine when he was nineteen. Braille devised his alphabet when he was twenty. Colt designed his revolver when he was sixteen. Keats wrote "On First Looking into Chapman's Homer" when he was twenty. Weber isolated sulphur sesquioxide when he was nineteen. Raphael painted the Granduca Madonna at twenty-one. Wolsey graduated from Oxford at fourteen. Maybe I was already old to be starting as a classifying biologist. Linnaeus began to learn plant names at four, and at eight he had his own garden where he grew all sorts of wild flowers and plants that he collected. Don't talk to *me* about making a commitment too early!'

Mr. BROADBENT. Go on, please—about the interview.

BARRY RUDD. Mr. Jones began asking the G-man about the various intelligence tests that had been given to me, and Mr. Cleary talked about his talent search. He gave my standings on the Minifie Gestalt Partial-Clue Puzzle and the Psycho-Kinesthetic Draw-Mama Test, and the Pankhurst Tell-Who, and the Olmstead-Diffendorff Game. Then Mr. Jones said, 'But what about his intelligence, Cleary?' Undistinguished, the G-man said. Low on the Olmstead-Diffendorff Game. Mediocre standing on two national-norm group tests. He rattled off scores and statistics; he seemed for a few moments to have stuffed percentiles and medians and average reliabilities and coefficients of data into his cheek pouches, as a red squirrel, *Scuirus hudsonicus*, secretes the meats of nuts.

Mr. BROADBENT. What was the child buyer's reaction?

BARRY RUDD. He asked if there had ever been a Binet or a Wechsler. The G-man said there'd been a Binet given in another school system, Treehampstead; but Pequot doesn't accept records from outside the district.

Senator MANSFIELD. Were you curious to hear your own I.Q.?

BARRY RUDD. I was feeling detached—as if all this talk had nothing whatsoever to do with me. For some reason I kept thinking about Dr. Gozar, who was the first person to make me realize that everything in this world isn't known.

Mr. BROADBENT. What happened next?

BARRY RUDD. It seems that Mr. Cleary had been scurrying around gathering ammunition to use on the child buyer, and he said he had a memorandum from Miss Perrin, and he handed it to Mr. Jones to read, and after Mr. Jones finished it he passed it to me. This thing did hurt me, because I like Miss Perrin.

162

Mr. BROADBENT. Can you remember the gist of it?

BARRY RUDD. I can remember every word of it. 'Barry Rudd is a lot brighter than I am. But he slumps in his chair, keeps his eyes down, chews pencils, and repels affection. Anecdotes as requested. (1) I put him on the list of blackboard cleaners, which thrills most of the children, but as soon as he saw his name put down he said, "Great!" in a very disgusted manner. (2) I wanted to show an audio-visual film strip in social studies but could not get the holes in the edge of the 16-mm. film to mesh with the little cogs in the projector. Barry stepped forward unbid and more or less pushed me aside and fixed it, but he did it with bad grace and went out of his way to make me feel stupid. (3) He let a cheese sandwich from his cold lunch stay in his desk and rot until it smelled intolerably. (4) I put my hand on his shoulder while talking to him. I like to touch my children, and most of them look as if they need to be cuddled, especially some of the hard-mouth Intervale boys. Generally my children are glad to be petted. Not Barry. He flinched and pulled away as if I had leprosy. It makes me feel queer when love is answered with hate. He can be cold and clammy, yet sometimes his eyes seem to be appealing for help.'

Senator SKYPACK. Mr. Broadbent, we should get ahold of that document. It ought to be entered here as an exhibit.

BARRY RUDD. As I was reading it, I thought, What does a teacher really know about his pupils? At fifteen Mirabeau, who baffled his family, was packed off to Versailles to be educated in the household of a M. de Sigrais. At the end of three months Sigrais announced to the parents that he'd remain the boy's jailer as long as they liked, but he couldn't do a thing with his mind.

Mr. BROADBENT. Carry on, please, with your account.

BARRY RUDD. The G-man said I had a certain richness of imagination but some carelessness in the handling of it; that I was uncritical on the whole. He said I had a sneaky streak, and glibness bordering on mendacity. He cited the answers I'd given on a form as to what I'd like to be when I grow up—and I'll confess, I had my tongue in my cheek that day. I was *fed up* with the G-man's everlasting boondoggling snoopery. I answered: One. Banker. Two. Forest ranger. Three. Christian Science Healer. That same day, I remember, I gave a lot of purposely mixed-up multiple-choice answers on sports, in an aptitude test, really just for the heck of it: that pucks are used in archery, fruit-basket is a kissing game, whist is played with pins, snap is played with mallets, and canvasbacks are a kind of tent.

Senator SKYPACK. You knew better?

BARRY RUDD. Of *course*. Canvasbacks—*Nyrocae valisineriae* —a kind of tent?

Senator SKYPACK. By God, I do think that's sneaky, Mr. Chairman, to just thumb your nose at the great institution of public education that way.

BARRY RUDD. Mr. Cleary referred to gifted students as 'the monster quotient' and kept talking about me as a 'deviate.'

Senator MANSFIELD. I noticed that was Miss Henley's favorite word, too, sonny. I don't blame you for bridling at that.

Senator SKYPACK. You got a better word, Mr. Chairman?

BARRY RUDD. While they were talking about their busybody old tests, I was having one of my regressive reveries—thinking that all my knowledge was innate; I'd been born with it. I've often been amnesic as to the source of my information, and I've just felt that I'd 'always known.' 'I just knew it.' When I used to believe in God I long had the image of facts and stories having been written in pencil on a sort of reel of microfilm made out of skin in my head by Him before I was born. I thought of God as being able to talk big and write *very* small.

Senator SKYPACK. Top off the rest of it, he's a blasphemer.

BARRY RUDD. I didn't intend any disrespect of your views,

164

Senator.

Mr. BROADBENT. Back to the child buyer and Mr. Cleary, please, Master Rudd.

BARRY RUDD. Mr. Jones began to heap ridicule on Mr. Cleary's talent search, and the G-man got talking in what seemed to me a confused way. 'The real problem is emotional,' he said. 'The child is disturbed. The blinking of his eyes—have you noticed that? That's not normal in a child his age. He's been on the brink. I've seen tears well up in his eyes. He's really afraid of Dr. Gozar. Well, I admit, Dr. Gozar's the dynamic type; everybody's afraid of her to some extent. But I've had to handle this boy with kid gloves. He blinks. I toyed with the idea of referring him to a psychiatrist but decided against it. I made my own psychiatric evaluation. The mother's the moving force. Look, I'm not the policy maker here. The administration makes the policy. What happens if every time a child comes to me and says, "I want to be on the talent chart," we put him there? There'd be repercussions, and I don't mean maybe. We've got standards. This child missed out on his fundamentals, some of them. He's got to learn to catch a ball. Be a *boy*. Besides, we can't spend all day on one pupil—we couldn't justify that to the Board of Finance, I'll tell you that. We feel there are other things in life besides biological research. That boy's one-sided. He knows little or nothing about associating with his peers. He isn't interested in girls. The boy has to learn to be a citizen and conform in some respects. No son of mine would be allowed to carry the kind of load Dr. Gozar puts on that child. We don't have the time of day in public school for cases that get too special. This is mass education.' And so forth. He just rattled on. Till Mr. Jones cut in and asked him what Mr. Cleary's own 'psychiatric evaluation' was that he'd said he'd made. 'This is rather technical stuff,' the G-man said. 'I believe that this boy, in reaction against the mother's psycho-cultural rejection-guilt-anxiety-overprotection cyclical pattern, is suffering from a rather clear-cut nipple fixation, together with a certain amount of vulva emulation.'

Senator SKYPACK. By gorry. What did Mr. Jones say to *that?*

BARRY RUDD. He said, 'Come off it, Cleary, don't hand me that Sigmund Fraud. Or Carl Jungle or Alfred Addled, either.'

Senator SKYPACK. That child buyer's really an enlightened fella, he doesn't stand for any nonsense, does he?

BARRY RUDD. I was taking some notes on the back of Miss Perrin's memorandum in a shorthand of my own that I'd devised, and when the G-man noticed me doing that he got very excited. 'See? See?' he shouted—as if my doodling along in that way, really just to occupy myself, proved that I was a mental case. Mr. Cleary began talking about my lack of social adjustment in school. He said I prefer the company of older people to that of my own age group, and he said that the 'regular guys' bully me.

Senator MANSFIELD. How did this make you feel—the two of them talking about you right in front of you, as if you were a sick cat or dog?

BARRY RUDD. I felt detached—mildly interested. When the G-man talked about my seeking out older people, I thought, 'So did Hegel, Descartes, Voltaire!' Not that I consider myself one of *them.* But John Sano *bores* me. And when the G-man talked about the bullies, I thought of the German apothegm, 'When Pythagoras discovered the theorem of the right triangle, he sacrificed a hundred oxen; since then, whenever a new truth has been unveiled, all oxen have trembled.'

Senator SKYPACK. You think you know more about his business than the Guidance Director, is that the size of it?

BARRY RUDD. I must say, Senator, for a so-called educator, Mr. Cleary has an odd way of grading mental abilities: A stupid person is one who lets himself be victimized; a gifted person is one who's shrewd. He thinks intelligence is cleverness. Since he thinks he's a 'realist,' thinks moral values are nothing but cant, he has the great advantage of not having to decide what he really believes—his morality is the cops, his golden rule is don't get caught. Yet, I've got to admit the G-man's honest; I mean to say, he sees himself as honest and other people see him as honest. Perhaps the two views make him, practically speaking, honest indeed, though they aren't the same. The G-man thinks he's honest because he can spot 'good' people and 'talented' people for what they really are—hypocrites and neurotics. He's so honest that a public display of genuine affection or loyalty or self-sacrifice is liable to make him feel sick at his stomach. When other people look at *him*, they see a man who's honest because he doesn't steal and because he sticks by his word even when he knows he's mistaken.

Mr. BROADBENT. This is the first time, Master Rudd, that we've heard you speak with real feeling. I take it you were not quite so detached as you've told us you were.

BARRY RUDD. My view is that I'm not maladjusted, I'm *intensified*. There's a difference.

Mr. BROADBENT. Let's get back to the interview. Tell us—

BARRY RUDD. The child buyer was getting more and more impatient. He was pacing up and down the room, and he burst out and said, 'Social adjustment isn't needed for research scientists. The more they prefer to be alone, the better off they are, and the better off science is. People in education,' he said, 'who *do* need social adjustment and often lack it, are simply obsessed with the subject.'

Mr. BROADBENT. From what we know of Mr. Cleary, he wouldn't take *that* lying down.

BARRY RUDD. He didn't. In fact he stood up, and I thought for a few moments we were going to have a boxing match—all about me! But suddenly the buyer changed his tactics altogether, and within two minutes the G-man had caved in. Utterly. I wish

167

you could have seen it. 'You told me the other day, Cleary,' Mr. Jones said, 'that you're a realist. Now, I suggest we get down to brass tacks. I'm a businessman. I'm here to arrange a business deal. It doesn't seem to be a particularly popular one, so my job is to make it popular, and I'm prepared to pay the price, or prices, of making it popular. This boy sitting here is something I want. I want him very much. I'm satisfied, knowing his I.Q. and having observed his performance, that he is a re-markable specimen—that he's one in roughly five hundred thou-sand in our population; in other words, he has one of maybe the three hundred rarest potential minds in this country. I want him, and I'm going to get him. And one person who's not going to stand in my way is *you*, Cleary. Because I know what your price is. It's a scrubby little wet rag of power that you want to hold in your hands. And I have it for you. It's an Assistant Superintendentship in Trent, in Fairfield County; one of the plush towns educationally, as you're well aware. Stan Preese is Chairman of the School Board down there, and he's a business-man and a realist, too—one who happens to have gotten himself rather seriously obligated to me and my firm. I can assert here and now that the job's yours. I know you don't care about the salary, but it's ten thousand five. The Superintendent is sixty-one years old, so the prospects are both excellent and practically immedi-ate. Now, for this price you're to support me whole hog—and that means be my legman, put me onto the soft spots and temptations of the people I have to win over, help me in every way you can to sew this purchase up. You're such a big realist, Cleary—is it a deal?'

Senator SKYPACK. By Christopher, he's a slick one!

Mr. BROADBENT. What did Mr. Cleary say?

BARRY RUDD. He didn't say anything. He blushed. A blush came out on his face like the slowly spreading and brightening glow of the coils of an electric toaster when it has been turned on. You could see him trying to fight the blush, but he was as helpless as Canute trying to halt the ocean tide; his realizing that a blush is involuntary, and that there was absolutely nothing he could do to stop it until it had burned itself out, made it come on the more brightly. He had given himself away! No matter how smoothly he spoke now, the buyer and I had caught him out. When his cheeks were hotly shining at the highest flood of the blush, I sensed that he felt, above all, a hatred for me.

Mr. BROADBENT. Did he accept Mr. Jones's offer then?

BARRY RUDD. He never did in words. Mr. Jones just took his blush as an acceptance of his bribe, and they started mapping out their next steps. Mr. Jones outlined the full plan of United Lymphomilloid on what they'd do with me, how first they would put me in a small room—

Senator SKYPACK. Now, wait a minute there, boy. That plan has been given to this committee by Mr. Jones in confidence, strictly off the record. We're not going to have you shoot your mouth off and betray his trust in us. There are newspapermen here. You just drop that line of chatter, hear?

Mr. BROADBENT. You say they planned their next steps. What were they?

BARRY RUDD. I don't know exactly. As they were talking they both seemed to realize for the first time that I was there as a human consciousness. Cleary never had gotten around to calling on me for support. Now both of them turned on me. Where, until a few moments before, I'd been watching a fascinating fencing bout, I now saw both épées leveled in line at me—and the tips weren't blunted, either. The two men were suddenly allies. Mr. Jones said, 'You'll excuse us now, Barry. You can run home—I suppose you had your nose in a book this morning; what were you reading?' I told him about the Voltaire. 'You can run home to Monsieur Arouet,' he said. 'Mr. Cleary and I want

169

to plot a little how to influence and change that stubborn little so-called mind of yours.' So I had no choice but to leave.

Mr. Broadbent. And I put it to you that this situation, after the interview—the two men joining ranks against you, as it were—led directly to your delinquencies of the following week. I put it to you that nobody else but Master Barry Rudd was at the bottom of the violence and delinquencies that ensued in Pequot, and that Master Rudd was motivated by the outcome of this talk.

Barry Rudd. That's a rather sweeping statement, sir—or perhaps I should say a sweeping misstatement.

Mr. Broadbent. I intend to prove it before we're finished with these hearings.

Senator Skypack. Can I have the witness a minute, Broadbent? If we're through with that part of the questioning.

Mr. Broadbent. Certainly, sir; I have no more questions on that interview.

Senator Skypack. Now, listen, boy, I want straight answers. You've already admitted you were in the lab the afternoon of the bombing—you and that delinquent punk. Right?

Barry Rudd. I don't think it's fair to Charles Perkonian to speak of him that way, Senator. He served out the full punishment under law for what he did, and he's working darn hard at his own rehabilitation.

Senator Skypack. I'll thank you to confine your remarks to answers to my questions, my boy. And, by the way, I'll pick my words and you pick yours. Now I want to put it to you directly. Did you make and throw that stink bomb?

Barry Rudd. No, sir.

Senator Skypack. You're not forgetting you're under oath. You know the meaning of the word 'perjury'?

Barry Rudd. From the French, *parjurer*, and originally from Latin, *periurare*, to forswear oneself, or, in other words, to swear to tell the truth and then tell a lie.

Senator SKYPACK. All right. You know what it means, and I assume you know the usual penalties for it. I'll repeat the question. Did you make and throw that bomb?

BARRY RUDD. I did not, sir.

Senator SKYPACK. Do you know who did?

BARRY RUDD. Yes, sir, I do.

Senator SKYPACK. Who was it?

BARRY RUDD. I'd rather not tell.

Senator SKYPACK. You know you're under oath to tell the whole truth, don't you?

BARRY RUDD. There is no greater truth than that I'd rather not tell.

Senator SKYPACK. Mr. Chairman, would you do me the kindness of directing the witness to answer?

Senator MANSFIELD. Now, look here, Jack, are you sure you want to make an issue—

Senator SKYPACK. You damn tootin' I want to make an issue. Was it that delinquent punk friend of yours, boy?

BARRY RUDD. If you mean Flattop, he isn't a punk, and as to the stink bomb I have no intention of informing.

Senator SKYPACK. Was it . . . was it that fellow Cleary?

BARRY RUDD. Are you crazy, Senator? He set up the meeting. He was on the stage with Miss Henley.

Senator SKYPACK. Was it that teacher? That Miss Perrin?

BARRY RUDD. I've already said that I don't intend to tell you who it was.

Senator MANSFIELD. Let's move on, Jack. You're not going to get any satisfaction out of the boy on this one. Is there anything else you want to ask about?

Senator SKYPACK. There certainly is. I want to ask about these dirty books he's been picking up at the public library. Tell me, boy, when did you first learn the facts of life?

BARRY RUDD. If you mean about the reproductive process in humans, I got the first basic information about two months ago.

Senator SKYPACK. Where did you pick this up?

BARRY RUDD. From my friend Charley Perkonian. We were walking home from the movies, a matinee, I remember we were going along Second Street, where there's a series of white picket fences, and Flattop was tapping a stick along the palings, and we got talking about the kissing in the film we'd seen, and how it sort of made you sick to the stomach, when suddenly he launched into kissing as a first step toward copulation—I mean, he used street language; I've acquired a more exact vocabulary since then out of books—and he described the whole process to me. His information, I later learned from my reading, was astonishingly accurate, except for one detail. 'Before a guy can start with a woman,' he said, 'he has to get her ready by he lets her shove her finger into a ring with a precious jool on it. Thing is,' he said, 'this has a lot to do with can they make a baby. They can make one pretty easy if the jool's a diamond, and you take and have a big-size diamond on the ring, about the size of a raisin, it's a pushover. I mean it's like rolling off a log, it's nothing.' I now realize that I went off on my geology kick just after that talk. I'd noticed mica shining in the rocks in the detritus along the river in back of our house, also down near Sandy Point where my father and Mr. Zimmer used to take us on picnics with the boat they made, and now I had a fantasy about fabricating synthetic diamonds, for men to use in this interesting way, out of the mica. I'd been crazy about cacti just before that, but they were wearing off, and the first thing I knew, I was off to the races with rocks. I was directed to a dentist in Tunxis who had a big amateur collection, and he gave me a lot of his extras. Then on two weekends Dr. Gozar drove me to the Agassiz in Cambridge and the Peabody in New Haven, and I saw a billion specimens of rock. I found some stone up on the ridge that crumbled into white powder, and I thought it might be gypsum, and I would 'discover' cement. My big adventure, though, was to go over to the old mica mine near Londonville, an open-pit mine which during the last couple of wars supplied mica for electronic uses. I had a prospector's pick, and I took out some rose quartz and garnet and some other pretty subgem stones. And mica. For men.

Senator SKYPACK. All right, boy. Now about these smut books you been getting from the public library. This Miss Cloud—

BARRY RUDD. To me things take on heightened reality after I have seen them on the printed page. Reading's just about the most important part of my life. We have a French conversation class at school, and when Miss Séjour asks, '*Que mangez-vous pour votre petit déjeuner? Qu'est-ce que vous faites dans la cuisine?*', the other kids answer out of the book, '*Je mange le dindon,*' or '*Je mange la tarte à la citrouille,*' or John Sano says, '*Je mange* peanut butter.' But I say, '*Je lise dans un livre de biologie.*' That's what I'd rather do than eat. Reading gives truth. I feel that, I really do. So whenever I come across something new, I want to read about it. Now. When Flattop talked about this new subject, there was an indefinable something—his knowing air, his controlled casualness, the curious feeling of intimacy I had with him while he was talking—that subtly made me realize that my approach to Miss Cloud for material on the subject would have to be circumspect. I understood later, when I'd read about adolescence, puberty, coming-of-age fertility rites among primitive peoples, and so on, that a particular reason for this being complicated in my case was that I have a physical age and a mental age which simply leap right across adolescence. On top of that Dr. Gozar had talked perfectly openly to me about reproductive phenomena, heredity in fruit flies and all, and I'd seen hamsters and termites born and hatched, but never a word about the process of fertilization. Now there were, from Flattop, mysterious suggestions of pleasure, of magic, what with the talk about diamonds, and even a whiff of right and wrong. So, to begin with, I kind of pussy-footed with Miss Cloud. But she's so understanding—she plunged right in and got me started right away on courtship rituals in fauna.

Senator MANSFIELD. And, by the bye, sonny, just what *does* the stickleback do?

BARRY RUDD. Oh, he's a rascal, but he's sort of pathetic, too. The three-spined stickleback, *Gasterosteus aculeatus*, is a little fish whose first dorsal fin and ventrals are dangerous pointed spines attached to bony shields of his endo-skeleton. He mates early in the spring in fresh water, in shallows. First he stakes out his home grounds and drives every other fish out of it. (This staking-out in the mating season is common to many creatures; Dr. Gozar once told me about a rose-breasted grosbeak, *Hedymeles ludovicianus*, that she'd seen pecking at his reflection in a window because he thought it was another bird intruding on his nesting area.) Anyway, the stickleback digs a hole about two inches square in the bottom, picking up the soil mouthful by mouthful, like a tiny steam shovel, and it piles thread algae and grasses in the hole, plasters them with some goo from its kidneys, and pushes them into a mound. Then it makes a tunnel by wriggling through. At that point he suddenly turns from pale gray to brilliant red and bluish white, and he begins to watch for fat females—they've got about a hundred eggs in them— and when he sees one he goes at her with a kind of zigzag dance, until she approaches him with her head up and her tail dragging, so to speak. He leads her to the tunnel, flops over on his side, inserts his snout in the nest, and waggles his spines at his girl friend. She gets the idea and when he gets out she goes in, with her nose sticking out one end and her tail out the other. He nudges her tail with his nose, rhythmically, bump bump bump bump, and she lays the eggs, and she slips out and he slips in,

174

and he fertilizes the clutch. Then he chases her away, and she better scoot or he'll bite her tail off! After a while he turns dark-colored and he hates everybody, male and female, and he fans water onto the eggs with his fins, and when they hatch out he worries himself sick over the babies; if one of them swims away from the brood, papa goes and brings him back in his mouth—

Senator SKYPACK. That's enough of that! So as I understand it, boy, you gluttoned yourself up with a lot of sex and smut at the free public library and then picked out a perfectly decent young girl, what was her name again, Broadbent?

Mr. BROADBENT. Florence Renzulli.

Senator SKYPACK. Renzulli, and in broad daylight, in the storeroom of the principal's office—

Senator MANSFIELD. Excuse me, Jack, but we're running along to lunchtime here, and I gather, Mr. Broadbent, from what you told me before we convened this morning, that you intend to develop this whole Renzulli incident at an early opportunity, is that correct?

Mr. BROADBENT. Right after our recess. We're all set on it.

Senator MANSFIELD. So if you don't mind, Jack, could we postpone—?

Senator SKYPACK. Just as long as we don't lay down on the job and cover up for this clever little devil here.

Senator MANSFIELD. Then we'll stand recessed until two o'clock.

(Whereupon, at 12:25 p.m., Monday, October 28, 19—, the hearing was recessed.)

AFTERNOON SESSION

(The hearing was resumed in Committee Chamber 202 at 2:20 p.m.)

Senator MANSFIELD. This committee will be in order. Go ahead Mr. Broadbent.

Mr. BROADBENT. I will call Mr. Willard Owing. Please bring him in.

Senator MANSFIELD. You're sworn before us, sir. Take your place, if you please.

TESTIMONY OF MR. WILLARD OWING,
SUPERINTENDENT OF SCHOOLS, TOWN OF PEQUOT

Mr. BROADBENT. We've recalled you to testify, Mr. Owing, because you have final administrative responsibility for the Pequot school system, and we intend to go into the Rudd-Renzulli incident here this afternoon, and we want to ask you, first of all, to describe what actually took place, as you understand it, between those two children.

Mr. OWING. I so enjoyed my visit with you Senators the other day. For the academic man to get out here in the hurly-burly of legislative life—it's heady, gentlemen, heady. I always say, 'A teacher's never too old to study.'

Mr. BROADBENT. If you please, Mr. Owing, when did the

Rudd-Renzulli incident first come to your attention?

Mr. OWING. These little episodes take place, you know, year in and year out. The important thing is to keep the sights high, keep your eye on the goals, don't forget that the schools' business is to manufacture citizens. First and foremost.

Mr. BROADBENT. Please try to follow my questions, Mr. Owing. Who told you about the Rudd boy being caught in school hours and on school property with the Renzulli girl?

Mr. OWING. I was saying at our Board meeting just night before last, you can't let a single incident loom too large in the foreground. Under law our schools are open at least one hundred and eighty-three days a year, and—

Senator SKYPACK. Broadbent, I want this shilly-shallying to stop. Let me have this witness a minute or two.

Mr. BROADBENT. With pleasure, Senator. And good luck, sir.

Senator SKYPACK. All right, Owing. Now, I want direct answers to direct questions.

Mr. OWING. As I said the other day, Senator, I'm here to help. In any way. Eager.

Senator SKYPACK. Who caught these kids?

Mr. OWING. At our Board meeting—

Senator SKYPACK. Na na na! None of that, Owing! I want an answer. Who caught these kids?

Mr. OWING. According to the first report I got . . . May I proceed, Senator?

Senator SKYPACK. Long as you're answering my question.

Mr. OWING. The first report I received reminded me of a dictum I first heard from old Professor 'Ink-Spot' Channing, in my sophomore year at—

Senator SKYPACK. Owing, I must warn you to answer my questions.

Mr. OWING. But, Senator, try as I will, you cut me off. You're constantly interrupting. I'm not accustomed—

177

Senator SKYPACK. You're not surrounded by a bunch of intimidated cross-stitch and rag-rug teachers here, Owing. I'll try again. Who caught these kids?

Mr. OWING. When you say 'caught,' it seems to me your emphasis is wrong, Senator. 'Surprised,' yes. 'Came upon,' perhaps. I'd accept 'found.'

Senator SKYPACK. I don't care what word you use, who caught them?

Mr. OWING. There's a matter of principle here, Senator. It isn't just semantics. If your public schools' authorities take the stance of—

Senator SKYPACK. All *right*, Owing. Who caught them?

Mr. OWING. Professor Channing's dictum really does apply at this point, and if you'll permit me—

Senator SKYPACK. No, I certainly won't permit you.

Mr. OWING. He first delivered the dictum one day—

Senator SKYPACK. WHO CAUGHT THEM?

Senator VOYOLKO. Excuse, Senator. Yield a minute?

Senator SKYPACK. I sure will. Brother!

Senator VOYOLKO. This Renzulli—that's an Italian name. Right?

Mr. OWING. Professor Channing pulled out his watch, a magnificent gold turnip, and—

Senator MANSFIELD. It's obviously an Italian name, Peter.

Senator VOYOLKO. I thought so. That's what I thought.

Senator SKYPACK. Let's get rid of this witness before my stack blows, Mr. Chairman. This is hopeless.

Senator MANSFIELD. I'm inclined to agree with you. Have you finished your questioning, Mr. Broadbent?

Mr. BROADBENT. I can't say I've even begun it, sir. I had hoped—

Senator MANSFIELD. You may be excused, Mr. Owing. I'm afraid you haven't been wholly responsive—

Mr. Owing. A pleasure, Senator. Please feel free any time. Down in Pequot we—

Senator Mansfield. Please stand down, Mr. Owing. We're a little pressed. . . . Mr. Broadbent?

Mr. Broadbent. Miss Charity Perrin.

Senator Mansfield. Take your place again, please, Miss Perrin.

Testimony of Miss Charity M. Perrin, Schoolteacher, Town of Pequot

Mr. Broadbent. Madam, we're questioning witnesses this afternoon on the incident involving the boy child Barry Rudd and his classmate Florence Renzulli.

Miss Perrin. I don't know why you call on me on that incident, sir. I don't know anything about it.

Senator Skypack. What do you mean, you don't know anything about it? Those kids are in your home room, aren't they? They're in your grade?

Miss Perrin. They are.

Senator Skypack. You're responsible for what they do in school hours, right?

Miss Perrin. Within reasonable limits.

Senator Skypack. And you try to tell us you don't know anything about this shameful incident?

Miss Perrin. I not only try to tell you that, sir, I succeed in telling you that.

Senator Skypack. I say you're those kids' teacher, you're directly responsible for what they did.

Miss Perrin. And I say you're talking through your hat, Senator Skypack.

Senator Skypack. What gives with this witness, Broadbent? She comes in here, she's little Miss Country Mouse on two occasions, and now suddenly she's like she's got a poker up her back.

Mr. BROADBENT. Dr. Gozar told us she might rear up and buck once in a while.

Senator SKYPACK. Well, I don't like it. Look here, miss, you better co-operate with this committee if you know what's good for you.

Miss PERRIN. Do you require me to lie under oath, sir?

Senator SKYPACK. I'll tell you something, miss. I wasn't at all satisfied with the way you stammered and yeehawed that other time here when I was questioning you about the stink bombing. Not at all satisfied. Mr. Chairman, I think we should pursue that further.

Senator MANSFIELD. We're on another topic right now, Jack.

Senator SKYPACK. All right. Now, miss, I want you to tell us what happened between these two kids. What was he doing to her?

Miss PERRIN. I don't know anything about it.

Senator SKYPACK. You think you're going to sit there and defy me, you got another think coming. I'll give you one more chance. Exactly what happened, this sex incident?

Miss PERRIN. I know nothing about it—except by hearsay and gossip.

Senator SKYPACK. I remind you, miss, of the initials U.C.N.T.

Senator MANSFIELD. Oh, now, Jack. That was twenty, thirty years ago. Let's not—

Senator SKYPACK. Do you remember those initials, miss? Or would you like me to air out your memory for you?

Miss PERRIN. They have nothing to do with the subject of these hearings.

Senator SKYPACK. I put it to you as a fact, and I ask you to affirm or deny the fact, that you were a ringleader of the Union of Clerks, Nurses, and Teachers in Pequot during the widespread strike here in the State back in—

Miss PERRIN. Do I look like what you call a 'ringleader,' Senator?

Senator SKYPACK. I warn you, I have full information on your part in that business, miss—and I happen to know something about that strike. I was kept out of seventh grade for four months on account of it, right in Sudbury. I have a personal reason to feel sore about it. If you want my advice, if you don't want this examination to get uncomfortable, you'd better go along with this committee and its sundry members.

Miss PERRIN. Were you truly 'sore' about being kept out of school for four months, at the age of twelve, or thereabouts, Senator?

Senator SKYPACK. I put a fact to you a minute ago. Answer the question.

Miss PERRIN. I have no intention of answering any such question.

Senator SKYPACK. *Answer the question.*

Miss PERRIN. My past life is my own. I will not be bullied.

Senator SKYPACK. We're talking about a case of . . . of sedition, miss.

Miss PERRIN. Senator, I think that during those four months of seventh grade that you were deprived of, you must have missed the unit of social studies that would have told you that it's no crime against the government to join a union. Have you ever heard of something called the right of association?

Senator SKYPACK. You know the history of that union as well as I do, miss, who got control of it and all.

Miss PERRIN. You're speaking of much later history.

Senator SKYPACK. It's the same union. Anyway, teachers are the one kind of people that don't have any business having a union. We put our little children in their hands—

Miss PERRIN. Mr. Chairman, I must protest. This hearing is supposed to be about the child buyer.

Senator SKYPACK. By gorry, Aaron, I'm not going to have a witness sit there and—

Senator MANSFIELD. Miss Perrin, I'm very curious about one thing. Your attitude has changed very markedly since your previous appearances here—one of them just this morning. Has something developed?

Miss PERRIN. I had lunch with Mr. Jones. I had a dry martini, and . . .

Senator MANSFIELD. And?

Miss PERRIN. I now think Barry should be sold.

Senator MANSFIELD. But you were fighting this harder than anyone else.

Miss PERRIN. I've changed my mind.

Senator MANSFIELD. What changed it?

Miss PERRIN. Money.

Senator MANSFIELD. *What?*

Miss PERRIN. Eight thousand five hundred and thirty-four dollars. I've worked as a teacher for four and a half decades, and I've scrimped and squeezed all my life, and when that much cash falls in your lap at one time, something happens! I've always dreamed of being free. And now I *am* free. This morning, Senator Skypack, I was putty in those horny hands of yours, because I was terrified of losing my job. Right now you can have it. I have money to live on long enough to take a good look around; teaching isn't the only work in this world.

Senator MANSFIELD. But, Miss Perrin. What about your beliefs?

Miss PERRIN. What beliefs? How can I be positive that Barry would be better off going through the Pequot schools than he would be going off to United Lymphomilloid? Or, to put it another way, Senator, would I be the first person in American history to shade his beliefs ever so slightly on account of money? I feel so *good*, Mr. Chairman.

Senator SKYPACK. I'm shocked and bitterly disappointed in you, miss.

Miss PERRIN. *You're* shocked, Senator?

Senator SKYPACK. My idea of a teacher was the last person in the world would do a thing like that. I mean, I remember when I was in school.

Miss PERRIN. Whereas a politician—well, one expects it of a politician, doesn't one, Senator? Even when he's elected to public office. The very word 'politician'—

Senator SKYPACK. I'm thoroughly disillusioned. Imagine a teacher!

Miss PERRIN. Want to know something? I found out a few pointers about myself from Mr. Jones today. That man can look right through your forehead and see every thought that's in there, and some ghosts and shadows you don't know are there, too; it's amazing. You've been trying to discredit me through that teachers' strike, Senator Skypack. Mr. Jones made me realize that in that whole mishmash I was a leader who tagged along behind. I was a patsy. I always have been. In the everlasting committee work we have in school I've always found some reason, ever since that strike, why I couldn't take on a chairmanship, but I've felt badly cheated if I wasn't allowed to do all the hard work and then give credit to someone else who didn't deserve it. Mr. Jones asked me about my student days, and I began telling how I waited on table to earn part of my tuition at Winship's Normal School, and how much—aside from the fact that watching people snap at their forks used to take away my appetite—I enjoyed the job; I was good at it; I was always right there with extra butter—I forced food on sated people like the keeper with the ramrod who feeds the lazy big snakes at the zoo. 'You're the Little Helper, aren't you?' the child buyer said. He said he bet I cried buckets when I saw a movie about Florence Nightingale or Dr. Kildare. I do! I do! I soak my handkerchief. I can't stand to criticize other people, for fear of hurting them, yet I always agree with criticism of myself—I guess I get some kind of gloomy kick out of taking it nobly, with a *mea culpa*. I never make demands. I never show off. Mr. Jones had me ticked off in every particular—he's got those brace-and-bit eyes! Hate storms, appease bullies, run away from quarrels. I'm *not good enough*, so I have these spurts of Ovaltine or beef broth or extra orange juice. Senator, you were dying to corner me about that strike. Sure, I was in charge of the Strike Committee in Pequot, but I was no more a leader of that strike than you are a statesman, sir. I'm not trying to deny anything; I just mean that people travel under false colors a lot of the time. This was the Depression. We teachers had a hard time. Six hundred dollars a year. Have you ever been hungry, Senator Skypack? Have you ever bitten your hand till it bled, to offset the pain of a knot in your stomach that came from not eating enough? I'll *bet* you haven't. Let me tell you, I suffered—not from hunger, I could stand that—but from pity: pity, on the one hand, for some of the kids from the Intervale section, whose families were unspeakably poor, and pity, on the other hand, for some of my fellow teachers who I imagined were worse off than I. I agonized so much everyone decided I must be some kind of saint, and they put me in charge—I mean in name only. I was the ideal front: I couldn't say no. What were you trying to prove, Senator—that I was some kind of radical? I'll tell you exactly what I was: I was trying to be agreeable. I even tried to be agreeable with the School Board. I wanted everyone to be happy, except for unworthy me. . . . I was about as much a leader as Barry Rudd is. By the way, did Mr. Cleary ever tell you how Barry got on the talent-search chart for leadership?

Mr. BROADBENT. No. How did he?

Miss PERRIN. They put him on because on a test form called the Give-and-Take Sociometric Peer-Rating Instrument he came out very badly on followership. *Ergo*, he must be strong on leadership.

Mr. BROADBENT. Mrs. Rudd told us that a certain Miss Bagas, his teacher in first grade, said he had splendid followership.

Miss PERRIN. He got over it, bless him—something I never did, until lunch today. Anyway, I think now *my* turn has come.

Mr. BROADBENT. Mr. Chairman, I'd remind you we've got a heavy docket here.

Senator MANSFIELD. Yes, let's move along. Thank you, Miss Perrin. I can't help saying, though, I tend to share my colleague's surprise that a teacher would take money like that to go back on her values. I feel let down.

Miss PERRIN. And I feel just great! Keep plugging away at the whole truth, Senator Skypack. And cheer up, Senator Voyolko. Tomorrow will be a less puzzling day.

Senator VOYOLKO. Tomorrow? What we got to do tomorrow, Mr. Chairman?

Mr. BROADBENT. Dr. Frederika Gozar. Bring her in.

Senator MANSFIELD. You've been sworn, Dr. Gozar; please take the witness's chair again.

TESTIMONY OF DR. FREDERIKA GOZAR, PRINCIPAL,
LINCOLN ELEMENTARY SCHOOL, PEQUOT

Mr. BROADBENT. We're trying today, Doctor, to get some information about the Rudd-Renzulli episode. Can you help us out on that?

Dr. GOZAR. Indeed I can, sir. Better than anybody. It was I who interrupted the little lambs.

Senator SKYPACK. By gorry, we finally struck paydirt.

Mr. BROADBENT. Would you be so good as to tell us what happened?

Dr. GOZAR. Surely.

Senator SKYPACK. You mean, no argument about it?

Dr. GOZAR. Senator, you look as if you were about to sit down to a T-bone steak.

Mr. BROADBENT. Proceed, Doctor.

Dr. GOZAR. Let's see, this was last Wednesday afternoon, during the sixth period. I had just completed my inspection of the furnaces and basement areas—something I do every day at two o'clock sharp—and I returned to my office. I should tell you that the main storeroom for school supplies adjoins my office; I got everything stowed in there thirty years ago, so I could keep a weather eye on withdrawals, and I'll warrant you, the Board hasn't ever been able to say that Lincoln was a wasteful school, I've seen to that. The first few minutes after I got back from the cellar I was preoccupied with something or other at my desk, and it wasn't till near the end of the period, which incidentally is a recess for Miss Perrin's room, among others—it wasn't till five minutes or so before the bell that I happened to look over on the floor by the storeroom door and saw something black, and I went over and picked it up, and it was a patent-leather Mary Jane.

Senator SKYPACK. A what?

Dr. GOZAR. A girl's shoe, with a little strap that buttons over the instep. . . . I then noticed a crack of light around the storeroom door, which was shut, and I entered. And there they were.

Senator SKYPACK. In the act.

Dr. GOZAR. I don't know just what act you have in mind, Senator. These are ten-year-olds.

Mr. BROADBENT. What was happening?

Dr. GOZAR. Whatever had been happening was over. We have a utility cart, on big casters, for the custodian to use for moving heavy loads, which is about three and a half feet long and has two shelves. Florence Renzulli was prostrate on the upper shelf, when I first flung open the door, and at the sight of me she

186

squealed and wriggled onto her side and doubled up and began tugging at her dress.

Mr. BROADBENT. And Master Rudd?

Dr. GOZAR. Master Rudd, as you call him, was standing at the foot of the cart, bent over Mistress Renzulli.

Mr. BROADBENT. What had he been doing?

Dr. GOZAR. Just a sec. We'll have to catch a glimpse of his regalia first. Barry was all in white, except for his hands. He'd copped one of the white gowns, one of those toga-like things, that the school nurse keeps in case she has to do an examination down to the buff; he must have sneaked it out of her cabinet. He had on a square white cloth cap, like the one the carpenter wears in 'The Walrus and the Carpenter,' according to Tenniel—I think he may have made it for the purpose. And he was wearing a handkerchief across his nose and mouth, bandit style. On his hands was a pair of red rubber gloves that I guess he'd brought from home.

Senator MANSFIELD. In other words, he'd been playing doctor?

Dr. GOZAR. Exactly. I guess he'd been giving Miss Renzulli a gynecologic once-over—something she may need for keeps at a younger age than most young ladies, I fear me. She's the most willing child.

Mr. BROADBENT. We understand you raised merry Ned over this incident.

Dr. GOZAR. To tell you the truth, I would have let it pass, but just at the wrong moment Mr. Busybody Cleary, having some overblown errand for me, walked in my office and caught a glimpse of Barry removing his rubber gloves and Florence straightening her clothing and me standing on the sidelines sending in the plays. Mr. Cleary, who's frightfully psychological, began to tremble and perspire, not out of concern for the girl, you understand, but because he saw he could make character for himself out of the incident, and I knew I had to take a firm stand out of plain self-defense. I know the town of Pequot. I could hear the palates already twanging as the gossip readied itself for flight from fence to fence. So that's how a trifle got to be a famous case.

Senator SKYPACK. You call that a trifle? A girl in that position on a table, all rumpled like that! Practically speaking, bare!

Dr. GOZAR. It was a trifle. Take my word for it. Either it was really scientific curiosity on Barry's part, or else—well, there was something odd about it: the location of this bit of research, right alongside my office, and the shoe lying there *inside* my office, as if it had been installed, like a small monument of some kind, right where there would be the most splendid public display. I don't know, something funny. In any case—a trifle. Except for the thrill our Guidance Director got out of the thing, which removed it from the trifling category.

Senator SKYPACK. I call this attitude shocking. Shocking.

Dr. GOZAR. Senator, your shock threshold is low down—like some other things about you. And while I'm at it, I think I'll give you another shock, sir, and I hope a taste of liberal education at the same time. Are you braced, Senator Skypack?

Senator SKYPACK. What now?

Dr. GOZAR. That stink bomb I've been reading about in the papers.

Senator SKYPACK. What about it?

Dr. GOZAR. I made it. And I threw it.

Senator SKYPACK. My God! And she calls herself an educator!

Dr. GOZAR. At least, I arranged to have it propelled.

Senator SYKPACK. If I was the town of Pequot, I'd fire you so fast.

Dr. GOZAR. Bzzt!

Senator SKYPACK. What was that? Why are you pointing at me? What did that sound mean?

Dr. GOZAR. That was a death ray going off the end of my

index finger in your direction, Senator. Bzzt! Bzzt!

Senator SKYPACK. I swan! I never seen a woman like this one!

Dr. GOZAR. Then why don't you subside and let a person talk?
You interrupt too much. And too foolishly.

Senator MANSFIELD. I must say, Doctor, I share my colleague's
astonishment. Why would a school principal do a thing like
that?

Dr. GOZAR. Do you really want to know why I did it?

Senator MANSFIELD. I certainly do.

Senator SYKPACK. *I* sure do.

Senator VOYOLKO. What she do? What the lady do?

Dr. GOZAR. If you'll be patient I'll tell you exactly what I did
and why. In full. Do you want to hear it?

Mr. BROADBENT. Yes, indeed. Proceed.

Dr. GOZAR. Then don't interrupt, please. Senator Skypack, you
see this lethal index finger? . . . Very well. . . . On Mr.
Cleary's solicitation I showed up at the lecture by the State
Supervisor for Exceptional Children. I knew Miss Henley's line
of blabber inside out, because I'd been listening to it for years
without thinking that it really affected me or the children in my
school. But this time I suddenly realized that all her gobblede-
gook had a direct connection with my Barry, and it began to
agitate me; I began to cross and uncross my legs and to fidget
in my seat. Her words acted on me as prickly heat or griping
bowels might. I was near the back of the auditorium and on the
side aisle—I always like to sit on the aisle in case I have to go
turn up the thermostats or call the riot squad or whatever—and
I noticed that one of the large windows along the west wall, just
to the audience's side of the stage, was open, because that day,
last Tuesday, was Indian-summery, warm, hazy, and muggy, and
with all those ardent humid teachers in there, it was close—so,
as I say, that window was wide open. And Miss Henley's effluvia
were suddenly too much for me, with a result that I had an idea

associated with that open window. And I got up and left.

Mr. BROADBENT. What time was this, please?

Dr. GOZAR. Miss Henley had been talking only about five minutes, because I know I worked up my charge awfully fast; I suppose it was four fifteen.

Mr. BROADBENT. Our investigator has established that the stink bomb was exploded at four thirty-eight. So what did you do in those twenty-three minutes?

Dr. GOZAR. Hold on awhile. You asked my motive. Before I tell you exactly what I did I want to tell you why I did it. Maybe even you will understand, Senator Skypack. . . . It had begun with a choking sensation, a feeling that I was being asphyxiated by Henley's outpourings, which were based on the notion that education is a science, that the process of learning is like a process of catalysis or combustion or absorption—observable, definable, measurable, manipulable; and that Barry— volatile, mysterious, smoldering Barry—is inert experimental material. But the idea of education as a science appalls me, really actively sickens me. There are some aspects of human social organization that simply cannot be defined and analyzed yet with the kind of precision that is the *sine qua non* of science. So I reacted to Henley with violent sensations. I felt as if I were drowning. And as if drowning I saw pass before my eyes certain images of my experience, which battered at my mind's vision seemingly to *prove* to me that education is non-science. Will you be patient and hear me out? Because I think this will help to explain my stink bomb, and lots more besides, lots about Barry's predicament, perhaps.

Mr. BROADBENT. Go ahead.

Dr. GOZAR. A long, long time ago some schoolteachers in the hills up in the northern part of the state held up in front of me that there was something better than sprinkling a stove with perspiration in a mill-town tenement block, that if you worked hard you could *accomplish*. Also they sold me, and my sister, too, on the idea that there is such a thing as vertical social mobility through education, and so my sister and I decided we'd have some of that. My sister's a year and a half older than I am, a full professor of biochemistry at Penniman Institute. She calls herself the uneducated half of the Gozars; she only has four graduate degrees, and I have six. Meg was one of New England's more famous women athletes in the early days, when women athletes were hampered by copious bloomers; nothing was supposed to show but the lowest part of the shinbone, even if you were competing in the hop, skip, and jump. Some people still take me for Meg, and I'm always flattered. Well. My mother was an ignorant immigrant woman who always put it up to her two daughters that if you tried hard enough you could do just about anything. I believed it then, and I still believe in it, and I talk it up energetically eight days a week. My first job was at age six: leading a horse to pull earth up out of a well that was being dug by hand. I had a paper route. I've always been obliged to do some things that are commonly reserved to the male sex. I graduated from eighth grade in a little one-room school in the foothills of the Berkshires. Father was a cow-and-vegetable farmer, a patient man who thought that if he just kept at it long enough, he'd be able to remove every single stone from a New England field; he was from Lithuania, he didn't know the stones were half a mile deep with just a pinch of clayey dirt sprinkled in for good measure. His persistence with his ever-willing team of oxen and his stone boat and his chain—the picture of him comes to my mind whenever I think *I'm* tired. Well, Father's farm went broke, and we missed a few meals here and there, but I've caught up on those in recent years, as you can see, and my sister Meg is even vaster than I am. Our school only went through eighth grade, and the nearest high school was thirty miles distant, so Meg and I struck a bargain with the teacher to start us off on something like a high-school education. She did. She was a fine inspiring lady named Danna French—one woman with eight grades and sixty people in her schoolroom, willing to take aboard two urchins who just wanted more. I've seen so much of that in schools in my time. She gave us a course in algebra and one in history, and in turn we helped her to do some of the cruder teaching. We also did coolie work—cleaned the place; and if you think I have powerful arms, they came originally from chopping firewood at Danna French's school. Meg and I were there that one year, then we made arrangements where we went to Galilee High School, thirty miles from home. We had to pay six dollars a month tuition, because they didn't have a district system to take care of us, and our room cost three dollars a month, and our food ran us six dollars a month. We didn't live too elegant on the tooth, but we weren't awful hungry. We worked various places; I remember I was some kind of sorter in a watch factory, and I assembled the two blades of shears. I must have put three hundred thousand pairs of scissors together with little screws. That was *tedious*—but when you took fifteen dollars a month out of your pay for fixed charges at one clump, you just had to get married to tedium, you were stuck with it. In the spring I helped with planting, in the fall I helped with the harvest. There was no stigma attached to hard work in those days. Danna French had held up the idea that if there was something better in the world, by gosh, you could go and get it. There were convenient places where my sister and I got work; there was a dairy not far from the school where we washed bottles. We had to start at four in the morning, but we got done before school. Out of twenty units of credit, I got nine A's and eleven B's. My sister reversed that. She was a better student than I. I tried to be as good a student as I could, and a good athlete, too. I wanted to look good to Meg. I still do. We had some great teachers who steered us both. Mrs. Ethel Le Grand. G. W. Sudland. Glenn B.

First. They were always holding up in front of you the possibilities of people to amount to something. When I got to college, at Silverbury, as I think I told you the other day, I decided on biology, and I took the two degrees, and then I settled out to teach, and so did Meg. And besides teaching I took on some of those jobs I was telling you about. One of them was in an iron foundry. It was an open shop, and I mean open—they put you doing whatever you could do, no matter what they were paying you. I was classified as a laborer, but at times I was doing molding, layout work, machine shop. One autumn I worked as an apple picker and saw them feed the people—they were itinerants, winos and bums, goodhearted broken folks—I saw the orchards feed these people on metal plates nailed to the tables, the knives and forks on chains; they washed up with fire hoses. All those years, whatever job I was on, I'd go to school on the side. Or maybe the job was on the side. I worked up an M.A. in biology in 19— at Springfield. Then I got a Ph.D. six years later at Colton College. I told you about all those semesters at Silverbury. Then after the second war I picked up an M.A. in history at Manchester College. After that I figured I was in the education business and it would be a good gesture to get me an M.A. in elementary education, which I did at Perkins State Teachers. And so it went. I've had two hundred and eighty semester hours since my Ph.D.—seven full years the way the credits usually go. This doesn't affect my salary; don't think *that's* why I did it. I'm planning now to get a master's in either physics or math so I can keep up with the Space Age, you know? Right now I'm taking a correspondence course in meteorology with Silverbury. In my leisure time I write Westerns for rags like *Highwayman* and *Big West*, though I've never been west of Albany; it's all from reading. Course I do it under a pseudonym, I don't want a scandal. Then I'm an amateur photographer. I point and shoot. I'm a *very* amateur musician, play the clarinet for the Valley Power and Light Company Marching Band. I've had four offers to be a permanent college professor—but no. I'm *me*. In spare times I go to track meets. I've made every state track meet in the last twenty-four years—even helped coaching a bit. It's on account of Meg, that's obvious. I take pictures, about thirty at each meet, of the finishes, on a four-by-five Speed Graphic, then I have the prints made and I send a copy to every athlete who shows, to the winner a copy and the negative—because somebody did that for Meg back in 19—, bloomers and all. It was a man named J. F. Van Palent, a Dutch preacher, with an old Graflex, and he sent Meg a copy of her breaking the tape in the hundred-yard dash. For the past couple of decades I've been sending copies like that—'this is of you and this is on the house.' Sometimes they write, and sometimes they don't. Oh, I could have retired four years ago. I wasn't interested. I can retire at seventy, but I won't unless they give me the heave-ho, because if I keep feeling as good as I do now, I don't think I'll ever want to stop learning and trying to hand on some of it. . . . Now do you see, gentlemen, why that stuff of Henley's about need reduction and reinforcement of rewards and restructuring the Gestalt field drove me to action? Do you begin to understand? How about you, Senator Skypack?

Senator SKYPACK. All right. All right.

Dr. GOZAR. All *right*. So now we get back to what I did in those twenty-three minutes between my leaving the lecture and the bomb going off. I flew like a hummingbird to Wairy High School, about a block and a half away from Lincoln, and I was feeling pretty ferocious; my old ticker was pounding a lot faster than my feet. I said hummingbird, though it's not an image that goes with my physique, to express speed, because I figured Miss Henley would talk about forty minutes, so I'd have to hurry. Speaking of pulse rates, did you know, by the way, that a hummingbird's heart beats six hundred and fifteen times per minute?

More than ten times a second? Barry found that out and told me it; we've had *fascinating* talks about the metabolism of birds. Anyway, I thought out my whole plan on the way to Wairy, and I charged up to the lab, and I found Barry and Flattop there— Barry was puttering around on some experiment, as he often does in after-school hours. I went right to work, and I never did anything with such dazzling speed. The two boys wanted to help me in whatever I was doing, but I wouldn't let them, because the law can take rather strict views of complicity, and Barry would just have slowed me down with his deliberate questions, anyway. I mixed ferrous sulphide and hydrochloric acid and a coloring agent in a globular vial in a matter of seconds. Then I took a large snap-type rat trap, and I—

Senator Mansfield. Why a rat trap?

Dr. Gozar. Back during the second war I had to fill in for a couple of months for a sick high-school physics teacher, and I did a lecture on ancient engines of war, such as the testudo, the battering ram, Greek fire, and so on. I developed a slinging mechanism on the snapping arch of a rat trap to show the centrifugal hurling principle of the trebuchet, and the spring action of the ballista and catapult. Furthermore, to exercise the brighter youngsters' math, I conducted a series of experiments to calculate the trajectories of objects of various weights as thrown by my rat-trap engine, and I had used these same globular vials containing varying amounts of water as my projectiles. I was therefore able to weigh my stink-bomb vial and estimate fairly closely how high and how far it would carry. It took me only about half a minute to rig a timing mechanism—a kitchen timer I keep in the lab for experiments, to whose pointer I attached part of a wooden pencil, so I could simply set the timer alongside the trap and in due course the pencil would swing down on the bait-trigger of the trap.

Senator Skypack. This woman's a Frankenstein!

Dr. Gozar. My maternal instincts, which haven't had much exercise in my lifetime, were turning out to be pretty formidable. It's the closest I've ever come, I guess, to imitating a mother tigress protecting her cub. I ran back to Lincoln, to the playground alongside the auditorium. I had to guess the interior distance from the window to the lectern, and, as it happens, I underestimated the distance by about eight to ten feet. I paced off the required distance outdoors, set my *engin volant* and timer, and shot back to my seat in the hall, and when I sat down I said in a loud whisper to my neighbor, 'What's she saying? Did I miss anything?' Pretending to be fascinated. 'I had to make a phone call,' I whispered. Cover-up.

Senator Mansfield. What did you set the timer at?

Dr. Gozar. My entire errand had taken not more than thirteen or fourteen minutes. It was a gamble just how long Henley would shoot off her mouth, but, not wanting the bomb to go off too soon after my return to the auditorium, I had set it for eight minutes. Eight minutes! They were like eight months. One nice ironic note. At about the seven-minute point, as I estimated, Henley took a crack at *me*—my harming Barry by singling him out for special help in the lab. 'Just you wait a minute, Henley,' I said to myself, 'you'll have my answer to that stinking statement.' And after one minute—beautiful! I saw the little sphere glisten as it arched through the window. It didn't quite make the stage, but fell on the floor in front. A delightfully pretty yellow-green smoke curled up over the heads of the audience in the front rows. It began to spread. People jumped up. I said in a loud innocent voice to my neighbor, 'What's happened? Did you see what happened? What's going on?' Then I saw Owing and Cleary running around with their arms over their heads and Millicent Parmelee Henley, B.S., M.A., heading for the wings with her hands to her face.

Senator Skypack. Are you completely finished, miss?

Dr. Gozar. I'll never admit I'm completely finished, Senator.

Senator Skypack. All I can say is, this has been one of the most disgusting, shameful, degrading exhibitions it has ever been my privilege as a State Senator to have to sit through and witness. I mean, here's an educationist, sitting here without once saying she's sorry, and she—

Senator Mansfield. I found it instructive, Jack. Didn't you, Peter?

Senator Voyolko. Who, me? What I want to know—what she want with that rat trap? I didn't dig that part. She trying to catch a rat or something?

Senator Mansfield. Never mind, Peter. In any case, Mr. Broadbent, we'd better keep things rolling. And thank you, Dr. Gozar. Most instructive.

Senator Skypack. Most disgusting! I mean, a person, we entrust our young people to a person . . .

Mr. Broadbent. I'll call Mr. Sean Cleary. Mr. Cleary.

Senator Mansfield. You're sworn, Mr. Cleary. Take your seat. Good. Now, Mr. Broadbent.

Testimony of Mr. Sean Cleary,
Director of Guidance, Town of Pequot

Mr. Broadbent. This afternoon, sir, we're discussing the Rudd-Renzulli incident. We understand you came in on the tag end of it.

Mr. Cleary. Yes, I did.

Mr. Broadbent. Would you give us your estimate—

Senator Skypack. We're beyond 'estimates' now, Broadbent. We need some rock-bottom facts here. Wouldn't you say, Cleary, that this was one of the smuttiest, cheapest incidents in the history of education in this State? The younger generation, the deadbeats we're breeding in this State.

197

Mr. CLEARY. Frankly, it was the adult, Dr. Gozar, who surprised me most when I first came on the scene. It was almost as if she was working toward some vicarious reward or climax.

Senator SKYPACK. We're not interested in her, we're interested in that criminal little boy. I want to know what you *did* about this crying shame.

Mr. CLEARY. First of all, Senator, I always try, when we have an incident involving a disturbed child, to get things out, get them talked about—not try to smother and hide them, because if you sweep oily rags off in a corner and cover them over you're just going to have spontaneous combustion and maybe a wicked fire. I therefore promptly called Mr. Owing, Mr. Wairy, Mrs. Sloat, Miss Henley, and Mr. Jones, and gave each of them a complete rundown on the facts.

Senator MANSFIELD. Sounds more like stirring up a hornets' nest than ventilating rags.

Senator SKYPACK. You wouldn't expect him to shush a scandal like that up, would you, Aaron?

Senator MANSFIELD. From what we've seen here, I'm not sure that calling Bill Sloat is exactly the way to clear the air of inflammable fumes. I suppose this led to that P.-T. A. meeting.

Senator SKYPACK. What else did you do, Cleary?

Mr. CLEARY. I summoned the boy and gave him a Standardized Testing Institute Mirror-Image Personality Inventory.

Senator SKYPACK. You wanted to see whether he was dangerous?

Mr. CLEARY. This test is a remarkable instrument. I would estimate that it gives the equivalent of a three-year psychoanalysis in about twenty minutes. It makes use of carefully framed psyche-symbol questions, all answerable by yes or no, such as, 'Are you sometimes cranky before ten in the morning?' and, 'When a person catches a nose cold, is it his fault?' The choices are significant, the results strikingly revealing.

198

Senator Skypack. And what did you find out about this cheap incident?

Mr. Cleary. It appeared to be a manifestation of transmuted Puritan libido-thrusts. The rubber gloves . . .

Senator Skypack. Let's not get high-flown, Cleary. Just a common garden-variety question. Was it good or bad?

Mr. Cleary. It was good (from my point of view) in that the boy's bad behavior tends to give Jones a good chance to bring a bad (from the boy's point of view) outcome of this United Lymphomilloid proposition. On the other hand, it was bad (for the child buyer) because the episode was really a good (in the boy, psychiatrically speaking) sign that he could do something bad to such good effect.

Senator Mansfield. Mr. Cleary, that goes quite some ways beyond double talk. That's quadruple talk.

Senator Skypack. What I would like to know is, how are you going to *punish* him?

Mr. Cleary. United Lymphomilloid—

Senator Mansfield. Don't I remember your telling us, Mr. Cleary, the first time you appeared before this committee, that there hadn't been time as yet for you to undertake psychological training? Do you think you're fully qualified—

Senator Skypack. That's a dirty, unfair question, Aaron. I seem to remember *you* said we weren't to manhandle our witnesses here.

Mr. Cleary. No, Senator, I'd like to answer the Chairman's question. I think it stems from ignorance rather than malice. The psychological tests we use in the schools today, Mr. Chairman, are so foolproof, the norms are so stable, the scoring is so automatic, the interpretation is so ineluctible, that you need have no concern over one man's array of graduate degrees. In short, sir, we *know* about these children. Please calm your nerves about my training.

Senator MANSFIELD. Another thing I seem to remember from your first appearance, Mr. Cleary, was your denial that the child buyer had done anything to influence you to help him. But we have heard testimony today that he is in fact finding you a new job.

Mr. CLEARY. There's nothing to deny in that! He's lining me up a job down in Fairfield County. Assistant Super. Big jump salary-wise, but of course I don't care about that part of it. It's just that a tadpole feels great when he sheds his tail and gets out of the slimy little pond he's been trapped in—know what I mean?

Senator MANSFIELD. You don't feel that there's anything irregular about this offer of his?

Mr. CLEARY. The significance of this kindness on his part, it seems to me, is in the way it shows his extraordinary perspicacity —his almost frightening powers of devination, clairvoyance. He must have some extrasensory ability, otherwise how could he have known that I had my restless shoes on?

Senator VOYOLKO. Mr. Leery.

Mr. CLEARY. Cleary.

Senator VOYOLKO. Mr. Whatever-It-Is. Where you go to school?

Mr. CLEARY. Perkins State Teachers.

Senator VOYOLKO. You play basketball?

Mr. CLEARY. As a matter of fact, I did.

Senator VOYOLKO. I thought so. See? I thought he did. Good and tall.

Mr. BROADBENT. If you gentlemen are finished with your questions—

Senator MANSFIELD. Jack?

Senator SKYPACK. I'm finished. I mean, you've got to crack down on these deadbeat kids, there's no other way in the world.

Senator MANSFIELD. All right, Mr. Cleary; thank you. O.K., Mr. Broadbent.

Mr. BROADBENT. Mr. Chairman, a few minutes ago Senator Skypack passed me a note that he wants to question the child buyer again.

Senator MANSFIELD. Do you still have him here?

Mr. BROADBENT. I think so. Yes, the committee usher indicates he's still out there.

Senator MANSFIELD. I would certainly want to honor the wishes of my eminent colleague from Sudbury County. Have Mr. Jones brought in. Thank you, Mr. Jones, for bearing with us again. Help yourself to the witness chair.

TESTIMONY OF MR. WISSEY JONES,
OF UNITED LYMPHOMILLOID CORPORATION

Senator SKYPACK. There's really only one question I want to ask Mr. Jones, and that is: Do you still want this boy, I mean after this business of stripping and pawing that little girl, the mortician's daughter, and all? Do you still want to buy him?

Mr. JONES. More than ever, sir.

Senator SKYPACK. That surprises me. That definitely surprises me. How could you want a cheap actor like that?

Mr. JONES. This proves he's alive. He's juicy. He's not one of your cobweb-and-lint intellectuals. Oh, this was encouraging, Senator!

Senator SKYPACK. Well, it beats me. That's all I wanted to ask, Mr. Chairman. But you got me with my mouth open, Mr. Jones, if the national defense requires a sneaky actor like that. I mean I'm not surprised about those moon shots fizzling out, the lag in rocketry.

Mr. JONES. You'll just have to take my word for it, Senator. The boy's value is enhanced.

Senator SKYPACK. Oh, I'll go along with you, sir. If that's the way you say things are. I'm going to stand by my promise to do everything I can to help you get him. Fact is, I'll be happier than ever to have him shipped out of this State.

Mr. JONES. I'm grateful for your expressions of support, Senator. I think I should tell you that they have just become rather urgently important to me. It would help me if these hearings could be brought to some fruitful conclusion as soon as possible. I had a telegram delivered to me a few minutes ago outside this chamber, and I believe it's pertinent to these hearings; I'll take the liberty of turning the wire over to your committee. Mr. Counsel, may I—?

Mr. BROADBENT. Thank you, sir. Shall I read it out, Mr. Chairman?

Senator MANSFIELD. I wish you would.

Mr. BROADBENT. It's signed HACK SAWYER. You might tell us, Mr. Jones—

Mr. JONES. Of course. Excuse me. Hack's the prex of U. Lympho.

Mr. BROADBENT. The wire seems to be a kind of purchase order, at least the first part of it. It reads here: DESIRE SOONEST DELIVERY TWENTY ADDITIONAL SPECIMENS STOP SHIP BY AIR STOP WE AUTHORIZE YOU TWO HUNDRED PER CENT INCREASE PURCHASE FUND STOP URGENT URGENT STOP REASON FOR HASTE SECURITY BROKEN RESULT THAT AMERICAN PANTOCYANDUM AND CILIO MILLS HAVE BEGUN PROGRAMS OF SPECIMEN PURCHASE AND EXPERIMENTATION EXACTLY LIKE OURS STOP ENTIRE STORY SPILLED TO MOMENTOUS THE WEEKLY NEWSMAG BY CILIO APPEARING NEXT WEEKS ISSUE WITH STORY EMPHATICALLY FAVORABLE TO U LYMPHOS INITIATIVE BUT ANTICIPATE OTHER COMPETITORS WILL INSTITUTE LIKE PROGRAMS AND CONSEQUENT PROMPT DRASTIC DRYING UP OF SUPPLY OF FIRST RATE SPECIMENS STOP CANNOT OVERSTATE PRESSURE BESTEST HACK SAWYER

Mr. JONES. So you see, Mr. Chairman. Senator Skypack. Senator Voyolko.

Senator VOYOLKO. Huh? Me? . . . Specimens, specimens. What they talking about specimens?

Senator MANSFIELD. It means children, Peter.

Senator VOYOLKO. Children! Why don't they say so? Nobody ever says what they mean any more these days.

Mr. BROADBENT. Could this wire be admitted into the record, Mr. Chairman?

Senator MANSFIELD. It will be part of the record. I so rule.

(The document referred to was marked 'Jones Exhibit No. 2,' and filed.)

Mr. JONES. You'll appreciate, gentlemen, these hearings have already detained me three days.

Senator MANSFIELD. What time is it? . . . It's already late in the day today, Mr. Jones, but I'd hope that with any kind of luck we can finish up here in one more day. Tomorrow. Two at the most.

Mr. JONES. Anything you could do to expedite—

Senator SKYPACK. Look, Jones, you say this whole scheme's coming out in the press. It states there in the telegram that the security is broken on the matter. I therefore want to renew my request to you to admit the off-the-record material you gave us the other day. This record doesn't mean much without that background.

Mr. JONES. Since this article in *Momentous* has apparently been drafted in a way so favorable to U. Lympho, I hesitate to chance spoiling it; I'm loath to jump the gun without checking.

Senator MANSFIELD. I might point out, Mr. Jones, on Senator Skypack's behalf, that our record won't be published by the State Printing Office for at least two weeks. There's no reason why the off-the-record material couldn't be held in confidence in our files until well after the dateline of the *Momentous* article and then be released to the State Printer.

Mr. JONES. I'd have no objection to that.

Senator MANSFIELD. I then order that the off-the-record matter presented by Mr. Jones to this committee in Room 417A of this building on last Thursday morning, October 24, be admitted to the record, on the basis just agreed.

Mr. BROADBENT. In extension of this ruling, Mr. Chairman, don't you think you'd better add that the matter in question was not recorded by the committee stenographer but is in the form of a memorandum by the committee counsel which has been reviewed by all members of the committee and by the witness?

Senator MANSFIELD. Right. So ordered.

(The document referred to was admitted to the record, as 'Committee Memorandum No. 1,' and is printed herewith.)

COMMITTEE MEMORANDUM NO.

Chairman MANSFIELD asked the witness to proceed in his own way. Mr. WISSEY JONES then deposed that the methods used by United Lymphomilloid to eliminate all conflict from the inner lives of the purchased specimens and to ensure their utilization of their innate equipment at maximum efficiency are and will be the following:

First, Period of Mental and Reflexive Reconditioning, Orientation, and Preparation. During this period, the length of which varies from one to six weeks, depending on the adaptability of the subject, each specimen is placed naked in a bare and confined chamber, six feet cubed, without exterior lighting, dimly lit within, so that the consciousness can take in nothing but the totality of barrenness of the setting. There is nothing. There is silence. There is nothing to do, except during one period of activity each day, when a single meal appears through a trap door and when feces can be removed if the subject desires and takes the step. The discomfort and rather extreme apprehension experienced by the specimen during the first part of this period, together with applications of the drug 'L.T.,' introduced through food, produce a complete elimination, or purge, of memory; all experience, education, knowledge are permanently cleared away, with no impairment whatsoever of the mind's acquisitive faculties and capacity for future new memory. As the mind goes blank, all thinking ceases, and the subject experiences a progressive feeling of warmth and relaxation. About three quarters of the way through this period, orientation is begun in the form of constant whispering which is piped into the chamber, barely perceptible at first, gradually increasing in volume and clarity, but never rising above an aspirated murmur, the content of which is entirely devoted to United Lymphomilloid—to the motherly, protective, nourishing qualities of the corporate image, and later to Her creativity, fecundity, and later still to Her great Mystery—the Miracle of the Fifty-Year Project. This whispering continues for several days and produces in the specimen a growing desire, which in due course becomes almost ecstatic, to be exposed to the image and to feel (the subject has forgotten he can think and therefore do anything besides feel) Her benignity and sovereignty, which the specimen apparently pictures as a kind of primitive comfort, a sort of swaddling. Upon its completion, this phase of preparation is followed by

Second, Education and Desensitization in Isolation. The specimen is removed from the Forgetting Chamber and is placed in a small but comfortable room, containing a hard bed, a table, a washbasin, and a toilet. (Toilet training is necessary, since the subject has forgotten, of course, how to avail himself of plumbing.) There are no windows in the room—in fact, the specimen will never again look out at the complexity of nature, which would only confuse him. Education now begins. A most important aspect of the United Lymphomilloid method is that the specimen shall have no contaminating (in a mental sense) contact with other human beings. All teaching must therefore be done mechanically—by the technique of whispering to which the specimen is already conditioned, by films and symbols projected against walls of the room, by recorded material infiltrated into the subject's hard pillow during sleeping hours, and by other devices so far too secret to discuss—Mr. JONES simply said that one of them involves, for example, hypnotic high-frequency vibrations. Reading is taught entirely by sound film. Gradually, as the student progresses (because of the emptiness of the mind at first and the possibility of excluding all irrelevancies, great and small, the progress is astonishingly rapid, so that in mathematics, for instance, which begins with adding one and one, the calculus is reached in five weeks of teaching, and logarithm tables are quite unnecessary), his life is made more comfortable. Television, radio, and books are introduced into his room, but the specimen is never exposed to anything that does not relate to the Miracle of the Fifty-Year Project. *The television programs he sees have all been specially taped for him and him alone, the radio programs specially recorded, the books specially written and printed and bound.* Everything the specimen learns has been built around the fecund female corporate image of U. Lympho. She is Truth. She is the Source and Secret of Life. She is the One and Only Television Sponsor. She becomes the motivating force for all activity—indeed, She, U. Lympho, becomes the Divinity. By slow and subtle training, in which rhythms of repetition play a great part, the specimen's relationship to Her becomes ritualistic. He begins to worship Her by solving problems—simple ones, to begin with, then increasingly trying ones. His whole life becomes an attempt to please Her by spurts of creative mental activity, which are seen as worshipful acts. This religion is, however, entirely intellective. Emotion of all kinds is eliminated as far as possible from the specimen's life, partly by keeping from his emptied mind all images and ideas that might stimulate feeling, and partly by a drug, enthohexylcenteron, related to the tranquilizers used in psychiatric therapy but specially developed by United Lymphomilloid researches to deaden all affective responses without, however, removing the elements of pain and joy in the specimen's new motivation—specifically, the particularly intense motivation to genuflect before Her, as it were, by problem-solving. This schooling period lasts about four months and is followed by

Third, Data-feeding Period. The specimen is now almost prepared to work for Her on the Mystery of the Fifty-Year Project —or at least on one isolated corner of the project. Into his mind is fed an enormous amount of data that will be needed in finding episodic solutions to certain problems in connection with the Mystery. Mr. Jones pointed out to the committee that it is common knowledge that electronic calculating machines have proved fallible because they are fed data by human beings. United Lymphomilloid reverses the process. The subject's human mind, capable of illimitable subtlety, is fed data by absolutely reliable and matter-of-fact calculating machines. (The machines are fed, in turn, by previously conditioned specimens.) The specimen's mind is now working so fast, and his motivation is so powerful, that this stage takes only about three weeks and is followed by

Fourth, Major Surgery. The subject is now perfectly prepared to do Her work. There are, however, two dangers. One is that through some inadvertence, unforeseen by the minds of technicians who have not been conditioned as the specimen has, scraps of information that are not wholly related to the subject's particular area of worship-solving may creep into his mind. The second is that he may develop emotions; it has been found that, despite the prophylaxis and enthohexylcenteron, extremely dangerous emotions may arise, apparently stemming from tiny doubts about Her, the source of which Project researchers have not yet been able to pin down. The specimen therefore undergoes major surgery, which consists of 'tying off' all five senses. Since the subject need not take in any more data, he has no further need of sight or hearing. Smell and taste have long since been useless to him, since he regards the intake of food as a mechanical process that he carries on only for Her sake. Only so much sense of touch is left the specimen as to allow him to carry on his bodily functions and 'write' on a Simplomat Recorder, a stenographic machine the use of which has long since become a ceremonial rite for the subject. Most specimens are also sterilized, though a certain few will be left their reproductive equipment in order to breed further specimens for the Project. It is thought that some of these breeders, after they have solved most of the problems arising from their data, will be retired to stud—the servicings for which will of course all be mechanical. The surgical period lasts about two months, whereupon ensues

Fifth, Productive Work. The specimen worships U. Lympho by offering up to Her solutions of incredibly difficult problems relating to the Mystery.

Mr. JONES then asked if there were any questions.

Senator MANSFIELD asked if all this wasn't a little drastic, and Mr. JONES replied that by the same token the results represented a major break-through in the development of the human intellect—as great and startling a break-through in its field as the one represented in another field by the first setting off of an atomic chain reaction in the lattice pile in the cellar of the squash courts at the University of Chicago in 1942. He would cite one fact to show the extent of the implications of the United Lymphomilloid method. This method has produced mental prodigies such as man has never imagined possible. Using tests developed by company researchers, the firm has measured I.Q.'s of three fully trained specimens at 974, 989, and 1005, whereas 100 is the median in the general population, and 200, estimated by the psychologist Terman to have been approached by only a handful of world geniuses such as Goethe, Pascal, and John Stuart Mill, had previously been considered the absolute tops. The company intends, incidentally, Mr. JONES said, to use as breeders only subjects who test for I.Q.'s at over the one-thousand figure.

Senator SKYPACK asked if this system wasn't prohibitively expensive, considering those special closed-circuit television programs, special books, and so on, and Mr. JONES replied that it was indeed costly, but that the firm had set its training facility up as an institution of higher learning, known as Hack Sawyer University, which is naturally tax-deductible, so that everything the company puts into it can be written off. Mr. JONES remarked that this feature might in due course have important beneficial ramifications for both private education and private enterprise in this country; they might, in effect, merge.

Mr. BROADBENT asked what the drug referred to by Mr. JONES as 'L.T.' was, and Mr. JONES said it was an herbal drug, of ancient origin, known as *Lethe terrae*, loosely, 'forgetfulness of this world.' Lethe on earth. He reminded the committee that in classical mythology Lethe was a river in Hades, the drinking of whose waters would produce amnesia, and he said this herbal drug was used in certain pre-Columbian sacrificial rituals in Peruvian mountain cultures—indicating, the witness remarked in passing, that some of the newest things in the world come straight from some of the oldest.

Senator VOYOLKO asked if Hades and Hell weren't one and the same, and Mr. JONES let the question pass.

Senator MANSFIELD asked how, if the specimens were permanently isolated and were given only small portions of the Mystery of the Fifty-Year Project to solve, the major parts of the necessary solutions would be brought together in the end, and Mr. Jones said he didn't want to talk too much about this, but, on account of the extraordinary development of the specimens' intellects, co-ordination was definitely being achieved by a process of telepathy between them—that when cognate solutions are reached by two specimens, *each becomes aware of the other's answers.* Senator Skypack asked whether this took place right through walls and everything, and Mr. Jones said it did, concrete walls.

Senator Skypack asked what the Mystery of the Fifty-Year Project actually is, and Mr. Jones said that that was a foolish question. He didn't even know himself. He believed it had to do with satisfying man's greatest need—to leave the earth.

If that was in fact the end and aim of the Project, Senator Mansfield then asked, how did Mr. Jones justify the claim that his purchase of Barry Rudd was for purposes of 'defense'? Mr. Jones said he justified the claim on the ground that the Project is being carried on by United Lymphomilloid under government contract. Besides, he added, in the present state of affairs the best defense might be departure.

The committee members thanked and heartily congratulated Mr. Jones, and the off-the-record session was brought to a close.

Senator Mansfield. Jack, he's your witness. Anything more?

Senator Skypack. Only this, and I ask it again: You're *sure,* are you, that you want this boy, after what he's done?

Mr. Jones. More than ever. Even before this happened, I regarded him as potentially one of the finest specimens I've yet found. Mr. Cleary told me the other day that the boy had been given an individual I.Q. test when he was in school in Treehampstead, and I took the trouble to ride over to Treehampstead on my motorbike, and I looked up the record.

Senator Mansfield. Did he do well?

Mr. JONES. Did he! He was five years and four months old at the time. The test was the Stanford-Binet. The examiner assigned him a basal age of six, and the boy made a perfect score at that level. He breezed through everything that the test demanded of a seven-year-old except to tie shoe knots. He got all of the eight-year-old items right, except that he did poorly, again, on co-ordination—did sloppily on finding an escape from a maze, because that meant holding a pencil. He got most of the nine- and ten-year-old questions right—at the ten-year level he was an eagle for errors of logic. On the twelve-year test he was still answering questions correctly, such as, 'In what way are the following things similar: *crow, cow, lizard?*' Only when he reached the fourteen-year-old test did the five-year-old boy fail everything. He was an assigned an I.Q. of one hundred eighty-nine. According to the Terman studies, this was approximately the I.Q. enjoyed by Bentham, Leibnitz, Macaulay, and Grotius, and is higher than those of Voltaire, Darwin, Descartes, Newton, and Lope de Vega.

Senator MANSFIELD. Was the family ever told of this? Does the boy know it?

Mr. JONES. Never. Of course not. An I.Q. figure like that is considered far too dangerous. In fact, the boy's teachers in Treehampstead were never told exactly what it was—only that it was 'quite unusual'—and no whisper of the figure ever leaked the nine miles to Pequot after the family moved.

Senator VOYOLKO. Wait a minute there, mister. *Crow, cow, lizard.* That's the ones you said, right? What's the story on that?

Mr. JONES. That would be easy, even at five, for Barry Rudd, for a future taxonomist. They're all animals.

Senator VOYOLKO. Who you think you're kidding? A crow an animal? Ever see an animal could fly? Ever see a cow fly, mister? Watch out if he does!

Mr. JONES. Barry could explain this better than I can, but

they're one each from the animal vertebrate classes of birds, mammals, and reptiles.

Senator Voyolko. Boy thinks cows can fly! He better get himself an umbrella.

Senator Skypack. All right, Mr. Chairman, I know all I want to know from this witness.

Senator Mansfield. Thank you once more, Mr. Jones. What next, Mr. Broadbent?

Mr. Broadbent. Charles Perkonian.

Senator Mansfield. Just sit down in that chair you were in before, sonny.

Testimony of Charles Perkonian, Minor, Town of Pequot

Mr. Broadbent. Now, Master Perkonian, we have information—

Charles Perkonian. Where you get this 'master' stuff?

Mr. Broadbent. We have information through our preliminary interrogations that you know all about Barry Rudd's indiscretion with Florence Renzulli. Is that right?

Charles Perkonian. All those fifty-buck words, you flammergast me. I mean holy Moses.

Mr. Broadbent. You knew about what Barry did to Florence —right?

Charles Perkonian. Everybody and his uncle talking about it.

Mr. Broadbent. I mean at the time—before it was public knowledge.

Charles Perkonian. The time? Man, I had the word way before it happened.

Mr. Broadbent. Barry told you his plan in advance?

Charles Perkonian. He told me? I told him!

Mr. BROADBENT. Please explain.

CHARLES PERKONIAN. It's my idea. The works.

Mr. BROADBENT. Exactly what are you telling us? Would you kindly give the committee the whole story?

CHARLES PERKONIAN. I given it. You stupid or something? I told you. My idea.

Mr. BROADBENT. How did this happen to come up?

CHARLES PERKONIAN. Rudd the Crud ast me.

Mr. BROADBENT. What did he ask you?

CHARLES PERKONIAN. He ast me what should he do.

Mr. BROADBENT. When was this?

CHARLES PERKONIAN. What's today?

Mr. BROADBENT. Monday, October twenty-eighth.

CHARLES PERKONIAN. Monday. What day'd he fool around, you know, when he was messing around with her?

Mr. BROADBENT. Last Wednesday, the twenty-third.

CHARLES PERKONIAN. Wednesday. So. What'd you want to know?

Mr. BROADBENT. When did Barry ask you whatever he asked you?

CHARLES PERKONIAN. What you say it is today?

Mr. BROADBENT. Oh, forget it. *Where* did he ask this thing?

CHARLES PERKONIAN. The lanes. We was watching Piggy Kowalski. You should see him, he's got this two-finger ball, arms is like Popeye the Sailor, shoulders when Big Daddy Lipscomb's got his shoulder pads on, you know what I mean?—like he could belt that ball down there like it's a cat's eye, fastest ball you ever see. Not him. He's got this slow banana ball. Slow curve, say twenty boards. He puts that sixteen pounds down so careful you'd a thought it's a powder puff he's dusting his old lady's bee-hind.

Mr. BROADBENT. What was Barry's problem? What did he ask you?

CHARLES PERKONIAN. He says to me this guy the funny hat I was telling you about, he's after him.

Mr. BROADBENT. The child buyer? So?

CHARLES PERKONIAN. So he wants to shake him, stupid.

Mr. BROADBENT. And he asked you what to do. What did you advise?

CHARLES PERKONIAN. Get in trouble. Anybody knows that. Only way you'll ever get out of trouble is get in new trouble. Then they forget about the other.

Mr. BROADBENT. You advised Barry to get in serious trouble in order to avoid being bought by Mr. Wissey Jones, is that it?

CHARLES PERKONIAN. Nobody wants a punk.

Mr. BROADBENT. The idea was to be caught? Deliberately?

CHARLES PERKONIAN. Want to know something? That's easier than to not get caught.

Mr. BROADBENT. And Barry liked the idea?

CHARLES PERKONIAN. He's not so dumb. You think he's dumb?

Mr. BROADBENT. You cooked up this thing with Florence Renzulli. Why did you pick on her?

CHARLES PERKONIAN. She never in her life knew to say no.

Mr. BROADBENT. You told her this was just to get Barry out of trouble?

CHARLES PERKONIAN. Nah. Nah. We tell her it's for kicks, see?

Mr. BROADBENT. And you planned out with Barry the whole doctor act?

CHARLES PERKONIAN. Nah, that's his idea. I don't like the doctor bit. That's his brain-child, he likes it. He says he can read up on it, this Miss Cloud's his pal down the lie-berry.

Mr. BROADBENT. And you then helped him persuade Miss Renzulli?

CHARLES PERKONIAN. I never did like that doctor idea. I hate

214

doctors, I'd like to punch 'em in the snozzle, I hate 'em. My idea, he should make like he's going to rape her.

Senator SKYPACK. My boy, how old are you?

CHARLES PERKONIAN. Twelve.

Senator SKYPACK. My gracious, boy, do you even know the meaning of the word 'rape'?

CHARLES PERKONIAN. Sure. It's cool. There's this guy, see, and he has this thing, and what he wants is, he wants to put this thing inside this other thing that this girl has, only in rape it's different, 'cause this girl, see, she *usually* wants this thing, I mean the you know, the thing this guy has, to be in this other thing that she has, only in rape it's different, she don't. I mean she don't want this thing—

Senator SKYPACK. Thank you, boy, I know what the word means. I'm astonished that at your age—

CHARLES PERKONIAN. Look, pop, us kids these days catch on all this stuff first thing. Like under teen age. I mean like Boy Scouts, 'Be Prepared.'

Senator SKYPACK. I trust you realize that we have laws.

CHARLES PERKONIAN. Aw, come on, pop. We don't never *do* any that stuff. We set there and talk about it.

Senator SKYPACK. That's good.

CHARLES PERKONIAN. Like I mean my friend Hairy Barry. Come the showdown, what's he do? Plays doctor. Doctor wants a little peek now. Nurse want a peek at doctor? O.K., nurse, just one peek. See if they's any rash. Stuff like that. Laws is for grownups, pop, you know that. People your age, that's where you need 'em. We're just kids.

Senator SKYPACK. Kids! Going around advocating delinquency!

Mr. BROADBENT. Mr. Chairman, this testimony puts a new light on the episode we've been discussing, and I think, if you agree, we ought to call the boy Barry Rudd.

Senator MANSFIELD. By all means.

Mr. BROADBENT. This would seem to explain his cryptic statement that he got into the incident with the Renzulli girl 'on account of Mr. Jones.' I will call Master Barry Rudd, then.

Senator MANSFIELD. You're excused, sonny. You were much more helpful today than last time, much more communicative. . . . You talked more.

CHARLES PERKONIAN. Hairy Barry he said to go ahead talk, sing away. So—

Senator SKYPACK. All right. Let's move along, young fellow.

Mr. BROADBENT. Bring the Rudd boy in, please.

Senator MANSFIELD. Take your place, Barry. Mr. Broadbent wants to ask you a few questions.

TESTIMONY OF BARRY RUDD, MINOR, TOWN OF PEQUOT

Mr. BROADBENT. We have just been informed by a witness under oath that your entire misadventure with Miss Renzulli was undertaken with the deliberate intention of being discovered, in the hope that your 'delinquency' would disqualify you from being bought by Mr. Wissey Jones. I ask you to affirm or deny this information.

BARRY RUDD. It's true.

Mr. BROADBENT. Would you please give us a full account of the events leading up to the incident?

BARRY RUDD. I had a problem. My problem was that I didn't like being for sale.

Senator SKYPACK. You mean your problem was that you wanted to chicken out on the national defense. That's more like it.

BARRY RUDD. As always, when I have a problem, I set about trying to find a solution. Now, I have learned by experience that there are three stages to solving a problem. First comes a period of rambling, when there's no sure destination, just meandering around in the underbrush of the mind trying to flush up ideas. This aimless beating around can be hard work for me, by the way, or seem like it. By Tuesday afternoon last week, after school, when I was sitting talking with Charley Perkonian at the bowling alleys—

Mr. BROADBENT. He told us you were watching a certain Mr. Piggy Kowalski.

BARRY RUDD. That's correct. It was Piggy Kowalski who triggered my solution, indirectly, at least. By that afternoon I was downhearted. Flattop and I had been in the lab earlier in the afternoon when Dr. Gozar had come storming in and had made her stink bomb—which I gather you now know all about —and there'd been something so ferocious about her behavior, she'd been so brusque with me, that I'd been forced to conclude that somehow things were going badly for me. I knew about the Henley lecture; I assumed that the meeting was going against me. Then at the alleys, as we sat watching Piggy Kowalski, Flattop let me in on the plan for the attack on our home, which was to be that evening, and my heart really sank.

Senator SKYPACK. Do you expect us to believe that—'heart really sank'—when you went right out and took part in the rumble yourself?

BARRY RUDD. I don't expect you to believe, Senator Skypack, that I'd take part in a rumble, as you call it, against my own mother.

Senator SKYPACK. The cops picked you up, didn't they?

Senator MANSFIELD. That's another story, Jack. One thing at a time, please.

Senator SKYPACK. All right. All right.

Mr. BROADBENT. Please go on. At the bowling alley.

BARRY RUDD. I told Flattop I was lonely. In his down-to-

earth way he asked me why, and I said it was because of my
eccentricity. He said that that was too long a word for him to
bother with, and I explained it, and he said if being that way
upset me, why didn't I get hep and be like everybody else? I
told him that Dr. Gozar had made me realize that the essence of
scientific creativity is disciplined eccentricity. Flattop said, 'For
God *sake!*' I said that she had shown me how, even on cut-and-
dried experiments and demonstrations in the lab, you could
learn more, perhaps discover more, perhaps get on the path to
true greatness, by not following the book too slavishly, by
breaking rules beautifully, as she put it. Flattop said, 'You mean
like Don Carter bowls the wrong way, with a bent elbow, looks
like he's got arthur-itis, so he wins the national championship?'
That was it, exactly. Flattop understands me. But I told him that
people who break rules are lonely; that Mr. Cleary had said I
was a quasi-foreigner in my peer group. Then the old catalogue
began riffling in my head. A few who were 'adjusted' occurred
to me. Voltaire—apparently an all-round fellow, admired and
beloved by his contemporaries in school. Thackeray—wonderfully social and good-humored. Victor Hugo—leader in the
boys' games. But there were so many others who were lonely or
rejected or overbearing. I told Flattop that Jeremy Bentham
was almost a dwarf, so he was left out of children's play, but,
having a mind of somebody twice his age, he treated all other
children as dunces. That at the age of twelve Benjamin Franklin
invented extension paddles for his hands and feet so he could
outswim his friends; he had to be better than *anybody*. That at
ten Mozart invented an imaginary kingdom, of which he
made a map—and of which he, of course, was king. That when
he was eight, Elie Metchnikoff, the Russian biologist, used to
pay children to listen to his lectures on the local flora. That before he was five, Thomas Chatterton presided over his playmates
as if they were his hired servants. Maladjusted, the whole kit and
kaboodle.

Senator SKYPACK. Didn't Flattop think you were a bit con-ceited for comparing yourself to all those people?

BARRY RUDD. No. He thinks they're just characters in tele-vision serials I've watched.

Senator SKYPACK. Including Benjamin Franklin?

BARRY RUDD. Sure. Sure. He used to watch *See It Now*. He told me once he thought Thomas Jefferson was cool—sort of like Phil Silvers, only not quite as funny; unlike Phil Silvers, he wore a wig; Phil Silvers could stand to use a wig, he said.

Mr. BROADBENT. Let's get back to solving your problem, please, Master Rudd.

BARRY RUDD. I hadn't talked with Flattop much about the child buyer, but now I suddenly began unburdening myself to him, and I told him what a nightmare it all was to me, and I asked him what in the world to do.

Senator SKYPACK. Asking advice of a no-goodnik who still smells of the correction home!

BARRY RUDD. He advised doing something bad. He said, 'They get feeling sorry for you.'

Senator SKYPACK. Wanted you to violate that poor little virgin girl.

BARRY RUDD. No, sir, he didn't have any specific suggestions at first, and we stopped talking about the problem altogether, and Charley was pointing out to me the delicacy of Piggy Kowalski's bowling style, so finicky for such a brute, he's a huge man, when I guess we both simultaneously noticed the floozy tattooed on Piggy's right arm in such a way—with her hands clasped behind her head and her legs straddling the biceps, tri-cepts, and brachialis muscles—that on the backswing and de-livery she did a sort of grind and bump. And that was where the second stage of problem solving came in. This is the phase of inspiration—when in the midst of a recess from work on the problem, while not thinking about it at all, a flash comes up from the depths of the mind which doesn't quite give the solution but hints at it. Looking at that tattoo, I very nearly had it! And by a curious coincidence Flattop must have experienced the same illumination at the same moment, because he exclaimed, 'Jeez, Hairy Barry, I got the answer. "I Was a Pre-Teen-Age Stickleback." '

Senator SKYPACK. So then you picked your victim?

BARRY RUDD. There followed the third phase of creative work. We knew we were on the right track, but we needed a period of consolidation, verification, elaboration. The basic notion was that I would break a rule beautifully, and get caught, that it would be with a female of the species, because we both sensed that here was where the rules were most deeply tribal. I would be not simply delinquent, I would be taboo. I would make my protest against civilization in terms as old as civilization itself. I give Flattop just as full marks as myself for this apt insight. You see, this is where Flattop, in his way, has a kind of talent. If only there were some way of harnessing it.

Senator SKYPACK. So now you want to put an ordinary J.D., a time server, on a pedestal!

BARRY RUDD. He deserves a pedestal, Senator. He'd be a worthy citizen if one could be found for him. Anyway, we discussed many details. For the central approach to my misbehavioral adventure I adopted a line of which Flattop disapproved: the gynecological approach. Flattop wanted a more elemental action, something meatier. As things turned out, I think he may have been right. My *crime passionel* turned out to be a flimsy curiosity. Here we sit politely mulling it over, when what I needed was to be clapped into Clarkdale. But be that as it may, I told Flattop that I had to follow my own natural bent, which was, alas, scientific rather than lascivious. I could read up on my approach at the library, with Miss Cloud's help—and later I did.

Senator MANSFIELD. How could you be sure you'd be caught?

220

BARRY RUDD. This again was Flattop's contribution, in large part. He had observed, during his frequent visits to the boys' bathroom, which is in the basement of Lincoln, that Dr. Gozar inspects the cellar installations of the school at two o'clock sharp every day, that her tour takes twelve minutes to the dot, and that afterwards she invariably returns to her office. I remembered the closet off her office. Florence Renzulli contributed the bit about planting her shoe in Dr. Gozar's office; Florence was most co-operative. I'm very fond of her, and very grateful. My time alone with her was fascinating. She has a mature development, prepubescence like young corn silk, excellent pelvis.

Senator SKYPACK. I see you're not repentant in the slightest degree.

BARRY RUDD. Repentant—no. Regretful—yes. Abashed that my little protest was so futile. It has, however, taught me something about adults.

Senator SKYPACK. Namely.

BARRY RUDD. Namely, that what is commonly called juvenile delinquency is largely ineffective as protest because it simply acts out things that grownups would secretly like to do. The horror adults felt at what I did appeared to be in direct ratio to their envy of me. Mr. Cleary was beside himself with rage. I don't think I ever saw a person gnash his teeth before. It's a sort of rotary sharpening process.

Senator MANSFIELD. Why did you want to be caught by Dr. Gozar?

BARRY RUDD. Because I knew that she's strict about things that matter—such as letting a book be damaged by rain.

Senator MANSFIELD. Any other questions, gentlemen?

Senator VOYOLKO. This Piggy Kowalski, he get that tattoo in the Navy?

BARRY RUDD. I don't know, but there's an anchor tattooed on

his left forearm. Entwined in a serpent.

Senator VOYOLKO. Anchor. See? I thought so. I thought he was in the Navy. You talk about national defense!

Senator MANSFIELD. If there are no further questions, gentlemen, I think the time has come to call it a day. Tomorrow, as I understand it, Mr. Broadbent, we'll take up the attack on the Rudd home.

Mr. BROADBENT. That's right, sir.

Senator MANSFIELD. O.K. We'll stand adjourned until ten in the morning.

(Whereupon, at 4:18 p.m., Monday, October 28, the hearing was recessed, subject to the recall of the Chair.)

TUESDAY, OCTOBER 29

(The committee met, pursuant to call, at 10:15 a.m., in Ordinary Session, in Room 202, Capitol Offices, Senator Aaron Mansfield presiding. Committee members and counsel present.)

Senator MANSFIELD. We will come to order. Again I must caution our spectators against disturbing our committee in any way. We intend to be orderly and expeditious here, and if there are any disturbances we'll be obliged to clear the room forthwith. Mr. Broadbent, you may go ahead.

Mr. BROADBENT. First, this morning, I'd like to call the boy Charles Perkonian. Usher him in, please.

Senator MANSFIELD. Sit down over there again, sonny. In a talking mood this morning, I hope.

CHARLES PERKONIAN. Barry says sing, I sing.

TESTIMONY OF CHARLES PERKONIAN, MINOR, TOWN OF PEQUOT

Mr. BROADBENT. Yesterday, Master Perkonian, the boy Barry Rudd testified to us that you gave him advance warning of the attack on his home, and you yourself made some broad hints in testimony here yesterday morning that the child buyer knew all about the assault beforehand. You remember that?

CHARLES PERKONIAN. Knew all about it? You can say that again. His baby.

Mr. BROADBENT. Are you suggesting that the child buyer engineered the attack?

CHARLES PERKONIAN. Like I said, it was his baby. Beginning to end.

Mr. BROADBENT. What makes you say that? How do you know it?

CHARLES PERKONIAN. What you think I got ears for? Flap off the flies?

Mr. BROADBENT. You heard something. What did you hear?

CHARLES PERKONIAN. The guy the flat hat, I heard him telling them fellas what to do, how to do it. A to Z.

Mr. BROADBENT. Where was this?

CHARLES PERKONIAN. Where was what?

Mr. BROADBENT. This conversation you overheard. These instructions.

CHARLES PERKONIAN. The drugstore.

Mr. BROADBENT. Ellithorp's drugstore?

CHARLES PERKONIAN. I don't know no names. The drugstore fella the stomach out to here.

Mr. BROADBENT. Mr. Ellithorp. Search your memory, Master Perkonian. Was this in Mr. Ellithorp's store?

CHARLES PERKONIAN. You're the one said that.

Mr. BROADBENT. The record will show that the alleged conversation took place in a drugstore in Pequot, presumably Ellithorp's. Please tell what happened.

CHARLES PERKONIAN. I already told. Stupid. Like I already told. The guy the flat fedora, cooking up the deal.

Mr. BROADBENT. How did you happen to overhear? What were you doing in the drugstore?

CHARLES PERKONIAN. Doing? Buying a bottle Bromo, my old lady got herself a head. Minding my own business.

Mr. BROADBENT. Where were they talking?

CHARLES PERKONIAN. In the back. I come in there after this bottle Bromo, nobody's around, the fat guy's usually got this white coat, like he's playing doctor like my pal Hairy Barry, anyway he's not there, nobody around. So I ease around behind the place he stashes all these bottles a medicine.

Mr. BROADBENT. And?

CHARLES PERKONIAN. Mumbo-jumbo in the back. The guy, the drugstore guy, he got this office in the way behind. I can hear 'em. So I crotch down, there's this trash barrel around the corner there, I crotch down where nobody can't see me, and I hear the whole thing.

Mr. BROADBENT. Who was there?

CHARLES PERKONIAN. I din see 'em, I only heard 'em.

Mr. BROADBENT. So far as you could tell from overhearing, who was there?

CHARLES PERKONIAN. I don't like to use no names. Gives me the heemie-jeemies, I ain't no squealer. Just those guys in there.

Mr. BROADBENT. We know the child buyer and the druggist were in there. Who else?

CHARLES PERKONIAN. These two hoody guys. You want I should stool on 'em or something? I don't go for that stuff.

Mr. BROADBENT. What was the child buyer saying?

CHARLES PERKONIAN. The whole deal. What time. Motorcycles. Pick-up truck. Baseball bats. How to open up the chimbley, side the house, pour this crap and stuff down it.

Mr. BROADBENT. Where did Barry come into all this?

CHARLES PERKONIAN. He dint.

Mr. BROADBENT. The police picked him up. You know that.

CHARLES PERKONIAN. You want to know about him, you ask him. I already talk too much. You get him in here, you want to know about him. Lay off from me on *him*.

Mr. BROADBENT. What was the purpose of the attack to be? Did you gather that?

CHARLES PERKONIAN. They was going to scare the living—

Mr. BROADBENT. Watch your language, now.

CHARLES PERKONIAN. Daylights. Anything the matter with daylights? What's so dirty about daylights?

Mr. BROADBENT. I thought you had something else in mind. Go on.

CHARLES PERKONIAN. Stupid. I suppose you think daylights is dirty or something.

Mr. BROADBENT. Go on, Master Perkonian.

CHARLES PERKONIAN. Jeez, a guy can't even say daylights around here. I ain't surprise you got a hatful a guys down Clarkdale. A guy can't say nothing till you come along and decide he's a criminal or something like that. You call this a democracy, a guy can't even finish a sentence he's in Clarkdale.

Mr. BROADBENT. You were saying about the purpose of the attack.

CHARLES PERKONIAN. I don't know. You got me so I don't want a open my trap, find myself down Clarkdale again.

Senator MANSFIELD. We're not going to do anything to you, sonny. Just go ahead.

CHARLES PERKONIAN. Well, I'd like to know what gives with this stupid jerk. Can't even say daylights. They going to give me a vote like anybody else, one these days. I'll bomb this jerk when they give me a vote.

Senator MANSFIELD. Never mind, sonny, just answer the question.

CHARLES PERKONIAN. How'm I supposed to say it? They got this idea they're going to scare the . . . the . . . Look at him! Just can't wait to ship me off to the correction house! They call it justice! . . . O.K., O.K. Supposed to throw a scare into mostly Mrs. Rudd, so she'll up and sell Barry like this guy the flat fedora wants to buy him.

Mr. BROADBENT. The attack was to intimidate Mrs Rudd?

CHARLES PERKONIAN. You accuse me the dirty words, I ac-

226

cuse you words a guy can't understand. You oughta watch TV, mister, learn to talk like a normal person the way they talk on the programs there. You can understand every single word.

Senator Voyolko. I agree with this boy. Wouldn't do you a bit of harm, Mr. Broadback.

Mr. Broadbent. You then joined up with the attack yourself at the appointed rendezvous?

Charles Perkonian. I don't know what you mean, that roundy-view, but sure I went along. Who wouldn't? It was going to be cool.

Senator Skypack. One more question, son. What do you think—should they sell Barry?

Charles Perkonian. Why not? What's to stop 'em? People don't have no choice. My pal don't want to go, that's just tough . . . Oh-oh. Mr. Daylights looking down my tonsils again, looking for dirty words. I was only going to say, Just tough luck. Barry don't have a look-in. Did they ask me, did I wanta go down Clarkdale? A free country, only trouble is, it don't work that way. Under twenty-one, it ain't always all that free.

Senator Mansfield. All right, sonny. Thank you.

Charles Perkonian. What's all this about, anyway? What's the fuss about? What's so special about Mr. Barry Rudd Esquire? Who ast me when they sent me down Clarkdale? Did they have these Senators and all this Mr. Daylights jazz then? I don't get the whole thing.

Senator Mansfield. All right, sonny. You're excused now.

Mr. Broadbent. I will ask for Master Barry Rudd.

Senator Mansfield. Take your place, sonny.

Testimony of Barry Rudd, Minor, Town of Pequot

Mr. Broadbent. Now, Master Rudd, yesterday you told us that on last Tuesday afternoon your friend Flattop informed

227

you about the imminent attack on your home. What did you and he do?

BARRY RUDD. What do you mean? Together?

Mr. BROADBENT. Flattop has testified here that he took part in the attack, and we know about the police apprehending you at the end of it. How did you and he enlist in the attack?

BARRY RUDD. You have the whole thing wrong.

Mr. BROADBENT. How wrong?

BARRY RUDD. About my role.

Mr. BROADBENT. Would you kindly give an account of the attack, then, from your point of view?

BARRY RUDD. As I explained to you, Charley Perkonian told me about the plan that afternoon at the bowling alleys. I went home about six o'clock. Father bowls in a league on Tuesday nights, and he'd already left for the lanes when I got home; we must have passed each other in transit—of course I was on foot and he was driving. It had been summery that afternoon, but it was suddenly turning snappy, I could see my breath as I walked.

Mr. BROADBENT. What did you do when you got home?

BARRY RUDD. I warned Momma and my sister Susan. I stood in the living room, still in my coat, hat, sweater, and gloves, and I tried to tell Momma all I had understood of what Flattop had told me. It was hard for me to get it out.

Mr. BROADBENT. What did your mother do?

BARRY RUDD. Momma got redder and redder, and then purple, and almost blue, until I thought she might have an attack of some kind and die. She was transformed. She was gradually transmogrified into something I had never seen before, as if she were going from larva to pupa—or, rather, the other way around, regressing from pupa to larva. 'Why, the sons of bitches!' she finally roared. 'The dirty lowdown sons of bitches!' I'd never heard such words from my mother's lips, and it seemed as if her body had changed and become coarser. From a proud, timid, genteel lady she had turned into a big, coarse woman, with a broad, florid face slashed by deep furrows across the forehead. Her hair, which is naturally curly, stood out in a bush all around. Her eyes were their usual remarkable clear light blue, but her mouth seemed thick and had no lipstick on it and was twisted. She wore a drab, beltless, dirty, hanging dress, and under it her bosoms hung long and huge, like the milch bags of *Capra hircus,* and out from short sleeves came two great, muscular, hairy arms. I'd never seen my mother look like that. I'd certainly never heard her shout the way she did, yet at first, rather than being frightened or mortified by her, I was overcome with pity for the big, helpless, cursing hulk she'd turned into.

Mr. BROADBENT. Go on.

BARRY RUDD. Suddenly she whirled and towered over me. 'How do I know you're telling me the truth? It's one of their slimy tricks—sending my little boy in here to scare me!' I was terrified that she would hurl herself at me and crush me in that mass of angry transformed flesh. Susan had begun to cry. 'The bastards came in here this morning with their sleazy threats, and they told me to call them up and give in to them—they said by seven o'clock—them and their bastardly deadlines and ultimatums; but they don't know Maudie Rudd. By Christ! Let them come, let the sod-hearted bastards come, I'll break every dad-blasted chicken drumstick in their dad-blasted white-meat bodies.' Then Momma burst into tears, and she fell in a heap on the sofa, and she wailed, 'Oh, Paul, Paul, why did you have to go bowling this night of all nights?' I was surprised to hear myself say, during a lull in her typhoon, 'Don't you think we ought to get ready for them?' Momma turned off the torrents, as if with a faucet, and she got up and surged toward me and looked as if she would fling those suddenly huge bear arms

229

around me in gratitude and affection, and I was just as fearful
of being suffocated by love as I had been of being squashed in
her fury, and she shouted, 'Dear Barry!' Momma lurched into
the kitchen, where, behind the display of linen, she evidently
looked at the clock, because she cried out, 'A quarter to eight!
The bastards! . . . First off,' she added in a quieter voice, 'I'll
put this wash away so we can have more room to fling around in.
Susie! Come here with the big basket. Susie! Lively!' Susan ran
into the kitchen. I took off my coat and hat and gloves but not
my sweater, because it was chilly in the house; the only heat in
the two rooms came from the kitchen stove—though both Susan
and Momma only wore cotton dresses. I went in the kitchen.
Soon all the clean things were mounded in a huge reed laundry
basket, and Momma took the rope down from its hooks and
threw it in a box in the corner, and once the linen was out of the
way I was hit by the mess in the room; I was saddened, so my
hands and feet felt heavy and I thought I'd cry, by the reali-
zation that Mother's gentility had all along been only a skin,
which she could easily burst and shed—a meaningless thing of
touches, like the pot of African violets, *Saintpaulia ionantha*,
on the window sill under the street-side window. The daybed
where I slept was unmade, and the things in the room were
cheap, crude, and battered, like Momma herself just then—
the iron coal-burning stove, the deep, low, galvanized sink for
both laundry and dishes, the dented pots and chipped plates;
the coal dust on the floor by the scuttle, the glasses on the
shelves mottled with soap-and-grease spots. I realized that
Momma really is a slattern. In the last few minutes she'd become one for me to see. Little to choose between her and Mrs.
Perkonian—sickening idea! I felt weak. Anyway, Momma began thinking out loud, and her thoughts were like thunder.
'The kitchen door to the street's O.K., it's like the door of a
damned old safe in a bank, let 'em try to crack that one! But

the door in the back. I've been nervy about it for months. We've got to back it up. Come on, Sue-sue. Come on, son.' And Momma led us into the living room and lifted one end of the ragbag sofa and roared to the two of us to grab the other end. 'H'ist!' Momma shouted, and we managed to get our end off the floor, and Momma heaved sofa and us and all toward the door. The thing was too wide to cram between the bureau by the door and the side wall, and it had to be canted up on its side, and not only clothes and magazines but also a thimble and two spoons and some change and other odds and ends fell onto the floor and scattered around like fleeing vermin, *Cimici lectularii* or *Periplanetae americanae*. We got the sofa jammed against the door. We went back into the kitchen. I asked, 'What if they came in a window?' Momma said the windows were all nailed. 'If they come in a window, they'll have to smash it first. If they do that, we'll just have to pick 'em off one by one. Let's see. . . .' Momma began to look around for a weapon. She took a broom from a corner and held it in the air and shook it, but it must have seemed too light; she handed it to me, and I clutched it as tight as I could. 'Aha!' she then shouted. 'I know what's loose.' She went to the kitchen table, lifted one corner, and pulled a thick leg out of its socket. She took it by its bottom end and swung it, and looked pleased. Slowly the table fell awry, with a sliding metallic sound of shifting kitchen cutlery. Susan suggested calling the police, but Momma was scornful of that idea. She said, 'Did you ever hear of calling the firemen before you set the house on fire?' The clock pointed to eight o'clock; the three of us in the kitchen fell silent. Then I had an idea. I asked Momma if we hadn't better turn the lights out. That way we could see them, and they wouldn't be able to see us—there was a moon out. 'You're a darling boy!' Momma said, but it didn't seem to me there was any real love left in her. We turned the lights out, and I thought of Father's long five-battery flashlight that he kept under his bed, and I ran out and got it and offered it to Momma. 'Keep it,' she said. 'You can use it to knock the brains out of them, such as they have. Give the broom to Sue.' We stood in the dark then. It was still within and without, except that Momma's breathing, which was beginning to be asthmatic because of her emotion, sounded like wind going intermittently through a *Pinus strobus*—

Senator SKYPACK. All right, boy, enough of that foreign talk.

BARRY RUDD. A white pine. After a long time she took the flashlight from my perspiring hands and shone it briefly on the clock, which said fourteen minutes past eight; she threw the beam then straight in my face, and she rasped, 'You little bastard, you wouldn't be trying to make a fool of Momma, would you?' She'd never talked to me like that, ever, and I would have cried, I guess, but she suddenly said, 'Bah! You're a good little boy,' and she snapped off the light and handed it back to me. We waited another eternity and then we began to hear something in the far distance, just a hum, at first, remote and low. Gradually the sound increased, until it seemed like a faraway flight of planes. 'That's them,' Momma whispered with a great wheeze. Then, speaking very loud, in a voice that made me jump, she said, 'We'd best have a lookout in each room. Boy, you stay here in the kitchen. Sue, you go in the bathroom. And I'll take my parlor, and Lord love the bastard that gets in there.' Parlor. It shook me to hear her use that word—a vestige of the gentility that had so suddenly peeled off her. You know about the appearance of that room, yet she always called it her parlor. Susan began to whimper. 'I don't want to go in there alone.' 'Git!' Momma roared, and Susan gat, sniveling and whining. I went to a front window. The moon was shining whitely now, and I could see the bright ribbon of the street beyond the porch and the sidewalk, and beyond that Mr. Zimmer's beautybush, *Kol-*

kwitzia amabilis, and his wayfaringtree, V*iburnum lantana,* and—
Senator SKYPACK. Now look *here.*

BARRY RUDD. For a moment I was seized by fear, and I wanted
to run into the back room and enfold myself in that strange
voluminous flesh in there, but just then the bathroom door
creaked, and Susan tiptoed out and came and knelt beside me
at my window. She had stopped crying, but when she settled
herself beside me she loudly snuffled. I gripped my flashlight,
and I whispered, 'I'll bean you.' The noise outside seemed un-
bearably loud now. There they came! I could see them off to
the right. First there were three or four motorcycles, then a small
truck, then a car, and some guys on bikes. The machines were
moving slowly, and the motorcycles' headlights flashed from side
to side as the riders kept their balance on the pavement. Susan
put her hand in mine; she was shaking like a passenger in a
rickety auto. The first machines had stopped, and I heard a voice
shout over the roar, 'Is that it?' And an answer, 'Sure, that's the
house. Them fake bricks and the chimney out the side. That's
it!' The convoy halted, and the riders dismounted and pushed
their machines to the Zimmers' side of the street and leaned
them on their stands. The truck parked a little down the street
to the left. The motors and lights were being cut off. I could see
about a dozen figures milling around the truck. High-school
kids, they looked to be. They all seemed to be talking in under-
tones. One of them stepped a few paces toward the house and
shouted to the others, 'Christ, lights all out. What if the old
bag ain't home? What the hell fun's an empty house?' I was surprised at how easily I could hear every word; I knew how thin
the walls were, but I still was surprised. I knew Momma must
have been able to hear in the back room, too, because now I
heard her mutter, 'What they'll call a person!' She let out a kind
of growl. Another boy called out that maybe she was in bed, and
still another shouted, 'You gonna get in it with her? What I

233

hear, she's got room for three-four of you, bub!" Because of my reading in Ellis, Curtis, Wharton, and others, I understood, of course, exactly what he meant, and I could picture it, and it gave me a queer and violent feeling I'd never had in my life before, to picture my own mother—but just then Momma let out a roar which, I swear, shook the pots in the kitchen: 'You just try to come in here and climb in the bed with Maudie Rudd, you knee-pants sophomore hoor-mongers. I'll give you a dose you didn't look for.' There was a second of silence, then the first boy shouted in mock-elegant tones, 'Lah-de-dah. The lady of the house is expecting guests!' At that the boys all started whooping and yodeling and making siren noises and laughing and scream-ing in falsetto voices like old maids. They swarmed around the truck and picked off it all sorts of things to make noises with—pans and wooden spoons, horns and megaphones, a drum, a watchman's rattle, a whistle, and a frightfully sour old trumpet which I saw flashing in the moonlight as one of the hoods played ridiculous taps. All the time Momma was swearing and Sue was giving out little miserable chirping squeaks like those of a fledgling bird. Two of the boys approached the house with a ladder and went in the alley alongside the house, and I could hear the scrape and thump of the ladder against the side wall, and then I heard a metallic banging at the tin chimney of our stove, and Momma shrieked out, 'If there's property damage, I'll skin your backsides one and all!' But there was such a clatter and whooping that I'm sure her challenge was lost on our as-sailants. A boy went into the alley with a bucket, and soon I heard a hissing and splashing as whatever had been in the bucket was thrown down the hot chimney pipe and ran into the kitchen stove, putting out the fire there. Soon the house was filled with a steam that had an overpoweringly foul smell on it. 'Skunks! Skunks! Skunks!' Momma shrieked. The trumpet blew a signal, and suddenly the noise all stopped, except for Momma's furious

234

tirade in the living room. The hoods all ran back to their truck and put down the things they had had and picked up some boxes and baskets and ranged along the street in front of the house. 'No windows yet,' a voice called out. A mournful blast came from the trumpet, and the boys began to pelt the house with things that made soft, squooshy noises when they hit. 'You can come back and paint this house tomorrow,' Momma shouted, 'you damned little schoolboy crab lice, you!' She was in a frenzy, and I could hear the heavy crashes of her feet as she ran back and forth in the other room. Soon the pelting stopped; the attackers apparently ran out of that sort of ammunition. 'By God,' Momma said, 'it's time for cops.' She ran with thudding steps to the telephone, which hangs on the wall by the back door; she must have reached for it over the barricading sofa. I heard her click the receiver once, then again, then rapidly many times. 'What a moment for the damnable telephone machine to go dead!' she shouted. I said, 'They probably used that ladder to cut the wires on the side of the house.' 'Ah, that's right,' Momma said. 'You're one of this younger generation, Barry, you'd know what these devilish young new-type bastards have thought up in their modernistic dirty minds.' Momma had come to the door of the kitchen, and she saw Susan, whom she had set to guard the bathroom. 'What are *you* doing in this room?' she screamed at poor Susan, and then she wailed, 'Oh, it don't matter, it don't matter,' and she went back into the living room and began to sob. A sentence she blabbered out hit me like a splash of scalding water. 'Barry! Barry! You've seen me the way I really am.' I saw the swarm of boys convene again at the truck, and this time each one came away with a baseball bat. I could hear some of them run into the alley beside the house, and some along it to the back, so they had us surrounded on three sides. 'What now? What now?' Momma said between groans and sobs, as she evidently saw boys appearing in the back yard. The boys in front got down on hands and knees and crept toward the house. I became very frightened, and I dragged Sue back to the wall of the room away from the street. Momma was weeping and moaning, 'Paul oh Paul oh Paul, I need you, Paul, Paul!' Then the trumpet blew a fanfare, like one when a king appears in a movie. With that the boys began their whooping again, and they leaped up, and with the baseball bats they smashed in every window on the ground floor of the house, all at once. Now Momma shrieked as if she'd been stabbed, and Sue began to cry again. The boys were laughing and shouting through the open windows, and they continued to pound at whatever glass remained in the sashes. I could feel cold air rushing across the floor and swirling in the room. I heard the hoods talking about coming in the house. 'Come on,' one of them shouted. 'All together!' 'No, no, no,' Momma cried. 'Stay out of here. I'll sell the boy. They can have the boy. Just stay out, for the love of God, stay out.' And she rocked off in a torrent of sobs. But some of the boys climbed in, anyway. Sue and I—we cringed against the wall. 'Where the hell's the light switch?' one of the voices asked. Then, 'Shut up!' a sharp voice shouted, and there was an immediate silence. In the distance a siren could be heard—the Zimmers told us later they'd heard the racket and called the police. Excited voices cried, 'Am-scray!' 'Cheese it!' 'Jiggers!' The mob began to pour out the windows faster than they had come in. 'I'll sell him, I'll sell him, I'll sell him,' Momma was shouting over and over in the kitchen. Suddenly I felt I couldn't stand any more of it, and I got to my feet and ran to the window where I'd been kneeling, and I jumped out, and I began to run, I didn't know where to, just to get away. The siren was wailing not far away, and down the road a searchlight was swinging its beam here and there. Motorcycle engines were starting up. The pick-up careened forward and swerved around in a U-turn and barely missed me as it hurtled along River Street in the direction away from the approaching police car. I was running blindly, as fast as I could. Another siren was coming. I was dimly aware of the first police car stopping and its doors flying open. Another searchlight was sweeping the street, and I could hear a third siren in the distance. I felt as if I couldn't run any further. I stumbled and fell face down; dust got in my lungs; I lay coughing and panting, and I shivered in the dreadful cold. Then a big hand was on my shoulder, and a flashlight was in my face, and a deep voice was saying, 'Well, well, well, here's the littlest rat of all. Why, this one's practically a mouse.' I could still hear Momma bellowing, 'I'll sell him, I'll sell him, I'll sell him,' back at the house.

Senator MANSFIELD. There, now, sonny, there's no need to cry.

Senator SKYPACK. He better stand down. Get him off there, Aaron.

Senator MANSFIELD. All right, sonny. That's right, Mr. Broadbent. That's better.

Senator SKYPACK. I can't stand to see a kid blubber like that.

Senator MANSFIELD. What next, Mr. Broadbent?

Mr. BROADBENT. The child buyer. Call Mr. Wissey Jones, please.

Senator MANSFIELD. Take the witness chair, please, Mr. Jones.

TESTIMONY OF MR. WISSEY JONES,
OF UNITED LYMPHOMILLOID CORPORATION

Mr. BROADBENT. You have been accused, sir, by a witness before this committee, of having planned and organized the gang attack on the Rudd home of Tuesday evening last. Do you admit to having done so?

Mr. JONES. 'Accuse'? 'Admit'? My dear Mr. Broadbent, you use words that suggest something reprehensible. I feel no guilt

237

about this little job of work. In fact, I'm rather proud of it.

Mr. Broadbent. You did, then, devise this attack and set it up?

Mr. Jones. Even the word 'attack' seems to me an overstatement of the case. 'Prank' sounds better to me. It was a business prank, by which I mean, it was not an idle joke.

Mr. Broadbent. Would you give us an account of your part in the incident, please, sir?

Mr. Jones. I turned over to you yesterday, and you read out loud to the committee, Mr. Broadbent, a telegram from the prex of U. Lympho expressing extreme urgency about getting my purchases of specimens completed. I will tell you that even before that wire arrived I had felt sharply the pressure of time. I was a man in a hurry. You will say fifty years—the expected duration of U. Lympho's Mystery—is a long time, two thirds of a man's life span, more or less. But, as you know, we live in a cutthroat world. What appears as sweetness and light in your common television commercial of a consumer product often masks a background of ruthless competitive infighting. The gift-wrapped brickbat. Polite legal belly-slitting. Banditry dressed in a tux. The more so with projects like ours. A prospect of perfectly enormous profits is involved here. We don't intend to lose out. That is why these extended hearings—

Mr. Broadbent. How was the attack, or prank, connected with what you're saying?

Mr. Jones. In this way. By Monday a week ago, the day before the prank, I had already spent four full days of work in Pequot, and I didn't seem to be getting anywhere. Usually it takes me only two or at most three days to conclude these deals, because, you see, your upper-middle-class families, where the high-I.Q. children mostly show up, need money much more desperately than poor families, such as the Rudds, do.

Senator Mansfield. How's that again?

Mr. Jones. Money is commonly thought of as a medium of

exchange, as a means of storing value, but in my work I think of it as a habit-forming drug. The more you've had, the more you need. For the addicted a large dose produces an ecstasy that is short-lived. Withdrawal, or even the threat of it, causes intense physical pain. Among those who are hooked I have no trouble at all extracting children in return for a jolt of the stuff. But people like the Rudds are often deeply afraid of heroin, morphine, cash, and other forms of dope, without really knowing how afraid of them they are.

Senator MANSFIELD. But I thought you told us that Mr. Rudd was eager to sell.

Mr. JONES. He didn't care about the money. He wanted the so-called luxury items. He knew deep down that it would be fatal to be rich, but to appear to be rich for a short time would be no more dangerous than having a sweet dream.

Mr. BROADBENT. So what did you do?

Mr. JONES. As you know, I had Cleary under my thumb, and I put him to work. My hunch—and I think it's proving to have been correct—was that my most important impediment was Mrs. Rudd, that if I could bring her around, the boy would follow, sooner or later. He might rationalize his decision, but when you came right down to it, you'd find it was a case of his being cleated to an apron string as strong as a tugboat's hawser. Cleary provided the clue. He told me about his first interview with Mrs. Rudd, when he was in fact arguing against the sale of Barry; he told me about Mrs. Rudd's confession of having spent her whole life trying to escape what she considered coarseness in herself, and how Barry had become the main prop in her charade. The first victim of fear is affectation; scared people can't hide their true natures, even from themselves. So the problem was: how to frighten Mrs. Rudd, but good; show her she hadn't escaped her basic self, and never would, Barry or no Barry. Cleary found out for me that Mr. Rudd goes bowling on Tuesday nights, and that would give us an opportunity to work on her without his support. I then devised the idea of an orgy of destructiveness on the part of some teen-agers—fun for the kids and hay for me. I asked Cleary who was Pequot's Mr. Fix-It. Every town has at least one: the guy who knows all the angles, the Republican who's thick as sin with the Democratic Town Committee, the man who can get it for you, who can squash tickets, knows the Chief. Paul Ellithorp, Cleary said. So I sent Cleary to him, to make the first approach, to put me in touch with the headquarters of the junior defacing element.

Mr. BROADBENT. You mean some high-school hoods?

Mr. JONES. I don't know exactly what you mean by that term. As a matter of fact, I asked for two or three boys, to be ringleaders, from good families, boys who'd had a sound record of breakage, ill manners, and rebelliousness. Sons of men who believe in firm discipline for the younger generation but not necessarily for themselves. Cleary set up an appointment for me with some boys who were just the thing, delightfully surly, in Ellithorp's office, and we had a grand time. It was like planning games for a party, all that capering with noise-makers and baseball bats and buckets of slops—like Blind Man's Buff, Bop the Boodle, Sardines. Joys of innocent childhood, discussed by my blackguard boys, of course, with terrifying frowns and disenchanted grunts.

Mr. BROADBENT. Yes, sir, we've heard about that conversation.

Mr. JONES. You have? From whom?

Mr. BROADBENT. From a boy who overheard you in the back of the store. A chum of Barry's, Charles Perkonian.

Mr. JONES. So that accounts for it!

Mr. BROADBENT. Accounts for what?

Mr. JONES. Did this child warn the Rudds?

Mr. BROADBENT. He did.

Mr. JONES. *That* explains Mrs. Rudd's recovery. At the end of

240

the attack she gave in—shouted over and over that she'd sell. But by the next morning she'd hardened up again. It must have been the lack of surprise that gave her a chance to become resistant to a certain extent. As to flu from a vaccine. Did she know I was behind it?

Mr. BROADBENT. Yes, she did.

Mr. JONES. Ah, well, there you are. That's how mischief climbs on mischief's back—the human tongue and ear come into play. I think the most merciful phase of our experiment with the specimens at United Lymphomilloid is the tying off of the senses. What serenity! What undisturbed virtue!

Mr. BROADBENT. Please go on with your story. Did you pay the high-school boys?

Mr. JONES. Heavens, no. The chance to destroy for a purpose was more than enough reward for them. After I finished making plans with them in the drugstore, Ellithorp came through with a brilliant suggestion. Why not call on Mrs. Rudd in the morning and give her a deadline—say seven o'clock in the evening, one hour before the gang was scheduled to arrive—for surrendering? This would lend added force to her alarm and shock at eight. I've always been astonished at how eager people have been to help me in my procurement work; I'm sure there's some secret here for the future of collective human effort, but I haven't quite figured out what it is. Anyway, we went; Ellithorp, who's a creditor of the Rudds', went along with me.

Senator SKYPACK. Jones, I have to call a halt here and congratulate you. I sure do admire a practical man.

Mr. JONES. Well, I thank you. I try not to be a fool.

Mr. BROADBENT. Sir, on the occasion of your first appearance before us, one of our committee, I believe it was Senator Skypack, asked about your collapsible motorcycle, and whether you personally took part in this attack, or prank, as you call it. At that time you denied any—

Senator SKYPACK. I wouldn't want to resurrect an old question like that, Broadbent.

Mr. JONES. The Senator succeeds in not being a fool, where I only try! . . . Don't take offense, Mr. Broadbent, I didn't mean to suggest that *you're* a fool. That was intended as humor.

Mr. BROADBENT. I understand perfectly. *Did* you take part in the attack, sir?

Mr. JONES. No, I did not. I leave specialized work to specialists. An office boy would have a right to be offended if I sharpened my own pencils—it's something he can do better than I.

Senator MANSFIELD. Have you ever staged an assault like this before, to help parents to make up their minds?

Mr. JONES. I rather pride myself on varying my approach to meet the unique requirements of each situation.

Senator MANSFIELD. But you have no compunction about what your mob did—about the cost to the Rudds of those windows, for instance?

Mr. JONES. I've offered the Rudds enough money for a lifetime of broken windows.

Senator MANSFIELD. You'd do it again if you had to?

Mr. JONES. Certainly. All's fair in love, war, and free enterprise. Only I'll tell you one thing: Another time I'd make sure a sneaky boy wasn't eavesdropping.

Senator SKYPACK. What I want to know, Jones, is: How are you coming along with Mrs. Rudd and that sneaky boy of *hers?* Are you going to get this deal closed?

Mr. JONES. Of course I am.

Senator SKYPACK. You sound cocksure. You making some headway?

Mr. JONES. I am. I'm glad to say that the mother has already come around, permanently, and I've got Dr. Gozar working on the boy right this minute, out there in the anteroom.

Senator MANSFIELD. You've got *Dr. Gozar* on your side?

Mr. JONES. I don't give up easily, Senator.

Senator SKYPACK. By George, he's a whiz!

Senator MANSFIELD. But how did you win them over?

Mr. JONES. I imagine they can tell you better than I can, sir. I'm not sure I really know myself—I've tried so many approaches on them.

Senator MANSFIELD. We'll certainly ask them. Mr. Broadbent, let's have in Mrs. Rudd and then Dr. Gozar. Thank you, Mr. Jones, you may step down.

Mr. BROADBENT. Bring Mrs. Paul Rudd in.

Senator MANSFIELD. The same chair, Mrs. Rudd. Yes, please.

TESTIMONY OF MRS. PAUL RUDD, HOUSEWIFE, TOWN OF PEQUOT

Mr. BROADBENT. Mrs. Rudd, how do you feel at the present time about Mr. Jones's proposal to buy your son?

Mrs. RUDD. I said at the beginning that the decision was really up to Barry, and I still feel that way.

Mr. BROADBENT. But personally? Yourself?

Mrs. RUDD. Speaking for myself, I wouldn't object.

Mr. BROADBENT. But you wouldn't actually give your approval to the deal unless Barry gave you the go-ahead?

Mrs. RUDD. That's correct. Providing Barry doesn't take too long making up his mind.

Mr. BROADBENT. Why do you say that?

Mrs. RUDD. There isn't all the time in the world. If we delay much longer, we're liable to lose out on the whole deal. The child buyer says he can't stay on one job forever.

Mr. BROADBENT. What has changed your mind, Mrs. Rudd? What has made you willing to sell your son?

Mrs. RUDD. My husband feels it would be the right thing to do.

Mr. BROADBENT. Is that the real reason? Mr. Rudd was for the

243

sale from the beginning, yet for several days you opposed him.

Mrs. RUDD. Well, I think it's a fine opportunity for Barry.

Mr. BROADBENT. Do you truly feel that? All those operations and everything?

Mrs. RUDD. It'll give Barry a chance to be alone and think. He's always complaining to us that we never leave him alone.

Mr. BROADBENT. But is that enough reason to sell your only son?

Senator MANSFIELD. Excuse me, madam, but I feel with Mr. Broadbent that your answers somehow don't carry complete conviction. May I hazard a guess at what swayed you?

Mrs. RUDD. I've told you, my husband, Mr. Rudd, thinks it would be best.

Senator MANSFIELD. Could it be, madam, that during the attack on your home last Tuesday evening you were thrown back into the state of crudeness—I think the word you used yourself to Mr. Cleary was coarseness—from which you had been trying to escape since your girlhood, and that—

Mrs. RUDD. I don't know what you mean. I came from a very good home. We never had much money, but my parents were refined—

Senator MANSFIELD. —and that your son Barry looked into your eyes, and it was as if he saw right through the gray tissue within to the back of your skull—an emptiness there—roughness—

Mrs. RUDD. I was brought up to read good books—gentle books. *Cranford. Northanger Abbey.*

Senator MANSFIELD. —and that you were ashamed to have your son see you as you felt you really are, and always have been, and always will be?

Mrs. RUDD. Barry respects my education. I don't know what you're talking about.

Senator MANSFIELD. Could it be that you fear that unless he

244

leaves you he'll be spoiled by you—not in the sense of being pampered, madam, but as a bad potato ruins a good one if they're left side by side in the barrel?

Mrs. RUDD. Honestly, sir, you're talking riddles. The one thing I fear for Barry if we let him go is that he'll miss the softening influences of a cultured home. Especially as things will be now.

Senator MANSFIELD. What do you mean by that?

Mrs. RUDD. Thanks to Mr. Jones, we'll be surrounded by the best works of man. I mean, he's going to give us the Five-Foot-Three-Inch Classics Shelf, in de-luxe imitation-leather bindings, and a subscription to the Upstream Book Society, where every month you can practically read right over the shoulders of Aubrey Winston, Pierre Berlioz, and Willing Lion, the judges, I mean as if you were in their own living room with those distinguished litterateurs' truly truly favorite books, and they send you an engraved invitation every month just to read in company with them, and the Sky-Hi-Fi Symphony Series, complete in sixty albums, and a composite stereophonic record player, and the Print of the Month, matted and framed, from the Modenheim Museum, and the *Drawn and Quartered Quarterly*, the digest of all the biggest Little Magazines, where you get hopelessness so condensed it's kind of thrilling, and you have to read it or you don't know what you're talking about, and a new television set—I'm not ashamed of this, it's part of our American culture—so we can view The Endless Mind, and Shortcuts to Longhair Music, and The United States Motor Company Shakespeare Half Hour. *And* a cleaning woman once a week. All the cultural opportunities I've always dreamed of!

Senator MANSFIELD. In other words, Mr. Jones switched his gift list on you. When did this happen?

Mrs. RUDD. He first proposed this new list yesterday afternoon, while Barry was testifying about that naughty Renzulli girl who got him in trouble.

Senator MANSFIELD. And what does Mr. Rudd think of this new list?

Mrs. RUDD. We've decided—I mean the child buyer and me— we've decided to let him still have that sports car. He loves to tinker. And those fancy brushes with the mechanical razor and music box, if he wants it, though of course he hates music.

Senator MANSFIELD. And you are actively trying to persuade Barry to give in?

Mrs. RUDD. One of the wise things my mother taught me was: When your children reach the age of discretion, don't interfere in their lives. Trust their judgment. And don't try to tie them to the newel post; there comes a time when you just have to let them free. . . . Anyway, Dr. Gozar's working on him.

Senator MANSFIELD. So we've heard. Any other questions, gentlemen?

Senator VOYOLKO. That TV set—that a eighteen-inch screen or a twenty-one-incher?

Mrs. RUDD. Twenty-one.

Senator VOYOLKO. I thought so. That fellow, the one buys the kids, he's not no cheap skate. Like the pro football games, on a twenty-one-incher you can see the plays develop, the belly series, the ride series, where your guard takes and mousetraps your defensive end, all like that. I'm real glad it's a twenty-one-incher, ma'am. I wouldn't advise you to barge ahead and sell the boy if it wasn't only a eighteen-inch screen. O.K., Mr. Chairman, that's all.

Senator MANSFIELD. Thank you, Mrs. Rudd, you're excused. Now, Mr. Broadbent.

Mr. BROADBENT. Dr. Frederika Gozar next, please.

Senator MANSFIELD. Yes, that's it, Dr. Gozar. Be seated.

TESTIMONY OF DR. FREDERIKA GOZAR, PRINCIPAL, LINCOLN ELEMENTARY SCHOOL, PEQUOT

Mr. BROADBENT. Witnesses here have informed us, Doctor,

that you now favor the sale of Barry Rudd, favor his going to United Lymphomilloid. Is this correct?

Dr. GOZAR. It is.

Mr. BROADBENT. We are most anxious to know the reason for your change of heart.

Dr. GOZAR. Of mind, not heart.

Mr. BROADBENT. You mean your feelings about the boy Barry Rudd haven't changed?

Dr. GOZAR. They never will. He's the finest of all my children, the thousands of children I've had in my thirty-eight years at Lincoln School. I love him very much. I'll be crushed when he's gone—though of course he'd be gone sooner or later anyway, by graduation; it's in the nature of things, we gain and we lose.

Mr. BROADBENT. Then why—? What did the child buyer give you, or promise you?

Dr. GOZAR. An honorary Ph.D. at Hack Sawyer University.

Mr. BROADBENT. And for that, for one more sheepskin—

Dr. GOZAR. Wait a minute. This isn't a bribe. He hasn't *offered* me a Ph.D. He bet me one. On my side of the bet I've put up a new turtle-neck sweater with the varsity letters H.S.U. on it, for him to wear when he rides his motorbike; I've promised to knit the cursed thing myself if I lose, and I loathe knitting—woman's slave labor! And if the child buyer wins, he will have earned his letter, believe me.

Mr. BROADBENT. What's the bet?

Dr. GOZAR. Let me tell you how it came about. I don't know whether you realize it or not, but out there in the anteroom, or outer hall, or whatever you call it, where you herd the witnesses while they're waiting to take the stand, we've been having sessions of our own ever since last Friday, tugging and hauling at each other and at Barry, trying to settle this thing, and I'll wager (I'm in a betting mood, sir) that our battle has been just as lively, and just as terrible, as your hearings. You know how there's that small wickerware table near one end of the gloomy room, with all the state pamphlets on it, on how to test well water, and how neighbors should establish common fences, and other such anachronistic pap, and between the table and the wall there's a settee, under the Governor's portrait? That's where Barry has been established the whole time. It has been like a royal levee. The rest of us have formed clumps around the room—three or four in one of the high windows looking out on Prospect Park, where the fat city squirrels play among the gum wrappers and empty cigarette packs glistening in the sun; another group standing under that mad brass chandelier in the middle of the room that looks like a tangle of golden rams' horns with little incandescent onions impaled on their tips. We've been lobbying and intriguing and debating. And Barry has sat there receiving one supplicant after another, with that impassive look on his face, giving no sign, simply listening. There's a kind of desperation in a long, long wait to hear your name called, and all of us were stripped down to our naked personalities. Papa Owing perspired gallons in his determination, if you could call it that, not to take a position. The great forceful Cleary has alternated between nourishing himself on the polish on the child buyer's boots and running the man's nasty little errands of corruption. Charity Perrin nodded and looked frightened but didn't budge an inch till she came back from lunch yesterday with the child buyer, as tiddly as a tufted titmouse; she was down the river; there were dollar bills sticking out of her ears. Anyway, *my* real crisis began first thing this morning, when I came in there with today's paper, and I'd done my stint in the lab before driving up, so I'd only had time for four cups of coffee, with a result that my blood was creeping like slush in a gutter in March, because this big frame of mine is hard to keep habitable, it really ought to be changed over to central heating. I sat alone in a window light and read about this hearing of yours yesterday afternoon, about the off-the-record matter on the United Lymphomilloid plan, what they *do* with these brilliant human beings, and then I looked over at Barry on the settee, with his mother patting his hand on one side (her hide's as tough as a turtle's shell, believe me) and the G-Man whispering in his ear on the other. At first, before the full weight of the United Lymphomilloid scheme landed on my shoulders, I sat there wondering whether you people are trying to prove something with these hearings, or whether you're just running down hares and pheasants. So much of government these days seems to be elaborate machinery for the ego-satisfaction, as I think Cleary would call it, of the elected. What do you really want of us the governed? . . . But I didn't last long on that line—because then it hit me. *Barry would beat their system.* Barry would show them they can't manipulate human minds like that. His steadfastness would break their backs. Oh, don't worry, I know that the roughest lesson about humankind this century has taught us is that mental breakdowns can be systematically produced to satisfy tyrants' whims. But this is the faith I have in Barry: He has the mind, and he has the fiber, to resist, to hold on, to remain himself. Barry's not just a routine cataloguist; he's more than a taxonomist. Don't forget that Aristotle worked on the classification of animals as a youth in Plato's Academy, but he didn't stop there. I have faith in Barry. He's the sort that could do very great things for this mortal world.

Senator Skypack. Know what I think? I think he's a silly, conceited boy. Probably going to be a homo. Turns my stomach, what we've heard him say.

Dr. Gozar. And you, Senator Skypack, are a Philistine. And Mr. Jones is worse: He's a Visigoth. But Barry, my Barry, he's one of those timeless ones, one of those who carry the human spirit-flame in them. My mentioning Aristotle makes me say what I've long thought—that Barry has that wonderfully sun-struck optimism, the love of existence, that the Greeks had and that gave meaning to their insatiable curiosity. This is why I think he can bring down the Goddess U. Lympho. He'll sit them out, and they'll find they can't make a calculating machine of him.

Senator MANSFIELD. But what about the drug, 'L.T.'? Can he resist that?

Dr. GOZAR. Ah, that's a worry. I've worried about that a great deal this morning while I was sitting with Barry on that creaking piece of furniture trying to give him my point of view. But here's what I think: To produce its effect, 'L.T.' must be essentially hypnotic, and, at least as far as the hypnosis administered by a human hypnotist is concerned, we know it isn't effective so long as the subject refuses to give over his mind. I believe it may be so with the drug. I believe it may. Barry can hold on. He can cling through that ordeal to the minimum notion that he is going to be a classifying biologist, that he's going to persist in this aim and break them, or Her, in the effort to make him ex-clude everything but *Her* from his life. He knows the phyla, classes, orders, and on down the line. He'll recite them to him-self a hundred times a day. He will *not* forget. He'll cling to the memory of a weasel gliding along, like the slippery hope in a thief's heart, beside a stone wall near a hen coop; the gaping mouths of baby robins, uptilted triangles, in a nest in dangerous springtime; a soldier termite undermining some man's slipshod carpentry with his sharp clamping jaws. He'll remember. I really believe he will.

Senator MANSFIELD. And if he doesn't?

Dr. GOZAR. If he doesn't, it will be a great loss. But not so great a loss as it might have been, were it not for the fact that Barry has been destroyed for all practical purposes in the last few days anyway. Talent is a hundred times as fragile as crystal from

Venice. It can't stand up under hammer blows of stupidity—least of all, those of stupid notoriety. Barry's finished as far as the world of Pequot and Treehampstead and what he has called home is concerned. Thanks to you gentlemen. So that the chance of something remarkable being salvaged at United Lymphomilloid seems to me worth taking. And if he fails, if he does forget, and if they do turn him into a machine, he'll be the best; he (or it) will have an I.Q. of twelve hundred, fifteen hundred. How the wheels will turn!

Senator MANSFIELD. Dr. Gozar, mightn't this position you've adopted be just what the child buyer wanted? Aren't you serving his ends?

Dr. GOZAR. How do you mean?

Senator MANSFIELD. It doesn't matter to the child buyer whether you urge Barry to go in order to defy or go in order to comply. All he wants is to get him, buy him. Don't you think the child buyer may have—

Dr. GOZAR. The devil! The dirty devil!

Senator MANSFIELD. How did you happen to make your bet with him?

Dr. GOZAR. That's why I call him a devil and a toad! I realize . . . About ten this morning, I'd had my first exciting reaction to the thought that Barry might resist, when Jones approached me—he watches faces closely, he says he studies foreheads, he must have seen the agitation under my skin—and he began talking—

Mr. BROADBENT. Excuse me, Doctor. Mr. Chairman, I've just been handed a note by the usher. It says the boy Barry Rudd wants to be heard.

Senator MANSFIELD. We'd better have him right in. Dr. Gozar, I know you'll forgive us if we excuse you out of hand. We'd better—

Dr. GOZAR. It doesn't matter. It was only about my idiotic

bet. I'm *such* a fool—but I still have faith in . . . They can't take away. . . .

Senator MANSFIELD. Yes, thank you. You may have the boy brought in, Mr. Broadbent.

Mr. BROADBENT. Barry Rudd.

Senator MANSFIELD. Take the chair, sonny.

TESTIMONY OF BARRY RUDD, MINOR, TOWN OF PEQUOT

Senator MANSFIELD. You wanted to tell us something?

BARRY RUDD. I've decided to go.

Senator SKYPACK. About time!

Senator MANSFIELD. Poor child!

Senator VOYOLKO. Go? Go? Where's he gonta go to? We finished with him yet?

Mr. BROADBENT. What decided you, Master Rudd? Why have you decided to be sold?

BARRY RUDD. It's funny, but I don't really know. One of the many things that passed through my mind out in that outer room this morning was a piece of misinformation they taught me in school. It was under Miss Songevine, in third grade. I remember the page in our social-studies book, and the words. I see the type in my mind now, under a sentimental litho of the *Santa Maria*, the *Pinta*, and the *Niña*. 'Until that time, men believed that the earth was a flat disk. If you sailed too far you would fall off the edge into Chaos. But young Christopher Columbus had the idea that the world was round. . . .' I suppose this was a benevolent simplification—nice short sentences with nice short words, and the equally nice notion that Columbus was the first man to think up a spherical earth, so he could discover America where all good school children live. It was too simple, and when, during my fifth-grade year, I learned the truth at the library, with Miss Cloud's help, I was *bitter:* that the spherical form of the earth was asserted by Pythagoras in the sixth century B.C., and that in 250 B.C., seventeen centuries before Columbus was born, Eratosthenes of Alexandria, knowing that it was a sphere, calculated its diameter to within fifty miles of the correct figure. Do you know the way he did it? It was ingenious—and childishly simple, as all great leaps of the mind seem to be. At a place called Syene the sun at midday was in zenith, straight overhead: he could see its reflection at the bottom of a deep, deep well. At Alexandria, four hundred miles north, an obelisk cast a shadow, which he measured at its longest point. By simple geometry, using the angle of the shadow and the four hundred miles as his clues, he found his answer.

Senator MANSFIELD. Has this anything to do with your decision?

BARRY RUDD. Maybe. I was thinking about it this morning. About my bitterness.

Mr. BROADBENT. Is it because your mother changed her mind?

BARRY RUDD. Mother's wanting me to go is the one thing that makes me want to stay.

Mr. BROADBENT. What arguments did your mother use with you?

BARRY RUDD. Momma's become genteel again since last Tuesday night—more than ever. After Father fixed the windows she cleaned the whole house, threw out stacks of her cheap magazines, made Father buy some deal bookshelves over at Hansen's, in Treehampstead, and she's taken my books out of the cartons they were in, under the beds and in the corners, and she's put them all out on the shelves. Her arguments with me? She hasn't really urged me very much, but she did say this would be a great opportunity for me to become, as she puts it, 'truly cultured.' Momma didn't read the account of the United Lymphomilloid experiment in this morning's paper as carefully as she might

253

have. She thinks Hack Sawyer University offers some kind of liberal-arts curriculum. Momma wants me to have the best opportunities. . . . I'll be homesick for Momma. I'll miss her. I love her more than I can say.

Mr. BROADBENT. You mention Tuesday night. Are you afraid? Did those hoodlums frighten you?

BARRY RUDD. Did you ever come across a poem called 'The Brontosaurus—A Sad Case'? It pictures the Brontosaur as a magnificent creature seventy feet long and four tons in weight, but

> 'As it was lacking in much brainium,
> It had a pitifully small cranium,'

and, the poem concludes,

> 'He was the giant of his day,
> But now his bones are on display.'

Mr. BROADBENT. I take it you're not afraid. Could you tell us—

BARRY RUDD. I'm not afraid, but I must confess that ever since a week ago last Thursday, when I took that walk in the woods down to Chestnut Burr Creek, from the moment I put my book down on that log, from the time when my brown friend *Mantis religiosa* turned his head as if on a swivel to look at me and then took off with a whir, like a helicopter, I've had a feeling that something—everything—was slipping through my fingers. I feel as if I've lost everything. Out there in that room this morning Charley Perkonian gave me the strangest looks. We were a thousand miles apart. I can't explain it.

Mr. BROADBENT. Is this why you want to go?

BARRY RUDD. Maybe, but I doubt it. Maybe it reduces the need to stay, but I can't see how it gives me any good reason to go.

Mr. BROADBENT. Are you going simply because you have no desire to stay?

BARRY RUDD. Maybe. Last night Momma was all steamed up—

254

finding fault with the schools. And I had the creepiest feeling— of being critical of her. I've never felt that way before; I think something must have happened to me that night when the hoods attacked the house.

Mr. BROADBENT. In what way did you feel critical?

BARRY RUDD. I felt the school people may have been put off by Momma's queer way of being half pushy, half timid. I'll give you an example. When I became five—we still lived in Tree-hampstead then—Momma took me to enter me in kindergarten at a school called Cotton Mather Elementary, and we were received by the school clerk. Momma's always been very much in awe of authority, and she thought this clerk was the principal, and Momma said, 'I think I have a son who is advanced for his age.' The clerk gave Momma an oh-my-God look, and Momma said, 'I suppose you have lots of mothers who think that.' 'You'd be amazed,' the clerk said. But the woman did go and get a primer, and she put it in front of me to read. I'd been plowing through news magazines and technical journals at that time, and I just laughed out loud at the silly book and wouldn't deign to read it. The clerk was polite and said, 'I'll certainly keep an eye on *this* one.' And Momma was satisfied with that—anyone could see, anyone but Momma, that the clerk was being sarcastic. That year all Momma got was a series of disquieting reports about my refusals to participate in Reading Readiness classwork and about my inferior hopping and skipping on the playground.

Mr. BROADBENT. But surely the teachers discovered you could read?

BARRY RUDD. They found out, after a fashion, but Momma feels that they were much more interested in the fact that I was maladjusted—as I guess I was, having 'I-see-Susan-run-Susan-run-run-Susan' rammed down my throat for six months.

Senator MANSFIELD. Don't you think the school people might be excused for thinking that *you* had been a bit in the wrong?

BARRY RUDD. I don't see that. What do you mean?

Senator MANSFIELD. I mean your laughing at the primer. After all, you had a chance to show that you could read and you didn't.

BARRY RUDD. I never gave that much thought. The book was so moronic, from my point of view at that time, I mean. . . . So Momma blames the schools, the schools blame me, and I blame Momma. It's a kind of circular motion, isn't it? Maybe some such circular linkage of forces, love and hate, love-blame and hate-blame, *philos-aphilos*, is what makes the world go round. Brings progress, war, adaptation—

Mr. BROADBENT. What about Dr. Gozar—did she persuade you this morning? Do you plan to hold out at United Lymphomilloid in the way she urged?

BARRY RUDD. Oh, no. Once I go, I'll go the whole way. It would be wonderful, but of course this is impossible—it would be wonderful if I could experience the United Lymphomilloid process twice, once co-operatively, and once fighting it. . . . You seem to want to know who persuaded me. . . . Everyone has changed. Why has everyone changed? Mr. Cleary—he used to have such contempt for me; he's been hovering around me like a brood hen, warm and protective. Miss Perrin has gone giddy, she's tried to argue me into leaving and she uses the funniest arguments. Dr. Gozar, my dear, open friend, is suddenly so conspiratorial, whispering with Mr. Jones and then whispering with me—about defying United Lymphomilloid. And Momma. So ladylike. But I can still hear the echo of her shrieks the other night. *'I'll sell him, I'll sell him.'* . . . I can't say I'm going in order to please *you*, Senator Skypack. . . . I guess Mr. Jones is really the one who tipped the scales.

Mr. BROADBENT. How? How did he influence you?

BARRY RUDD. He talked to me a long time this morning. He made me feel sure that a life dedicated to U. Lympho would at least be *interesting*. More interesting than anything that can happen to me now in school or at home—now that everyone has changed. Or perhaps it's that they've come out into the open as themselves. . . . Fascinating to be a specimen, truly fascinating. Do you suppose I really can develop an I.Q. of over a thousand?

Senator MANSFIELD. So the child buyer found a way to corrupt you, too, did he?

BARRY RUDD. Corrupt? What do you mean, corrupt? Is it corrupt to want to be interested—to want to use your mind—to want to be *alive*?

Senator MANSFIELD. I don't suppose a person who has succumbed can be expected to recognize the coin that has bought him. I.Q. points! How absurd! . . . Does it occur to you, sonny, that the child buyer has driven a wedge between you and your mother?

BARRY RUDD. Not at all. I told you I love Momma. The child buyer has been most generous with her.

Senator MANSFIELD. You like him, do you?

BARRY RUDD. Very much. Why shouldn't I? He respects intelligence. He wants intelligence on his side.

Senator MANSFIELD. I wonder what else the child buyer wants. What he wants altogether—for himself, I mean.

BARRY RUDD. I think I know. I can guess. I feel I know him now. I think he wants to be accepted as a specimen. I believe he hopes that his good work as a child buyer will earn him the right. He must know he's old for a specimen, and I can assure you he has no illusions about his brilliance, but his devotion is pure. He believes in U. Lympho. He worships Her already. Do you know what I think he wants most of all?

Senator MANSFIELD. What is that?

BARRY RUDD. I think he wants more than anything to go into the Forgetting Chamber.

Senator MANSFIELD. Do you really think you can forget everything there?

BARRY RUDD. I was wondering about that this morning. About forgetting. I've always had an idea that each memory was a kind of picture, an insubstantial picture. I've thought of it as suddenly coming into your mind when you need it, something you've seen, something you've heard, then it may stay awhile, or else it flies out, then maybe it comes back another time. I was wondering about the Forgetting Chamber. If all the pictures went out, if I forgot everything, where would they go? Just out into the air? Into the sky? Back home, around my bed, where my dreams stay?

JOHN HERSEY was born in Tientsin, China, in 1914 and lived there until 1925, when his family returned to the United States. He was graduated from Yale in 1936 and then attended Clare College, Cambridge, for a year; upon his return from England he was private secretary to Sinclair Lewis during a summer. His first novel, *A Bell for Adano*, won the Pulitzer Prize in 1945. Since 1947 he has devoted his time to fiction and has written *The Wall* (1950), *The Marmot Drive* (1953), *A Single Pebble* (1956), *The War Lover* (1959), and *The Child Buyer* (1960).

Mr. Hersey brought to *The Child Buyer* more than a decade of interest in American public education. He has been a member of a local school board and of a town school-study committee; chairman of a state committee on the problems of gifted children; member of the National Citizens' Commission on the Public Schools; delegate to the White House Conference on Education; member of the National Citizens' Council for Better Schools; and consultant to the Fund for the Advancement of Education.

September 1960

A NOTE ON THE TYPE

THIS BOOK was set on the Linotype in ELECTRA, designed by W. A. *Dwiggins*. The Electra face is a simple and readable type suitable for printing books by present-day processes. It is not based on any historical model, and hence does not echo any particular time or fashion. It is without eccentricities to catch the eye and interfere with reading—in general, its aim is to perform the function of a good book-printing type: to be read, and not seen.

The book was composed, printed, and bound by KINGSPORT PRESS, INC., Kingsport, Tenn. Paper manufactured by S. D. WARREN Co., Boston. Typography by VINCENT TORRE; binding design by CHARLES E. SKAGGS.

C 1

Hersey

Child buyer.